I scrambled out of the scrub onto the open, moonlit crest and straightened, gasping for breath. Then I heard hooves and turned. A rider had been coming along the crest in my direction and, seeing me, had spurred his horse into galloping attack. Ignoring his lance, he drew his sword, leaning sideways to strike. My hand seemed to move in slow motion— drawing my stunner, raising it, pointing, thumbing. His horse nose-dived, hitting the ground so heavily I swear I could feel it through my feet. The Saracen hurtled over its head in a billow of robe, moonlight flashing on sword. I zapped him too, as he skidded. He stopped not ten feet from me.

He was dead of course. On high intensity at such close range, I'd really curdled his synapses. I took his shield; I'd need one when daylight came.

JOHN DALMAS
RETURN TO FANGLITH

BAEN BOOKS

RETURN TO FANGLITH

Copyright © 1987 by John Dalmas

A Baen Books Original

Baen Publishing Enterprises
260 Fifth Avenue
New York, N.Y. 10001

First printing, August 1987

ISBN: 0-671-65343-1

Cover art by David Mattingly

Printed in the United States of America

Distributed by
SIMON & SCHUSTER
1230 Avenue of the Americas
New York, N.Y. 10020

Dedicated to
my good buddies:
Sally Thielen
and
Ruth Sokoloff

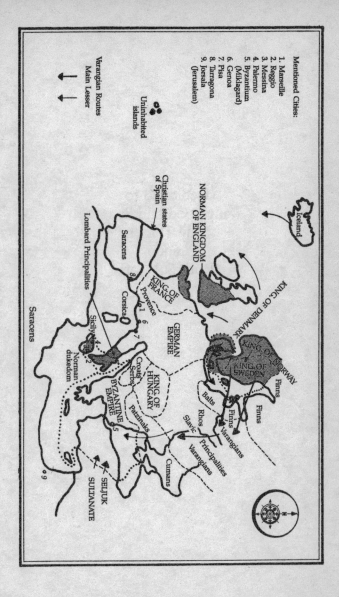

Mentioned Cities:

1. Marseille
2. Reggio
3. Messina
4. Palermo
5. Byzantium (Miklagard)
6. Genoa
7. Pisa
8. Tarragona
9. Jorsala (Jerusalem)

Varangian Routes
Main Lesser

Uninhabited islands

Iceland

NORMAN KINGDOM OF ENGLAND

KING OF DENMARK

KING OF NORWAY

KING OF SWEDEN

Finns
Finns
Finns

Balts

Rhos
Varangians

Slavic Principalities

Varangians

Cumans

SELJUK SULTANATE

Patzinaks

Croats
Serbs

BYZANTINE EMPIRE

KING OF HUNGARY

GERMAN EMPIRE

Norman dukedom

Sicily

Corsica

Provence

KING OF FRANCE

Lombard Principalities

Saracens

Christian states of Spain

Saracens

Saracens

PART ONE

ESCAPE FROM EVDASH

ONE

I wasn't actually undernourished, but we'd been on tight rations, and more or less hungry, for fifty-seven days. Which is something you can get used to, but not what I think of as ideal. In space you can't stop off at a friendly nearby restaurant or food store. The nearest planets are likely to be parsecs* away, and have a couple of Imperial frigates flying sentry around them, with chase craft ready for launch. We'd had more than enough of those.

Now Fanglith lay beautifully blue and white, primitive and savage, only 40,000 miles off our starboard window with, so far no sign of a picket ship on our instruments. Which were good ones, as you'd expect on a stolen naval patrol scout.

I wasn't sure what we could hope to accomplish there; we had no plans. But just then, food was what I was mainly interested in.

"I never expected to see this place again," I said, more to myself than to Deneen or Bubba or Tarel. We'd been lucky to get away alive the first time. But sometimes fate—whatever "fate" is—hits you when you're least prepared. And when it does, it can be with three or four punches, one after another.

We'd been 646 parsecs from Fanglith, on a wilderness trek in the Snowy Range Preserve, when the first

*A parsec equals 3.258 light-years.

3

punch hit. Bubba was the first to notice. At that point, all that the rest of us noticed was Bubba. His big wolf's head raised, alert, attention fixed, looking off west.

Deneen, my sister, put down the seared hind leg of a burrow pig. "What is it, Bubba?" she asked.

He didn't make a sound; didn't look at her. His attention was all on what he heard, or maybe what he was receiving telepathically.

Then the rest of us began to hear it, too. It was so low-pitched, it was as if we felt it before we heard it—a deep bass thrumming, barely audible. Yet somehow it seemed very loud—loud but far away. Uncle Piet and Bubba got to their feet, the rest of us a half second behind, and we all trotted through the trees to the edge of the cliff a hundred feet away. From there we could see southward across the foothills, toward the Valrith Plain.

"So it's happened," Piet said softly, as if talking to himself.

What we'd heard was a Federation battleship. Make that an Imperial battleship—things had changed. I stood there in my moccasins, staring. It must have been more than a quarter mile long, cruising across the clear morning sky two miles or so above the foothills, and maybe three miles south. It answered a question we'd been talking about a few days earlier.

"Let's go home," Piet said.

It took us very little time to break camp and leave, all without conversation. We had almost nothing to carry—no sleeping bags, no cooking gear, no tent. Each of us, except Bubba of course, carried a small blanket, a heavy belt knife, a spark wheel for starting fires, a tinder box, a sharpening stone, a self-made backpack, woven at Piet's instructions from the inner bark of a tree, and a water bag made the previous butchering season from the boiled-out gut of a fatbuck. We were being as primitive as we knew how—or as Piet knew how.

I doused the fire with a minimum of water—it was a small one—then stirred the coals, wet ashes, and dirt with a stick to make sure it was out. Tarel wrapped what was left of the burrow pig in its flayed-off pelt and stashed it in his pack. Jenoor untied the cords we used to set up shelters, and put them in hers. Like the packs, the cords were inner bark, cut into thin strips. They'd be hard to replace if we lost them, because it was late summer now, and the bark wouldn't strip off the trees anymore.

We were ready for the trail in about two minutes, maybe three. No one needed to ask what next. We'd go down to Piet's floater and fly home, hopefully to mom and dad and Lady and the pups. After that. . . . We'd see.

The Snowy Range is beautiful, but hiking out, I didn't pay much attention to aesthetics. The country was rugged and mostly forest, there was no established trail where we were, and we were hurrying. When my attention wasn't on picking the route—I was the pathfinder that day—I had things on my mind. All of us did, I guess.

We'd been three weeks in the Snowy Range on a survival-training trek—part of the training Piet was giving us. Piet isn't really our uncle; he's more of an "honorary" uncle. He'd worked with our parents back when dad and mom had been members of the underground on Morn Gebleu, the executive planet of the Federation. Dad and mom had taken Deneen and me away from Morn Gebleu when we were little, to bring us up on Evdash, a world that was safer and a lot more democratic—an old colony world, well outside Federation boundaries.

They'd started training us seriously for the resistance after we'd come back from our crazy, unintentional—adventure, I guess you could call it—on the forgotten prison planet, Fanglith. Piet had come to stay with us about a year later. He'd been a lot of places and done a lot of things, and became another trainer. One of the places he'd been—he'd hidden out there a couple of years—was a world where the intelligent species was a two-legged felid type with a primitive hunting/fishing culture. He'd learned things there about living in wilderness conditions that the known human worlds had lost long before, and he'd been teaching us the basics.

By Bubba's standards, our wilderness skills were still pretty poor, of course. Espwolves had been pack hunters before their planet banged heads with a comet. Only a few dozen of them got evacuated with the human colonists there. Bubba had been pretty much grown already—old enough to have learned the skills of an adult wolf.

Espwolves are more than just telepathic. They're intelligent, with mental processes a lot like humans'. You kind of half forget that sometimes, because they look so much like any large canid species, and because they don't say much.

That's right—some of them can talk. Bubba had taught himself to speak Evdashian, more or less. By combining telepathy with intelligence, he'd analyzed words and speech patterns, and their meanings. Then he'd substituted certain sounds he *could* make for the human speech sounds he couldn't.

His approximation of Evdashian wasn't easy for him, though, so he wasn't much for small talk. Because he belonged to a telepathic species, his brain probably didn't even have a speech center, and his mouth and throat weren't built for talking. His grammar was adequate, but rough—anything to keep it brief—and he usually avoided words that were hard for him, but with practice you could understand him. Our family had no trouble at all.

Anyway, a month earlier, the news had come that the Federation had declared itself "The Glondis Empire." That wouldn't make a lot of difference on Federation planets. Since the Glondis Party had taken over the Federation government, a few years before I was born, they'd run it more and more as a Party dictatorship.

But the declaration of empire would make a big difference to us. Our parents and Piet talked a lot about politics in front of us and to us; it was part of our continuing education. And they'd agreed that if it was now formally calling itself an empire, then the Party must feel about ready to start taking over the outlying independent planets. It would be just a matter of time before they got to us.

Evdash had been colonized by refugees the last time the central worlds had been an empire, four centuries ago. Most of the so-called colony worlds had been settled by refugees at one time or another. The central worlds have a tendency to go imperial now and then, and an empire usually became a dictatorship after a while, if it wasn't one to start with.

Our way out of the wilderness was mostly downhill—about four thousand feet downhill—but that didn't mean it was fast or easy. We hiked through old forest with lots of blown-down timber to pick your way over or around, and down ravines littered with boulders and fallen trees. Toward noon a thunderstorm came through, booming and banging, and we stopped to wait it out in a thick dense glaru grove that would keep us dry if it didn't rain too long.

As we crouched there, Deneen looked at Piet. "The Empire didn't wait long, did it?" she asked.

It was a statement more than a question. A few evenings earlier, around the cook fire, Jenoor had asked Piet how long he thought it would be before the Empire took over Evdash. He'd said probably within two or three years.

"You don't suppose there's been much fighting, do you?" Jenoor asked, looking at me.

I looked at Piet. He was leaving it to me. "I doubt it," I told her. "A few skirmishes, maybe. Fly a million-ton monster like that over the largest cities on Evdash, and ideas about defending the planet evaporate in a hurry. That battleship has got more firepower all by itself than the whole Evdashian navy. I'm just glad it's down here in the atmosphere and not out a few hundred miles bombarding the surface."

The rain had begun—fat drops in myriads assaulting the leaves above, overlaying the swish of wind-ruffled treetops with sibilant rustling; intermittent rolls of thunder drowned them all. Occasional shattered droplets touched my face with mist, and the air smelled of ozone.

"Tell us what you're thinking about, Deneen," Piet said.

I turned to look at her. She was frowning, more grim than thoughtful.

"I wonder how long they've been here. They could have taken over two weeks ago, or longer, and where we've been, we wouldn't have known it." She turned to me. "And if it's been that long, we won't find mom and dad at home. They'll have taken off somewhere to avoid the political police."

That was obvious. I just hadn't looked at it yet. It was also food for thought. Whether we found our parents or not, the question was where we'd go. There was probably an Imperial flotilla guarding the planet to keep people from leaving. And the Empire would be developing an informer network, of course; they'd already had a spy network. So if we tried to lie low, we'd probably be uncovered sooner or later.

Of course, the Imperials might have just arrived, and our parents might still be safe at home. Dad knew the ropes on this world better than just about anyone—probably better than Piet. He'd operated as a business consultant here on two continents, and had a lot of underground contacts, too. He had resources I didn't know existed.

The rain lasted just long enough for Tarel to get out the burrow pig and pass it around for a few bites each. Then, not even wet, I led off again. By mid-afternoon, landmarks told me we weren't too far from Piet's floater. Bubba assured us there was no one near it—that was just one advantage of having an espwolf—and in a quarter hour we were there.

Six of us, with our gear, didn't leave a lot of room in the floater's boxy body. Piet raised her above the trees and started for home. The first thing Deneen did was turn the radio on. The programming was not the usual. For a few minutes, all we got was Federation, now Imperial, patriotic music, no matter what station we tuned to. Then some guy speaking Standard came on and gave a brief news rundown—mostly stuff on changes in laws and regulations.

That told us how the Empire figured to run things— they weren't even broadcasting in Evdashian. The languages were enough alike that people on Evdash could pretty much understand Standard, and I would have bet that the Empire had declared a law against speaking our own language.

When Deneen and Bubba and I, and our parents, had gotten back from Fanglith more than two years earlier, we'd resettled on the northern continent. Federation spies had found our previous home. Dad fixed up an old farmhouse, and about a year later Tarel and Jenoor had come to live with us. Their parents had joined the resistance on a Federation planet named Tris Gebleu, and had them smuggled to Evdash, where they'd been placed with us. They were twins Deneen's age—sixteen. Soon after, Piet came to live with us. Add Lady and the two pups, and you get a pretty full house.

Half an hour in the floater brought us close to home, but Piet didn't simply land in the yard and punch the hooter. He flew past about half a mile north at 3,000 feet, while Bubba scanned the place telepathically. Someone was home all right, he said—two someones—but they weren't our parents. They were two human males, playing cards while they waited for their detector to buzz.

My gut knotted. Had mom and dad escaped or been hauled away? If they had been arrested, chances were that Lady and the pups would be hanging around nearby, living in the forest. But if they'd escaped, they'd probably all have left together. Telepathically, Bubba found no sign of Lady or the pups around, so my guts relaxed a little.

Where we lived, the country was three-quarters woods. Our house was near the edge of the farm clearing, with a sod road going by it. Piet put down in the woods about a mile away. Leaving the others with the floater, Bubba and I took off at a trot, his esper senses alert. When we got near the clearing, Bubba, in his rough grunting version of human speech, suggested I stay back. I knew it was good advice, but I didn't like to leave everything to him, so we continued together to the clearing's edge, creeping on our bellies the last hundred feet, keeping to cover, until I could see the house and our big shed. The shed doors were open and the cutter was gone, but the floater was still there.

That could mean that my parents had gotten away, or it could mean that the police had impounded the cutter. My guess was that they'd gotten away. Otherwise the police, if they were smart, would have left the cutter in the shed to fool us, maybe after taking out the fuel slugs. They probably wouldn't know our canid was an espwolf. There are lots of different kinds of canids from the known worlds, and espwolves are rare. As far as we knew, ours were the only ones on the continent. Our friends thought Bubba was just another big exotic canid with ordinary abilities.

In a family like ours, you learn very young to keep certain kinds of things a secret.

Bubba started crawling backward, and I did the same. When we were out of sight of the house, he got up and trotted off without saying anything. I knew where he had to be going, and followed him. When we'd moved here, dad had put a waterproof box in a huge old hollow tree, where messages could be left in emergencies like this.

It paid off: there was a package in the message box and a medkit on top of it. I took them out, and Bubba and I headed back to the others.

We opened the package at the floater. There wasn't a lot in it—several data cubes and a message cube. One by one we checked the cubes in the floater's computer, the message cube first. It was dated seven days earlier. An Imperial flotilla, standing off Evdash, had demanded surrender, and a force of fifth-column commandos, with the collusion of traitors in the national police, had taken over national police headquarters. With us not due back for eight days, our parents had no choice but to leave without us. "We'll try to meet you later on Lizard Island," mom had said, "and leave Evdash from there." Try. Later. All in all not very reassuring. And it didn't say where they were going or for how long—probably for good reason.

The other cubes were a mixed lot: an astrogation cube; a "miscellaneous" cube that included, among other things, a learning program and a linguistic analysis program—I'd had good use of both of them before; a couple of library cubes; and a copy of the family's planetary coordinates cube with everywhere we'd ever flown on Evdash.

There was also one other: a copy of the old contraband data cube we'd used to find Fanglith. When I saw that one on the menu, I got goose bumps. I also became aware that Deneen was looking at me. I wondered if it affected her at all the same way. She'd always been "Miss Objective Practicality."

An astrogation cube and the contraband data cube! Umh! The knot returned to my gut. "Well," I said, "if they don't meet us, it looks as if they expect us to leave the planet on our own, somehow or other."

Although, how we could do that without a cutter . . . "Let's sit here till dark," I suggested. "It'll be safer traveling then. With the coordinates cube, we won't have any trouble finding Lizard Island at night."

I could feel part of my attention stuck on the contraband data cube. On Fanglith, actually. And from Deneen's expression, hers was too. "I'm not going to be surprised if they don't get to Lizard Island for a month or more," I went on. "Obviously, they've got something to do first, or they'd have gone there already, not 'later.' And they'll need to wait until things quiet down, because a cutter's a lot more conspicuous than a floater and a ton more likely to attract trouble."

Of course, they might not get there at all.

The floater's main door was open, letting in the late sun. I was sitting in front, with Deneen and Piet. Tarel was in back, looking sober and saying nothing. He was generally pretty quiet and serious. Beside him, Jenoor was quiet, too. She wasn't generally quiet like he was; in fact, she was often pretty animated. But just now she was worried.

Jenoor tended to look up to me because I was older and had the Fanglith experience under my belt, which was fine with me. We'd told people that she and Tarel were our cousins, so of course it hadn't been okay for me to take her around. But I had it in mind to propose to her after she reached legal age, and when I could support her. Looking up to me the way she did, it seemed to me she'd probably say yes. Anyway, she hadn't shown much interest in other guys, although they'd been pretty interested in her.

Meanwhile, living in the same house with her hadn't always been the most comfortable thing in the world. She was too good-looking.

Deneen considered her pretty special too—had even asked me once if I'd ever thought of Jenoor as a future wife. When I admitted I had, she said she was glad to see her brother showing good taste. Deneen was more critical than our parents about whom I took out. She didn't issue her seal of approval very often, even though they were just dates. And as for getting serious—she said that considering the kind of future I could expect, I needed "a wife of similar purposes and comparable ability."

She was right, of course. But how could we know for sure what someone's purpose was—one of our friends at school for example. I was sure no one there knew ours.

At the floater we sat around or napped for a couple of hours, until it got dark. I thought a little about Lizard Island. That was our family name for it; all the chart said was "Great Central Shoal," and showed a string of dots along it to indicate little islands. Lizard was inconspicuous, all right. I wondered what it would be like in a hurricane; hopefully I'd never find out.

I was in the pilot's seat. Piet sat in the seat next to mine. He was like dad—ready to let me handle things myself if it was something I could.

"Let's go," I said. I keyed the Lizard Island coordinates into the computer, and we took off. At 3,000 feet

I put her on automatic pilot and we headed southeast for the broad, shallow Entrilias Sea, keeping track of the radio and the traffic monitor, which was on high sensitivity.

The knot was gone from my gut. For whatever reason, I felt as if everything was going to come out all right.

TWO

The floater didn't have an infrascanner—it wasn't intended for anything more than family-type use—but the stars give more than enough light to see Lizard Island when you're right above it at 200 feet. It appeared to be about two hundred yards long and half as wide, but it wasn't really, because part of what looked like island was a fringe of mangrove trees that stood in the water around its edges.

"It's little, isn't it," Jenoor said.

"Small enough that no one pays any attention to it," I answered. "Small and out of the way. It's one of the biggest in a string of low islands like this, and they're a navigation hazard—the high points of a long shoal—so ships stay well away."

"How do we land?" asked Tarel.

"Carefully and by daylight. There's no clearing, so we'll have to slip down between trees."

I could feel that Tarel and Jenoor had more questions but were holding off, hoping someone else would ask them. Questions like, how do we live down there? Deneen knew, of course. Our family had been here once before, not long after we'd gotten back from

Fanglith, establishing a refuge in case we ever needed one. We'd stayed for several days, getting a feel for what it would take to live there.

We definitely hadn't set up a vacation home or anything like that, but we'd hidden a plastite chest with a shovel, hammocks, fishing lines, hooks and spears, a pair of books on edible fish and plants of the Entrilias region, a little water still and a good-sized pail, a couple of insect repellent-field generators, a pint-size geogravitic power tap (very expensive), and Rigidite plastic sheeting that was highly flexible to start with but would get semi-stiff once it was wetted. There was also a small beam saw.

Nearby we'd buried a lightweight skiff about eight feet long and three feet wide, for fishing.

Meanwhile we had an hour or so before dawn—longer than that before it would be light enough to land—so I got in back to catch a nap. I hadn't been sleepy, so I'd stood pilot watch most of the way. I still didn't feel sleepy, but I was willing to bet I'd go to sleep, once I lay down.

I was right. I lay down and closed my eyes, and it seemed like only a minute later when I woke up. We were moving, settling downward. It was already light, almost sunup, and Deneen was at the controls. Treetops were rising past the windows. A couple of light thumps and brushing sounds marked our passage through their branches; then there was one last little bump and we were on the ground. Everyone else piled out, but I closed my eyes again, "just for a few minutes." When I opened them next time, the chest had been uncovered and the shelter built. I got out of the floater all sleepy-eyed, and Deneen looked at me.

"Well, brother mine," she said, and handed me the shovel. "You're just in time to dig up the boat for us."

After I'd dug the boat up, I took the beam saw and cut a little canal through the mangrove prop roots so she could be floated out to open water. The beam saw wouldn't cut under more than a quarter inch of water, so Piet and Tarel and I had to use our heavy survival knives for a lot of it. It was slow hard work, and I was disgusted before we were even close to finished. Then Deneen and Piet went fishing. Fishing was going to be very important. The only food we'd brought with us was the remains of the burrow pig, and all we'd find on the island, I knew, was a little fruit, a lot of little lizards, and insects that were mostly too small for food.

With Piet and Deneen off in the boat, that left me to finish setting up camp with Tarel and Jenoor. Deneen had done well as far as she'd gone. The shelter was a large lean-to, and she'd laid a pole on its sloping roof to form a sort of groove before splashing water on the Rigidite to harden it. This would gather the rain, which would run into the plastite chest—our cistern—which we could cover when it wasn't raining, to keep out the bugs. *If* it rained. By the looks of things, this was the dry season.

Meanwhile, if dad and mom arrived, they'd never be able to bring the cutter down through the tiny gap Deneen had coaxed the floater through. Correction, I told myself—not if, *when*. *When* they arrived. I might as well cultivate a positive attitude. But it didn't feel very real to me. *When, if, whatever*, I thought. Be prepared. I needed to fell a couple or three trees, but not where they could fall on the shelter or where the debris would be a problem. Or where our camp could be spotted through the little hole they'd leave.

It wasn't as if I had any reason to expect someone to scrutinize this tiny islet in the middle of the Entrilias, but time was one thing it looked like we had lots of, and it made no sense to skip simple precautions.

So with the beam saw I lopped off a couple of stout saplings and sharpened an end on each, for pushing with. Then I picked trees to cut down—three of them in a row that would leave a thin, inconspicuous gap long enough for the cutter. The forest was thick enough that a tree cut from the stump would tend to hang up in other trees instead of falling, so I had had to shop around a little for one that looked as if it would go all the way down. After seeing which way it leaned, I had Tarel and Jenoor put their push poles against it on the opposite side, digging the points through the mass of tough vines that coated the bark. Then I cut it with the beam saw, and when it started to fall, they both pushed as hard as they could. Brushing through surrounding branches, it picked up momentum and smashed to the ground.

The second and third trees were simpler. Each leaned toward the opening made by felling the one before, so there was a good place for them to fall. When all three were down, I cut them into pieces small enough that we could move them. They weren't what you'd think of as big trees; the soil here was too sandy and infertile. But before we were done dragging and throwing the pieces out of the way, all three of us were soaked with sweat, and I knew we'd be stiff in the morning.

It helped that Tarel was as strong as he was. He wasn't much more than average height, but he was broad and chunky. Overweight, actually—even after three weeks of survival training had melted off maybe twelve or fifteen pounds. He was one of those people who tend to be naturally, genetically fat. I knew for sure he wasn't a big eater. But he was one of the strongest kids I've ever seen—quite a lot stronger than me—and I'd been one of the strongest guys in school when I'd graduated this past spring.

After we'd gotten a landing place ready, I set up the geogravitic power tap for our insect repellent field and, if necessary, our water still. When Deneen and Piet came back, an hour after we were done, I showed them what we'd accomplished. Meanwhile they hadn't had a lot of luck fishing, but the two edible fish they'd caught were big enough to feed all of us, including Bubba.

It looked to me as if our problem on Lizard Island was going to be mostly a matter of coping with monotony.

THREE

I was right about the monotony, but somehow it wasn't that unpleasant. Two of us would go out in the skiff each day to fish, and stay out till we had enough. It could take most of the day, or only a few minutes, but commonly it took less than an hour. A couple of times, early on, we got nothing, but as we learned the fishes' feeding habits, it went a lot better.

Besides fishing, there were just two other jobs: Every hour or two, someone had to fetch a pail of sea water and pour it in the still. Yes, this was the dry season. The other job was gathering what fruit there was. Most of the time, there was nothing that needed doing.

The food was the worst part, and even that we got used to. We ate our fish raw to get the maximum vitamins from them, because there wasn't much edible fruit in the dry season. Most of the plants timed their fruiting to take advantage of the rains. Bubba at least got a little variety by eating lizards. The rest of us left the lizards alone. They were too small and bony, and too hard to skin, to be worth it for humans. Bubba, on the other hand, ate skin and all. I suppose his stomach acid dissolved the bones.

Somehow or other, it wasn't as bad as it sounds—not the boredom or the food.

To pass time, we drilled hand-foot art—both the combat and gymnastic parts of it. Piet wasn't willing to be the drill instructor—he said Deneen should be, that

17

her technique was amazingly good. I'd known she was good, I just hadn't realized how good. We'd been trained in it since we were little kids, one reason we're both such good all-round athletes.

Tarel and Jenoor had never heard of hand-foot art till they'd come to live with us. It's been illegal, and pretty much a secret practice, most of the time for a thousand years or more. As a result, on most worlds, people didn't know there was such a thing. Jenoor had picked it up fast; like Deneen, she was a natural athlete. Tarel was slower at learning things that took coordination, and the necessary flexibility had come slowly for him too. Now, though, with more time to work on it, he was starting to get good enough to really feel some mastery, and with confidence, his movements became surprisingly quick. Combine that with his strength, and he was turning into someone you'd do best not to fight with. He was actually getting lean, too, partly from the food.

He was still very mild-mannered. I wasn't sure what it would take to make him violent, but there was bound to be something.

You couldn't practice hand-foot art all day, of course; it was too strenuous. Two sessions a day, about an hour each, was plenty, so the first month was about the longest, slowest one I'd ever experienced till then. The closest thing to it had been traveling to Fanglith two years earlier. That had been fifty-seven days of reading and sleeping. Here we didn't dare use the floater's computer for recreational reading because we needed to conserve the fuel cell. For some reason known only to Consolidated Floaters Corporation, computer operation required that the whole system be on—at least on idle. And, of course, floaters don't have the kind of fuel slugs that cutters do.

We got so we slept a lot.

I thought about Jenoor more than I should have. Not that I got fixated on her or anything, but I couldn't help thinking, now and then. We fished together a lot, we were always around one another, and no one wore much in the way of clothes. It was generally hot, and a great chance to get a tan. A couple of times I was pretty close to making a pass at her, but managed not to. Partly, I was afraid she'd say yes. And if we got something going, no way could we keep it secret, which Tarel might resent, and maybe Deneen—just what we didn't need in exile on a tiny little island. And I was going on nineteen, with responsibility to more than my own druthers.

But partly, maybe I was afraid she'd say no. From what I'd read about Tris Gebleu in social geography, people there took a lot of things more seriously than we did, including sex, and I didn't want her to think I was some kind of horny creep.

Anyway I kept it cool.

It helped that she'd told me once I was like an older brother to her. She and I had gotten along really well from the time they'd come to live with us; I'd always enjoyed having her in the family.

Generally the five of us would sit around in the evening and talk while it was getting dark. One of the topics was what we'd do when dad and mom arrived and we left Evdash. That was always the stated situation—*when* mom and dad arrived. But beneath it was the unspoken *if*—if they arrived.

We'd all listened in on discussions between mom and dad and Piet about what they might do when, someday, the Empire started taking over the colony worlds. They would check out the more remote of the so-called "lost" colonies, in what was referred to as "the deep outback" —worlds scattered thinly around the fringes of known space. The idea was to find the best ones to establish hidden rebel bases on. And there was always the implication that the rest of us would be part of it if we wanted to.

One of the problems would be to get the lost-world locals interested. Generally they wanted nothing to do with off-worlders, beyond maybe getting replacements or parts for some equipment they couldn't make locally. In the deep outback, people were self-reliant and not much interested in off-world problems—until maybe those problems became theirs, too.

They were referred to as "lost" colonies because ships seldom went there, and mostly they had no ships of their own. Some of them may not have been visited more than once a generation. They were so poor economically, and so far from civilization and trade routes, that the Federation had been no more interested in them than they were in the Federation.

So they'd have little to contribute to the Imperial treasury or trade, and hopefully the Empire would decide to ignore them. Or some of them, anyway. The cost/benefit ratio of taking them over and controlling them would be high, and the Empire was bound to have troubles closer to home.

Of course, we couldn't be sure that that's how the Empire would look at it.

On Lizard Island, about the first thing we did each evening was listen to a newscast on the floater radio— the only time we turned it on. It was always in Standard. After a couple of weeks, a local announcer was used—we could tell by his accent. Apparently, the occupation administration was phasing in Evdashians they felt they could trust. By the end of a month, judging by the news, things had settled into a new routine on Evdash. The mass trials were over, the public executions had taken place, and thousands of political prisoners had been shipped off-world to forced-labor camps on mining planets and the like.

We didn't hear Klentis and Aven kel Deroop mentioned among the names of people executed or arrested. They'd been prominent in the old days, in the resistance back on Morn Gebleu, and we agreed that they'd be mentioned if captured.

So far things had gone about the way we'd expect, with the Glondis Party in charge. Their idea was to make everyone too scared to resist. But you could pretty much depend on it that a majority now hated them, and in time the Empire would explode—as soon as anyone got a good strong revolt rolling somewhere.

Of course, that might take a long time to happen.

We all agreed that our function would be either to

help brew the revolt inside the Empire, or build a base outside—in one way or another to help bring it down. The only alternative acceptable to any of us was that the Empire might somehow evolve into a decent place to live. History said it wouldn't, especially under something like the Glondis Party. We'd see what happened, and meanwhile we'd prepare for the revolution.

After six weeks I began to fret about my parents. Not many of the things I could think of that might be keeping them were very cheering, given how things were now on Evdash. So I brought it up one evening while we digested our raw fish. Actually, the way I put it was: "Piet, how long do you think it'll be before dad and mom show up?"

His eyes turned to me without telling me anything. "How long do you think?" he answered. I should have known he'd say that.

"Things take as long as they take," I said. "But knowing mom and dad, they won't take any longer than they have to. I guess what I was really asking was, how long should we wait before we leave without them?"

"Leave for where?" Deneen asked. "This isn't my favorite place, but I can stay here a year if I need to. Or anyway as long as the floater's fuel cells have power enough to take us where we decide to go."

"Right," I answered. "But if dad and mom don't show, we'll have to make some kind of move on our own, sooner or later."

I glanced around at the others. Piet was interested in what I'd do with the subject. Tarel looked solemn, his eyes shadowed in the dusk. Jenoor looked serious and neutral. Neither of the two had ever shown any tendency to get involved in decisions. They were young, though no younger than Deneen, and in a sense "outsiders" because they were latecomers in our family.

"Have you got any thoughts about this, Tarel?" I asked.

I hadn't really expected a positive answer, but he surprised me. "Unless your parents get here," he said, "the only way we'll get a space cutter is to steal one—a naval cutter of some kind. The occupation forces probably confiscated all the private cutters they could find out about."

"There might still be some private cutters around," Jenoor put in, "belonging to Evdashians who are part of the Imperial spy network. And private cutters ought to be easier to steal than, say, a patrol scout on the ground for servicing."

I couldn't feel optimistic about the prospects. It was one thing to talk about going out and establishing rebel bases, but doing it, or even getting out there, would be something else. I looked at Piet, who'd been sitting there listening and saying nothing. "What do *you* think?" I asked him. I could swear he laughed behind those quiet eyes.

"You're doing fine," he said. "Keep talking. I wouldn't be surprised if you came up with something."

I didn't, though—that night or any other. I didn't know what Piet might have in mind of course, but none of the rest of us came up with anything.

I was fishing with Jenoor a few weeks later when the end of the dry season arrived. We found out the hard way. Fortunately, we were fairly close to the island, on the west side, usually the upwind side when there was any wind. We seldom went more than a couple of hundred yards from it, for safety's sake, and the water two hundred yards from the island was only four feet deep or so, green in the tropical sunlight. It was shallow enough that we used spears occasionally, when a fish came near enough to that strange object floating on the surface.

We could have gotten out and waded, but we wouldn't of course, because one of the fish species around there— the javelin fish, which was sometimes five or more feet long—was known to attack swimmers. The idea was for us to eat fish, not vice versa.

It was early afternoon, a better time for spotting fish than when the sun was lower. Usually we would see fish from time to time—more often than not, the fish we caught were ones we saw feeding. We'd cast a little way in front of them and let them come up on the lure.

This day we were seeing none at all; it was as if they'd all moved somewhere else.

We'd noticed occasional thunderheads for several days, building far to the west in the afternoons, but none had come near. We'd have welcomed a good rain, just for the change.

Jenoor and I were both facing east to reduce the glare effect on our eyes, and hadn't noticed how near the storm had gotten until we heard the thunder. Jenoor had just hooked our first fish after two hours of nothing. We both turned; the thunderhead wasn't much more than a mile away, with a thick dark wall of rain coming down from it to the sea.

We weren't smart enough to be worried, and returned our attention to the fish. As she played it, perhaps forcing it more than usual because of the rainstorm coming, swells started to raise and lower the skiff. I'd already reeled in my own lure, to keep my line out of her way as she worked her fish. Now I picked up a paddle. The storm was approaching faster than I'd expected, and I felt my first misgiving.

"Horse him in," I told her tersely. "If the line breaks, it breaks. I think we'd better get to shore before that thing hits."

She nodded, raising her rod tip and cranking harder. That lasted about ten seconds before the wind hit. It was colder than I would have thought, and almost too hard to be air. With the water as shallow as it was, the sea responded quickly; within seconds the swells became waves that threatened to swamp us.

"Break the line and let's get out of here," I yelled. Jenoor yanked, and the line and rod went slack. Gripping the paddle, I began to dig for the island with it. That's when the first big wave hit, and we turned over.

The water seemed deeper than usual. The wind was piling it up, and it was up to my shoulders. I knew Jenoor didn't swim very well, and my first thought was to find and get hold of her, but I couldn't see her. *She's on the other side of the boat*, I thought, *or under it*. Somehow I'd come up on its upwind side. The next thing I knew, she surfaced a few feet in front of me, swimming clumsily, as the boat righted itself. It was full of water.

I struck out for it, and that's when I discovered that the big wave hadn't been big at all. The next one was the big one, and steep because the water was so shallow. It lifted us both, but we went up and down almost in place, because it wasn't breaking yet. The skiff, on the other hand, got carried thirty feet farther from me. The next wave was close behind and bigger still, and it was breaking. I just had time to grab Jenoor when it crashed over us, carrying us tumbling and confused in the general direction of the island. I was scared to death I'd lose hold of her.

I wasn't even sure the waves would take us to the island, because we'd been on the windward side, but off toward the south end. With my free arm, I tried to swim to my left. The next breaker caught us and drove us forward again, sprawling and out of control, and then we were in waist-deep water. My arm was around Jenoor. I lurched to my feet, helping her up. We were inside the breaker line now, not more than a couple of hundred feet from the mangroves, about even with the island's tip. I could see the skiff, awash but still upright, sideways and seventy or eighty feet ahead of us. The wind and waves were pushing it a lot faster than we could wade or swim, and unless we were luckier than I had any right to expect, it was going to miss the island and go out to sea.

Let it, I thought, and kept wading toward the island with my hand clamped around Jenoor's wrist. There were, after all, priorities, and I could always make a raft.

The rain hit then like a wall, and the wind slammed our backs, knocking us off our feet for a moment, while a rip current tried to take us past the island. But the water was shallow enough that once our feet found the bottom again, the rip couldn't sweep us away. In a minute or two, whipped by hard-blowing rain, we were clambering through and over the prop roots at the edge of the mangroves. We didn't stop until we were on solid land, scrambling as if something was after us.

Then we just lay on the ground for a minute, holding on to one another. The rain fell on us as if there weren't any treetops overhead, and we didn't get up until I realized I was starting to feel a lot more than just protective of Jenoor.

The wind hardly penetrated the forest, but it sure whipped the treetops. They were all bending southeast. The rain was incredible. When we got to camp, our cistern, the plastite chest, was already full and running over. All five of us crouched inside the shelter, no one speaking for a while. Finally Deneen said two words: "The boat?"

"Gone," I said. "We're lucky we didn't go with it."

She nodded and reached over, squeezing my hand.

After a few minutes though, we stopped feeling awed by the storm. Or maybe the word is intimidated. "No boat," Deneen said. "Maybe it *is* time to think about leaving this place. We could get pretty hungry trying to live on lizard."

"We could make a raft," I said. "But maybe this storm is just the first of a season of them." Again I turned to Piet. "What do you think?"

"We've been waiting ten weeks," he said, "almost eleven. And I've got a contact or two who might have a lead on a cutter."

I knew when he said it that he wasn't feeling optimistic.

"But let's give Klentis and Aven another five days, at least," he finished. "If they don't get here by then, we'll try our luck."

FOUR

The storm lasted about an hour, then stopped almost as suddenly as it began, leaving us with sunshine, and water dripping from the trees. If we were to stay another five days, we'd need to keep fishing, so I went out and cut poles to make a raft with. Then, it still being our day to fish, Jenoor and I went back out. There were no more thunderheads to the west, but we stayed within a hundred yards of the island anyway. The raft wasn't as quick as the skiff, and we had only push poles to move her with.

We were lucky we'd had four sets of fishing tackle.

If the fish had given us almost no action earlier that day, this time we had more than we needed within half an hour: a pair of sand moochers more than thirty-five inches each.

That evening, instead of talking about stealing a cutter, we talked about where we'd go in it. Piet told us about a planet we might try—one that dad had favored. He called it Grinder.

"It used to be a mining world," he said. His voice was quiet, as soft as the twilight that let us see his face but hid his expression. "There used to be deposits of very high quality heavy-metal ores in the crust. But after a few centuries they were mined out, and Grinder was too far from anywhere to make ordinary ores worth mining. By six hundred years ago the mines had shut down. Most of the people left then, but some stayed, hunting and farming, and gradually it turned into a hideout for smugglers."

"You think it would work as a rebel base then?" Deneen asked.

"It's as promising as any." He paused as if deciding whether or not to say what he said next. "Both your parents favored it, so it's the place they're most likely to go if they get off Evdash."

If they get off Evdash. It was the first time Piet had even implied an *if,* and the words ended the conversation. We sat together in the silent gloom for a minute or more longer before anyone moved. Then Tarel got up without saying anything and went out to his hammock. A moment later Deneen went to hers, and then Jenoor, my eyes following her. That left only Piet and me squatting in the shelter, and when I turned to him, his eyes were on me.

"Piet," I murmured, "I need to talk to you. Privately."

"Go ahead."

"I need more privacy than this," I said, and got up. Piet got up too, and followed me as I walked to the floater. It was parked outside the repellent field, so we got in and shut the door quickly to keep most of the bugs outside.

"Okay," he said when we'd both sat down, "let's have it."

"I want you to marry Jenoor and me. You're the senior member—the leader and magistrate in this community. If you say we're married, we are."

"You've talked to Jenoor about this?"

"No. I wanted to get your agreement first."

"How old is she?" he asked.

"You know how old she is. She's sixteen. And a half."

"What's the legal marriageable age for a girl on Evdash?"

"Eighteen. Seventeen with a parent's consent. What's the legal age in the Federation? The Empire?"

"Eighteen. Sixteen with a parent's consent."

"Or a guardian's?" I asked.

"Or a guardian's."

"So there's no natural law that says eighteen. Only legal arbitraries that some past legislatures passed."

"Not all laws make sense," he replied. "But they're the stuff of civilization. Unless a law is actually destructive and can't be changed, it ought to be obeyed. Decent laws, even if they seem a bit foolish, are what keep a society from coming apart."

His words surprised me. I hadn't expected them from someone who'd been a rebel most of his life. I could see what he meant though, even if I felt sure it didn't apply in this case. I sat there waiting for something to come to me that would convince him, but all I could think of was how I'd felt when Jenoor and I had gotten ashore that afternoon, safe from the sea, and I'd lain there with my arms around her. It had felt like my heart was in my throat, and I'd wanted to keep her safe forever. Among other things.

Piet was the one who broke the silence. "All right. So let's say I'm her guardian now; I guess I am. Give me a reason it's all right for you two to get married."

"Okay," I answered slowly. "First let's assume she's willing; that she wants to. Evdash is part of the Empire now, so legally, sixteen should be old enough, if we consider you her guardian and you give your permission. And next, we're outside the law, so we can't go to some courthouse and ask them to marry us. We couldn't if we were thirty, so age isn't the issue. Only whether she wants to and whether you're willing."

"Why not wait?" he said. "You're not the kind who lets his gonads rule his life."

There was no denying that sex was part of it, but only part, though I suppose it added a lot of the urgency to it. And like I said, I felt protective of her. But I also felt fond, and—I just wanted to be with her as her husband. I didn't really have the language to describe it.

It also occurred to me that now Piet's questions were more to make sure I'd thought it through myself. That probably meant he'd say yes, "Why not wait?" I said, answering his question. "Because in two weeks there's a good chance we'll all be dead. And we could have had two weeks together by then."

Piet turned the door handle. "Ask her," he said. "I hope she tells you yes. Five to one she does."

We shook hands on it and got out. When I'd closed the door, we walked together through near night the twenty yards to camp. I almost went over to her hammock right then to ask her, but I didn't. Hers was between Deneen's and Tarel's—they were only about six or eight yards apart—and I wanted my proposal to be private.

Sometime in the middle of the night it rained again. Not a downpour like we'd had that afternoon, but a pretty good rain that chased us all out of our hammocks and into the shelter. So of course we had to bunk down on the bare ground—not the most comfortable sleeping, especially with Bubba smelling like a wet canid. He read my thought and chuckled, a sound so human you'd have to hear it to believe it.

In the morning we could cut vegetation and pile it in the shelter for beds. The repellent fields would keep it from getting full of insects and other arthropods. But the hammocks, which were made of fine-mesh netting, were cooler and generally more comfortable than piles of weeds would be. So the best solution seemed to be to keep on sleeping in the hammocks and only take shelter as needed—hopefully not often. I couldn't see any practical way of slinging hammocks inside the shelter.

Maybe, I told myself, we'd been too quick to leave our hammocks. We didn't wear much to sleep in anyway, and as long as the rain wasn't too cold . . . And the hammocks were made of "Skin-Soft" synthetic, so they didn't soak up water.

Which brought to my mind the matter of privacy if Jenoor agreed to marry me. We had a second repellent field, so we could have our hammocks away from the others, but they were too small and unstable for double occupancy. And as for separate shelter if needed . . . This definitely seemed to be the rainy season. The best possibility seemed to be the floater, if we moved it a little farther away. The floater would get around the problem of hammock stability, too. At the very beginning, Piet had said no one would sleep in the floater because everyone couldn't, not comfortably, and he wasn't going to give anyone, including himself, special privileges. Besides, hammocks were cooler.

But Jenoor and I would be married. If she said yes. And he'd treat that as a different situation, I was sure.

I went back to sleep feeling pretty cheerful, considering our long-range prospects.

The next morning had a good feel to it. It even smelled good—not dusty any longer, but fresh—and I was glad the rainy season had arrived. We all had a hand-foot workout and then Deneen and Tarel went fishing. Piet sat on a log stool—we'd sawed five blocks from a log to use for seats—and began working on a new carving. He was the best of us all at turning a piece of wood into something artistic. It would have been my day to keep the still supplied with salt water, except that now we had rainwater—all of it we needed.

It was Jenoor's day to collect jonga fruits, beat them thoroughly with a hammer, and put them to soak, to soften for tomorrow's breakfast. The way to pick jonga fruits is to take a pole with a heavy survival knife lashed to it and find some you can reach from the ground or from some branch you could climb on. Then, with the pole and knife, you saw or hack at their tough stems till they drop off. She had picked up the pole and her old plaited packsack and was leaving camp when I fell in beside her.

Bubba had fallen in on her other side. *Not all right, Bubba,* I thought to him. He knew what I had in mind. *This isn't going to be easy for me. If you have to eavesdrop, do it from somewhere out of sight, okay?*

He flashed me a quick grin and veered off casually to explore some interesting smell. As if there was any spot or critter on Lizard Island that he hadn't examined a dozen times already.

"Okay if I walk along with you?" I asked Jenoor.

She smiled sideways at me. "Sure. Glad to have you."

"I've got something in particular I want to talk to you about."

"All right." She looked interested, and something more. I really didn't know what to say next, or rather, how to say it. *Will you marry me* would make sense of course, but it seemed kind of abrupt and inelegant.

"What I want to say is—it's a question." I stepped in front of her. "Jenoor, will you marry me?"

So much for elegance.

. She looked at me seriously, not turning her eyes down shyly or anything like that. "Of course I will, Larn. I've been hoping you'd ask one day. I can't imagine marrying anyone else; I haven't since the first week Tarel and I came to live with your family."

"You mean it!" I said. It seemed a wonder. "You really mean it!" I stepped back from her and looked around for something to sit on; my knees felt a little weak. But there wasn't anything handy.

"Who'll marry us?" she asked.

"I asked Piet if he would, last night when he and I went to the floater. He's the one we look up to here—sort of the magistrate of Lizard Island. He questioned me about it pretty closely, and then he said he would, right here on the island, if you agreed. He even said he hoped you'd say yes. And I've already solved the problem of privacy."

It suddenly occurred to me I was talking too much, too fast, and I stopped.

She answered slowly. "Of course. The extra repellent field and the floater. Piet would let us use the floater, under the circumstances."

I nodded.

"When would you like the wedding?" she asked.

"How about—this evening? Just before supper."

She nodded thoughtfully. "That sounds good." Then she leaned the pole against a tree beside her. "Is there . . ." This time it was her turn to be a little embarrassed. "Is there something we should do now to seal the agreement?"

I stared. She was so darned pretty. I put out my

hands. She took them and we stepped together and kissed, long but gently. Then she stepped back.

"I'm going to like being married to you," she said. "And I want it to last a very long time. Until . . . As long as circumstances allow. But now I want you to go back to camp, and I'll go cut some jongas. It's best if we don't spend all day together."

"Right," I said, and started back to camp. She'd handled the whole scene as if she was twenty-five years old, I told myself. I'd known she was mature for her age, but she'd been incredible.

Suddenly I flipped out and did a run of three hand-springs right there in the forest.

Back at the shelter I told Piet what Jenoor's answer had been. He accepted it matter-of-factly and didn't even smile. To my surprise, that bothered me. It was as if I wanted him to pump my hand and congratulate me or something. Then it occurred to me that I'd once heard mom mention something to dad about someone she called "Gwennith"—as if this Gwennith had been married to Piet, or anyway been someone special to him. And as if something had happened. But I'd never heard anything more. In the rebel life he'd led, with the political police always looking for him . . . She might have been killed or imprisoned, or they might have had to separate and never found one another again. I was sure Piet would have been a heck of a good husband. He had all the qualities.

The thought bothered me for a while. Then, as if he'd read my mind, Piet put down his whittling and, smiling, reached out a hand to me. "Congratulations," he said as we shook. "You've got excellent taste in women. And she's got excellent taste in men. I hope you have lots of years together."

A woman. That's what she was, a sixteen-year-old woman. And that "lots of years" would begin today. Tonight. If there was anything I wanted, it was to make her happy. It would help that my parents had been the kind of role models they'd been: considerate, sharing, affectionate, willing to talk things out and to let each other be themselves.

I felt confident, both for the long run and about tonight. In lower middle school I'd heard a couple of guys describe their dads telling them the facts of life. It had amounted to a short biology lecture. But when dad had told me the facts of life, he'd included discussion of rights, comparative emotions, courtesy and consideration, tenderness, and two-way communication, so I couldn't imagine things working out any other way than fine. Maybe—maybe Jenoor and I would even settle down on some world and spend our whole lives there, maybe operating a training camp in hand-foot art.

I spent the next hour building daydreams on that theme, until Deneen and Tarel got back with a string of fish. The fork-tailed streakers had been feeding. They were small, but about the tastiest species we ever caught there. Even Bubba preferred them.

A little later Jenoor came back too. She'd not only cut jongas, she'd taken the time and trouble to pick about three cups of tiny pink thrimberries—the closest thing to delicious that Lizard Island had to offer. Thrimberries were so small and so sparse, and the bushes so prickly, that none of us had tried to pick any quantity of them before. It hadn't seemed worth the trouble. When she arrived, we stood together in front of the others and announced our engagement—the shortest engagement I'd ever heard of.

It was Deneen who did the whooping—old cool-headed Deneen, who'd always seemed to take everything calmly. She whooped and squealed and jumped around like an enthused eight-year-old, and kissed us both while Tarel stood there watching without saying anything. Then she said she was going to *bake* the fish they'd brought back—that we'd just have to put up with heat damage to vitamins and amino acids for the sake of festivity. And anyway the thrimberries would make up for the vitamin loss.

It was Piet's and my turn to clean the fish, while Jenoor and Tarel took clubs and started hammering the jongas on a flat place I'd cut once on a large log.

Deneen went to the debris of dead branches and twigs where I'd cut the three trees that first day, and brought back pieces that were dry enough to burn. Then she dug in her pack and took out her tinder box and spark wheel. We'd only had fire once or twice before on Lizard Island; fire made smoke and light, which theoretically might be seen if anyone was flying past. Besides which, until yesterday's rain, the island had been dry and dangerously flammable. But this day was special, and before long she'd built a small fire, piled tall.

When Piet and I had the fish cleaned, he got up and moved the floater off between the trees to a place some hundred and fifty feet from camp.

Finally the fish, wrapped in large wet leaves, were buried beneath coals. Then Piet looked at Jenoor and me. "Are you ready?" he asked.

I nodded, my face sober, my heart starting to thud. I heard Jenoor say "yes" in a small voice.

"All right," Piet said, and stood up. "We'll do this without rehearsing. The two of you stand in front of me."

We did.

"Tarel, you stand beside Larn. And Deneen beside Jenoor." He watched while we lined up. Then he looked us over and nodded.

"Good," he said. "Start of wedding. Larn, Jenoor, a marriage is a lifetime commitment—a commitment to love and help and care for each other. It is a two-way arrangement that becomes unethical if it is allowed to get lopsided—if it becomes too much take on one side and too much give on the other.

"Marriage is also a commitment to trust, and to be worthy of trust.

"Larn, you must know what a marriage should be; you've seen how your parents treat each other. Jenoor, I don't know your parents, but I've seen the kind of people you and your brother are. I'm confident that you too know what a marriage should be. A marriage resembles any close friendship, but in addition it has special responsibilities, and it should have special love.

"Now. Larn, bearing all this in mind, do you promise to be a good husband to Jenoor forever?"

My throat felt as if a whole jonga was stuck in it. I could hardly believe how normally the words came out when I said, "Yes, I do."

"And Jenoor, bearing all this in mind, do you promise to be a good wife to Larn forever?"

My eyes moved to her as she answered. "Yes, I do."

Piet nodded as if in approval. "Then I pronounce you man and wife." His serious expression changed; he grinned. "You may kiss each other."

We did. Softly and not too long. When we stepped apart, I looked at Tarel. He looked more serious than ever. And Deneen? She was grinning a foot wide, even though her eyes were watery.

Then Piet reached into his pocket and handed us what he'd spent much of the day making: Two pairs of hearts, perfectly carved, the hearts in each pair joined at the edge. And on them, engraved with a straightened, filed-down fishhook point, were our names. He was still grinning at us as we made sincerely appreciative noises.

We wrapped our gifts together in an old undershirt, and while Jenoor stashed them in a corner of the shelter, I turned to Tarel again. I couldn't tell what he was thinking.

"Tarel," I said, holding out my hand, "I want you to know I'll be the best husband to Jenoor that I know how to be, and that I'm glad to have you as my brother-in-law."

He nodded without smiling. "I know you will. And I'm glad to have you as my brother-in-law. You're the best brother-in-law I can imagine."

I think I must have blushed; no one mentioned it, but that's how it felt. He'd surprised me, and I felt like he must have gotten me mixed up with someone else. I mean, I generally think I'm pretty good, but the best brother-in-law he could imagine? That was more than I was ready for. I didn't know what to say back, so I gave his hand a couple of extra shakes and hoped someone would say something to get me off the hook.

It was Bubba who did. Tail waving slowly, he'd been standing behind Piet watching, as if making sure everything was done right. "I think you guys make good family," he said to me now. "When Lady and pups find us, I tell pups one of them should adopt you."

Deneen applauded that, and Piet and Tarel joined her. Then, with a stick, Deneen dug the fish out of the coals and we ate. It had started to get dark when we finished, so I went and hung Jenoor's and my hammocks on the other side of the floater, then set up the second repellent field. Afterward the five of us kept the fire going for a while and sat around it, talking without saying much. I was feeling a little nervous; nothing serious.

Finally Deneen stood up and stretched. "I don't know about anyone else," she said, "but I'm going to bed."

"Sounds like a good idea," said Piet. He too got up, and with him Tarel.

"Yeah," I said, and standing, turned to Jenoor. "Time to go, while it's still light enough to find our way."

I helped her up, her hand small but strong in mine. Actually, it wasn't going to be a really dark night. Donia, the major moon, was close to full, and the forest roof was less than solid. Hand in hand we walked toward the floater. The lump did not return to my throat. This evening the world felt right to me, even in a sector ruled by the Empire.

FIVE

It wasn't one of Evdash's traditional ten-day newlyweds' trips to Paradise Valley and Sky Falls, or Lake Indigo, Cloud Island, and Ocean City—anything like that. We had four days on Lizard Island, with duties as usual, such as they were. But they were the happiest four days of a life that had already been happier than most. I couldn't believe how lucky I was.

Lucky in spite of daily rainstorms, one of them as violent as the one that almost killed Jenoor and me. Whoever was fishing kept part of their attention on the weather. And where before everything had been really dry, now everything was dank. The fresh smell of the first days with rain changed to mold. Even our clothes began to smell of mildew.

No one was really surprised that our parents hadn't shown. A cutter flying in the atmosphere would be detected in minutes, maybe seconds, and one in Evdashian space probably almost as quickly. So if they tried moving around in the cutter, the odds were they'd be picked up or blown up in a hurry.

To casual eyeball observation, they might go unnoticed for a while in heavy traffic, especially if there was a mixture of cargo carriers and public transport—units much bigger than personal and family-size floaters. But the police would notice fast. Even floater traffic had to be way down; the radio talked about tough travel restrictions and a limited curfew. And judging from the newscasts and the general Glondis way of doing things, they wouldn't be relaxed soon.

Piet talked with us about the prospects of getting our hands on a cutter. The resistance movement in the old Federation had long predicted a Glondis takeover of the colonies, of which Evdash was one of the most prosperous. Of course, Evdash had had its own branch of the Party—a very minor party here then—and the resistance had infiltrated both the Party and the Evdashian military, just to keep track of what was going on.

Piet had actually been a regional chairman of the Glondis Party on Evdash! Until he'd made a slip that was sure to get him uncovered before long. So he'd arranged an "accident," and disappeared.

Some of that was new to us, especially the part about Piet. The point was that he had resistance contacts, or he had had, in the Party, the Evdashian military, and the public at large. But he didn't know who was still alive and in place, or whether any of them was in a position to help.

On the fifth night after the wedding, we all got up at first dawnlight. After a breakfast of jongas and raw fish, we loaded everything we wanted to take with us into the floater. There wasn't very much. By the time we lifted through the forest roof, the sun sat red and swollen on the watery horizon. The treetops were spotted with flowers now—white, pink, yellow, violet—brought out by the rains. Piet stopped for a minute while we took in the view. Then he punched in a navigation sequence that would take us to a point near Delta City, a seaport. There he'd slip us into the general traffic corridors. If nothing went wrong, we'd head up the Jarf Valley from there, for Jarfoss, the town where Evdash's main naval station was located. He hoped to contact friends there, and get enough information to plan with.

"Who knows," he said. "Maybe we'll even get a line on Klentis and Aven there." I didn't allow my hopes to build, but it did make me feel a little better.

It seemed to me, when I let myself look at the situation, that we had almost no prospects of getting a space cutter. But then, our chances had looked even bleaker when Deneen and I had been on Fanglith. Now we had two and a half years' additional experience. The Fanglith experience was worth about ten years all by itself, not in data so much as in getting grooved in on operating in dangerous situations without much information. Doing the right thing—or *a* right thing—at the right time; or at least not doing something fatally wrong.

To cut down the risk of detection, Piet ran just above the water the whole 423 miles to the coast. There he joined the sparse early morning traffic—mostly cargo carriers but with a mixture of public transports and private vehicles. We were a pretty scruffy bunch. Piet and I had beards, something rare on Evdash, and Tarel's was starting to show too. The only clothes we had, dirty and mildewed, hadn't been properly washed since we'd put them on more than fourteen weeks earlier. To prepare ourselves for civilization, we'd used the hairbrushes Deneen and Jenoor had carried when we'd left home, but that was it.

There weren't as many police floaters in traffic as I'd expected to see though, and none paid any attention to us.

Finally, near the naval station, Piet turned into an approach pattern to an outlying officers' housing area, set in a matrix of dark forest and light green meadows, of recreation grounds and parking lots and shopping centers, of streets lined with houses whose roofs were red and green and cobalt, of emerald yards with pale blue swimming pools.

It was very nice. I wondered what Imperial troops thought of it—troops from the paved and crowded highrise population centers of the central worlds. Presumably the people stationed here were still Evdashians.

Piet had said the top command positions, with their personal staffs, would be filled by Imperials now, and there'd probably be a garrison of Imperial Marines here for intimidation purposes. But the principal forces, such as they were, would be Evdashian—the same people as before, acting under new commands and policies. There'd have been some changes, of course. Officers thought of as especially hard-nosed Evdashian patriots would have been shot or imprisoned as examples. Their replacements would be people who seemed willing to carry out Imperial intentions. And a few would be eager to prove how loyal they were to the Empire.

Of course, some of them—people who seemed to just be trying to adjust and get along—would actually be resistance people, or potential resistance people. And so would some of the apparent turncoats who were singing the Imperial song and giving the Imperial salute. That's where our hopes lay.

Our first contact was going to be critical. We had to find a friendly who could help us clean up and get civilized looking, because the way we looked now, we were ripe for stopping and questioning. If we were stopped, we'd say we were just getting back from a hiking vacation, but that would hardly be convincing. We had no useful identification, and at least fourteen weeks' wild growth of hair to explain.

The streets here were grass, neatly trimmed. Piet dropped down low over one of them, then skimmed along as if he knew exactly where he was going. After a few hundred feet he turned smoothly, pulled into an attached garage as if he parked there every day, and put us down on the concrete, leaving the floater-field generator on. I didn't know whether he'd picked this place just because the garage door was open, or whether he knew the people who lived here.

"Larn," he said, "take the controls. If anything happens to me, you're in command."

"Right," I said.

He got out and I moved into the pilot's seat. Looking like something washed up on the beach, he walked casually to the connecting door, but before he could knock, it opened. Behind it was a woman in a summer house suit, with a blast pistol in her hands.

For just a moment she stared at Piet, then without saying a word, lowered the gun. He thumbed toward us. She shook her head and murmured something too quietly for us to hear, then reached to one side and the garage door closed behind us. If anything went wrong now, we couldn't make a quick getaway, but that didn't seem to bother Piet. She disappeared, closing the door behind her, and Piet stepped back over to the floater.

"She has company," he said softly.

"What's she going to do?" I asked.

"Knowing Dansee, she'll think of something."

The situation felt about as uncomfortable as it could get. Knowing almost nothing about what was happening inside, I hadn't the foggiest idea what to do, so I just sat there while Piet stood next to the floater door. From beside me, I could feel Jenoor's hand on my forearm, resting lightly, not gripping. Looking behind me I saw Tarel, his hands fisted. Beside him, Deneen watched intently the door the woman had closed behind her. Bubba probably knew what was going on, but whispering wasn't one of his abilities.

Nothing happened for the slowest several minutes on record. Then we heard voices outside the garage door—women talking and laughing. It sounded as if they'd just come out of the house. One of them seemed to stay in place while two others became more distant. Then the talking stopped, and we heard a house door close. A minute later the woman appeared in the door again, grinning this time and without her blaster.

"Get in here," she said, not trying to be quiet now, and held the door for us. Piet went first, the rest of us trooping after. As we passed, she looked us over, then closed the door behind us. She came across as a nice-looking middle-aged lady who still did something or other athletic. She herded us down a hall and into a kitchen, where we stopped. "Piet," she said, "I'd hug you if you looked a little more sanitary." She indicated the living room with a head motion. "I'm reasonably sure my visitors didn't suspect anything. They were sitting with their backs to the window; I was the only one who saw you float in."

"What did you tell them?"

She chuckled. "That Jom had told me not to leave the garage door open again. Which was true, as far as it went."

"How did you explain the blaster?"

"They never saw it. It's my kitchen gun. Who are your young friends? Or can't you tell me?"

He hesitated a second. "Why not? Dansee Jomber, this is Mr. and Mrs. Larn kel Deroop—Larn and Jenoor. These are Deneen kel Deroop, and Tarel Sentner. And Bubba. Bubba's a kel Deroop too. Those are their real names incidentally."

She was studying Bubba. "Is Bubba an espwolf?"

"Right."

"Well, that's got to be a big plus-point." She sized us all up. "I can see what you need first, unless you're famished. There's a shower in the basement and a complete cleaning facility upstairs. Just choose up who uses what. When you're done I'll have something edible for you and start cutting hair.

"Best you hustle now. I'm not expecting anyone else till Jom comes home about half past fifteen, but then, I wasn't expecting my earlier guests either.

"Where are your other clothes?"

"M'dam," said Piet, "there are no other clothes. These are it."

"Mmh! All right, get at it. Throw what you've got on into the hall. I'll dig up something temporary and put your old things in the cleaning drum as soon as I have a chance."

Piet and Tarel went into the main-floor bath, while Deneen went with Jenoor and I into the basement guest apartment. I offered Deneen first chance at the bathroom there, and minutes later Dansee Jomber came down with clothing.

"These'll do for now," she said, putting them on the couch. "We'll worry about fit later." Then she turned and went back upstairs. Deneen didn't take more than six or eight minutes in the shower, and when she was done she left, while Jenoor and I got ready and showered. We scrubbed each other pink and then, wishing we had more time, put on the clean clothes and followed the others upstairs.

By that time Deneen was giving Bubba a cleaning.

An hour later we'd been fed and herded back to the basement—a safety measure in case any unexpected visitors came by. We took all our camping stuff with us from the floater. In the basement we got barbered, and by that time our own clothes were clean and we put them back on. They looked surprisingly presentable now for field clothes. Dansee had used clippers on Piet's and my faces when she'd cut our hair, and Piet and I, and Tarel too, debearded with Jom Jomber's facial kit. After that we killed time reading and napping until, late that afternoon, we heard a pair of heavy male feet start down the stairs.

Piet and Jom Jomber didn't discuss very much in front of us. Instead, after a few minutes they left in the Jombers' floater, saying they weren't sure when they'd be back. I got the idea that they didn't want us to know anything we didn't need to—the old "need-to-know principle"—in case we got arrested. What you don't know, no one can get out of you.

After they'd left, Dansee Jomber baked sweetcrisps and made hot meloren, and asked us about our weeks on the island.

We were so used to sleeping half the clock around that we went to bed well before midnight. Jenoor and I were put in the Jombers' spare bedroom, while Tarel and Deneen slept in the basement on a bed and a couch. Bubba was happy with a pallet on the floor.

It was sheer luxury to be clean and comfortable and alone together. I'm glad I didn't know what would happen before daylight.

According to the dresser clock, we'd slept about three hours when Piet woke us. He tossed two Evdashian Marine uniforms on the foot of the bed and told us to get dressed fast. Now was our chance, he said, and if we missed it, we might not get another.

If they'd been Imperial Marine uniforms, what happened probably wouldn't have. But those weren't available—at least not on short notice.

Mine had a holstered blast pistol and stunner on the belt. So did Piet's and Tarel's. Piet also carried a blast rifle and wore a senior sergeant's insignia. Jenoor and

Deneen, besides belt weapons, carried attaché cases attached to chains around their necks. It was as if we were their escorts.

There was even a guard canid control collar and leash for Bubba, barely big enough to fit around his wolfy neck.

In ten minutes we were ready. No one told us anything—no one even talked except for a few brief, low exchanges between Piet and Jom—till we left in Piet's floater. As Piet piloted, he briefed us, and brief was the word. We'd be meeting a guy, an Evdashian marine noncom who'd be driving a marine floater. He was a courier with a pass authorizing him to enter the scout park—the small landing field where naval scouts were parked when not on station. This guy knew which craft were ready to fly.

What he would try to do was *drive* into the scout pool, something his pass didn't authorize. He'd claim to have high-security packages to put aboard one of the scouts.

Our man was waiting for us in the employee parking lot at the local utilities central, a civilian agency. Piet's floater didn't emit the proper identification signal and would have been shot out of the air if we'd tried to fly it into the air space of a military installation. Piet parked a hundred feet from the marine vehicle, got out, then stood pretending to talk to us through the rear window. That was the signal. A few seconds later the marine floater drifted over, stopped, and we got in.

In the back of the marine floater was a box with a handle at each corner. The marine told Tarel and me to take out our blast pistols and hold them conspicuously in our laps; that was how courier escorts would carry them. Gate guards would check us, and we were to make and keep eye contact with them while they looked us over; it would be expected of us.

At the field we were stopped at two security gates. At each, a marine guard came over to the floater while two others stood nearby with blast rifles ready, pointed in our direction, guard canids at heel. After questioning our driver briefly and examining his pass, the guard looked into the floater, taking in our uniforms and weapons. At each gate the guard's hand lamp paused on Jenoor and Deneen. In the Evdashian Marines, women were almost solely clerical personnel. And besides, both Deneen and Jenoor looked awfully young.

Their attaché cases may have helped, but I believe it was Bubba who cleared us. At each gate, after the guard's lamp beam dipped to examine him, the guy waved us through. Our having an apparent guard canid made us real to them.

Finally we were in the scout pool, moving down a broad service lane a foot or so above the pavement. Our driver stopped about twenty-five yards from the nearest scout, a forty-five-foot patrol scout. The area was lit more than I liked, by lights on tall poles around the perimeter of the field.

"That's it," the sergeant said, jerking a thumb in the direction of the scout. "Piet, get out with the canid and stand about ten yards in the other direction. Keep looking around, but act bored. And light up a weed; it'll make things look relaxed."

"I don't smoke."

"Have one of mine. Here's my lighter." He turned to Jenoor and Deneen. "You two walk with me. And you two," he added to Tarel and me, "follow us with your sidearms in your hands, looking as if you're guarding us. But not as if you're worried. Could be no one's actually watching us, but we need to look as if what we're doing is entirely according to regulations. Nothing sneaky is going on, and nothing tense—nothing worth paying attention to. Got it?"

Tarel and I answered yes in unison, and we started out. At the scout, our marine put an ID plate in the slot and the door opened. We got aboard. The marine took a hand lamp off his belt and, without turning it on, put it on the deck.

"Don't turn on any ship's lights, not even inside," he said. "That *would* draw attention." He looked at Tarel and me. "And I don't want any needless activity out here either, for the same reason, so you two stay aboard." He turned to Jenoor and Deneen. "Come on."

With no more than that, he stepped down the ramp onto the pavement again, the girls close behind. My guts tightened; something about this didn't feel right. I told myself it was being separated from Jenoor and Deneen in a situation like this, and I watched them cross the pavement to the floater. There the sergeant apparently said something to Piet, because Piet, with Bubba beside him, walked over to them with his blaster still at the ready.

The marine got into the floater, then backed out, pulling the box I'd noticed. Again I could hear his voice, quiet but fast. He took the handles at one end and the girls took the handles at the other, and they started toward the scout.

Beside me, Bubba growled. Then a floodlight beam speared through the night to bathe them in brightness. From across the field a loud-hailer called for them to stop. They did, for just a moment, then started for the scout, still carrying the box.

The guard tower didn't use its blasters. Maybe they thought the package was contraband and didn't want to destroy it. Instead, projectile weapons ruptured the silent night with bitter racket. Bullets struck the side of the scout, and both Tarel and I ducked back out of the open door. Scant seconds later, Deneen and Bubba came dragging the box.

"Close the door!" she yelled as they came through it. "Close it now!"

"No!" I cried. "The others!"

She screamed in my face. "The others are shot! Close the door!"

Instead I dove for it, blast pistol in hand, and started down the ramp. Then strong hands grabbed the back of my jumpsuit. I twisted. It was Tarel holding me, and I yelled at him. The heel of his hand slammed me in the forehead. Lights flashed in the space behind my eyes, and for a moment there was only blackness. I was vaguely aware that someone, Tarel, was dragging me back into the scout, and that the projectile weapons were firing again. Inside, Deneen was sobbing and cursing—I'd never heard her do either before—and I opened my eyes. She had the hand lamp, and seemed to be hunting for the door controls. I got back up and lunged clumsily for the door, but Tarel slugged me again, on the back of the neck this time.

When my eyes opened, the door had been closed and the power unit activated. A cabin light was on. Deneen was at the controls and Tarel was standing over me. I just stared. She must have found the force shield controls, something our family cutter hadn't had, because through the windows I could see flashes as blaster bolts dissipated their energies in flickering sheets around us.

The basic controls operated like those on our family cutter. Abruptly we rose, climbing in mass-proximity mode, wrapped by the drive field in a mini-space of our own that divorced us from any inertia relative to real space. In seconds, we were beyond blaster range.

Tarel looked at me with the strangest expression I'd ever seen on a person. "They're dead, Larn," he said. "They're dead. There was nothing you could do for them. They're all dead."

Then his face crumpled like plastic melting in a fire, and silently he started to cry. All I could do was stare, while my guts withered inside me.

SIX

Jenoor:

When the shooting began, the sergeant went down at once. I turned and saw Piet stumble to his knees, so I dropped my corner of the box to try to help him. I didn't take more than a step, though, when I felt a bullet smash into my foot, and I fell forward onto the pavement. I scrambled the last eight or ten feet to him on my hands and knees, I'm not sure why. Maybe I thought I still could help him somehow, maybe drag him to the scout.

But by the time I reached him, he was lying on his back. I'm pretty sure that he'd been hit some more; he'd been shot almost in two at the waist. All I could do was lie there, half on top of him. I think I was crying then. The automatic projectile weapons were still making a terrible racket across the field, their bullets smacking and whining all around. It seemed impossible that I was still alive, and I expected to be killed any moment. That went on for a long time—maybe as long as a minute. The bullets only stopped when the blaster bolts started sizzling.

Scared as I was, somehow I raised my head enough to look toward the scout. The ramp was in, the door was closed, and I could see that the cabin was lit. Someone had activated the force shield, because the energy of the blaster bolts was flickering around it like some weird aurora. It seemed to me that they might actually get away—whoever had made it to the scout— and I felt jubilant. As I watched, it lifted, then almost leaped upward, the blaster fire following it, still sheathing it in flickering light until it passed out of sight half a minute later, too high to see anymore.

Then I was filled by a sense of abandonment more terrible than anything I'd ever imagined.

But that lasted only seconds, replaced by a sense of—I guess resignation is the best word for it. I closed my eyes and laid my head down on Piet's shoulder. I realized that my hands were in a pool of what had to be his blood, and also that my foot didn't hurt. There was a feeling there, but it wasn't what you'd call pain yet. I knew there'd be enough of that when the shock wore off. I also knew that someone would come out pretty soon and I'd be arrested. And executed sooner or later.

After another minute I saw a small utility floater coming out low, and I laid my head down again and closed my eyes. I heard it settle right beside me, and a man spoke in Evdashian. "I saw her move," he said. "We'll put her in on bottom and the other two on top of her."

Then I felt two men grab me by the knees and under the arms and load me into the open back of the floater.

"If we're caught . . ." I heard the second one say.

"We won't be. From there they don't even know how many are down out here. She was lying on top of the big guy."

Then I heard them grunt, and a moment later a heavy dead weight was put down on top of me. "Sorry," the first voice said. After another moment there was a third body. Next I heard a light thump, and opened my eyes enough to see Piet's rifle lying on the deck. The two marines got in the front and drove off, seeming to keep within a few feet of the pavement.

"Suppose someone comes out and looks?" the second voice asked.

"Then we unload the girl with the other two, like it was what we had in mind all along. But they won't. We'll unload the two dead ones and I'll get back in as if that's all, and take her away. You stay there."

The floater slowed and lowered to the pavement, and the two men came quickly around and removed first one body, then the other. I could hear another voice coming toward the vehicle.

"Are they dead?"

"They seem to be, sir. I'll take the truck over and clean out the back before the blood dries."

"All right," the new voice said, "do it. But don't take all night." It sounded as if it was right by the tailgate. He almost had to have seen me and pretended not to.

A moment later the floater lifted and moved away. I opened my eyes again; the blast rifle was gone. A minute later the truck set down. I opened my eyes and saw that we were beside a large shed. I heard the marine move away. In another minute he was back and lowered the tailgate. Under one arm he carried a dark bundle—a small plastic tarp; in the other hand was a broom. He saw that my eyes were open.

"I'm going to hide you," he told me. "In a waste bin.

You'll have to tough it out the best you can until some-body comes to get you. It'll be a few hours."

He flopped the half-unfolded tarp next to me on the truck bed, then rolled me onto it with an apology, wrapped me in it, and with a grunt got me over his shoulder. He wasn't big, but he was pretty strong. Inside the tarp I couldn't see a thing. He carried me a dozen steps, then I heard a lid raise on squeaky hinges. I felt myself roll off his shoulder, and landed on a jumble of what had to be lignoplastic containers—boxes and bottles. The lid lowered again, and I wondered if I'd get enough air in there. I decided I probably would; it wouldn't be airtight. If it seemed like I was going to suffocate, I'd wiggle loose and prop the lid up a little with something. Meanwhile I'd stay the way I was.

The marine had risked his life to save me; both of them had. And maybe their officer too. And I'd thought the Evdashians were docile because they'd given up their world without fighting! I imagined an empire sprin-kled with people like them, learning better and better how to undercut their masters.

Then I imagined him hosing the truck bed and scrub-bing it with the broom, the blood of Piet and the marine sergeant—and maybe some of mine—mixing with the water to flow into a sump or something. Then he'd drive back as if everything was normal.

My foot was beginning to hurt. The shock was start-ing to wear off.

I dozed anyway, drifting in and out of sleep without knowing for how long, a sleep mixed with pain and feverish dreams. But through it all I kept thinking: *I must not groan. I must not groan. Someone might hear.* And that if I was discovered, the two marines who'd saved me would be executed.

I didn't come wide awake until I felt the bin being lifted. A mechanism screeched, jerked, and I felt my-self being tilted. Then I was sliding, and fell into what had to be trash. Pain stabbed my foot like a knife, and I tasted blood where I bit my lip to keep from screaming. Most of the contents of the waste bin seemed to land on top of me, and I passed out.

The next thing I knew the trash was shifting again. Not very much; it was as if the trash truck had tilted, its load sliding. Then the movement stopped, and faintly, through the tarp and trash, I could hear a man talking.

"Motor pool trash, eh? You better not have anything in there that'll damage the chopper again."

"Take it easy, Frelky," another voice said. "We just haul it, we don't pick through it. If someone dumps an old electric motor in a bin and it busts up your chopper, that's no fault of ours."

Next I heard the truck's beeper as it rose and swung away. A minute later I felt someone digging the trash out around me. Two arms wrapped around me as if I were a bundle and pulled me free, then dragged me a little way, which hurt my foot. I felt my feet drag over what seemed to be a door sill, then I was laid out on a flat surface and rolled over twice. I could see.

I was on the floor of a small, unlit office shack. A heavy, older marine corporal in fatigues knelt beside me. On the other side a voice spoke, and dimly I could see a sergeant standing there in what seemed to be early dawn.

"Check her pulse," he said. "See if she's still alive."

"She's alive. She's looking at me right now."

"Where are you hit?"

I realized he was speaking to me. "In the right foot," I said. My voice was so weak, I was surprised he could understand me.

"You've got blood all over the front of you."

"It's Uncle Piet's," I told him.

He didn't say anything for a few seconds, then: "Wrap her up again."

While the corporal in charge of the trash processor began to roll me up in the tarp, the sergeant added, "I'm taking you to a safe house. There'll be somebody there who'll take care of you."

I felt them pick me up together and carry me. They put me in what seemed to be the luggage space of a small floater—a staff car or something. A minute later I felt it take off, and I passed out again.

SEVEN

Larn:

While Tarel stood weeping above me, my mind cleared. Four of us were still alive; I include Bubba in my count of people. If we could just stay that way, someday I could find out who did the shooting back there . . .

Tarel turned and stumbled toward the washroom, and I got up. I'd have liked to help him—his hard hands had saved me from myself twice in maybe a minute— but what he needed was a little time alone.

Just aft of the exit door was the gunnery control station; I recognized it from holodramas I'd seen. But by the time I could hope to figure it out and learn to use it, we'd be dead or possibly "safe" in FTL mode. Once in FTL I'd have plenty of time to work with it. So I walked over to Deneen and sat down in the copilot's seat.

From the side, her jaw looked set and her eyes intent. There was no sign that she knew I'd come over, though I'm sure she did. I looked the instrument panel over; most of it, though not all, was familiar from the cutters dad had owned. Neither Deneen nor I should have any trouble flying it, and she was doing fine.

She'd have to take us out the better part of a million miles before shifting to FTL mode; otherwise, the stresses would tear the ship apart.

In spite of everything, dying wasn't something I wanted to do for a while, and neither did Deneen, I was sure.

52

Neither had Piet a few minutes ago, nor Jenoor. Nor the marine sergeant who'd laid his life on the line to help us get away, and lost it.

I told myself I wouldn't waste the chance they'd given us.

The array of stars I could see through the wraparound for'rd window didn't mean much to me, so I turned my eyes to the instrument display. We were already 6,3 miles out; the right-hand digits were a blur, and even the tens were changing too fast to read. At the hundreds position, a 4 replaced the 3 almost at once, followed quickly by a 5, then a 6. Pretty soon, I told myself, the hundreds would be changing too fast to read, too. Short seconds later we turned over 8,000.

I wondered if it was possible we might get away unattacked. There had to be patrol craft on picket around Evdash, between the hard radiation belts, probably piloted by some of the more reliable people the Imperials could identify, or maybe by Imperials themselves. They were sure to have been warned by now that we were outbound fugitives. There were monitor screens above the window that ought to show any approaching hostiles, if I could figure out how to turn them on. Without them, we couldn't take evasive action.

Not that Deneen or I was anything approaching a fighter pilot, but we ought to be able to do something. It might make the difference between getting away and getting blown out of the sky. Without the monitor screens on, all she could do was keep accelerating at maximum for mass-proximity mode, the computer holding us on the curving course that gave us the greatest momentary distance from Evdash.

Above the more familiar console section was a sort of shelf with key rows that probably controlled things such as the monitor screen, but they were marked only by initials or symbols. *Let's see,* I thought, *if I can call up a keyboard diagram on the computer*.

But first I reached for something I did recognize— the radio switch—and turned it on. Through the weird distortion effect of an accelerating mass-proximity drive, a demanding voice spoke from it, ordering:

". . . at once, we will destroy you! Fugitive scout! If you do not . . ."

Deneen's hand reached up and cuffed the switch on her side, overriding mine and turning it off. She didn't even glance over at me. "I'm flying this," she said tightly.

"Right." I could see her point: she didn't need the distraction. We both knew what our situation was, and all we could do was try to run through it. Letting threats pour into our ears wouldn't help, and she could do anything at the control console that she thought needed done.

The accent had been Evdashian, though. That had been apparent, even through the distortion. And despite the threatening words, that was at least a little bit encouraging. The pilot might not be as zealous to kill or capture us.

I looked around for Bubba and didn't see him. Had he run back outside for some strange reason before Deneen got the door closed? It didn't seem possible; he was one of the most rational people ever born. But it was out of character for him to go hide somewhere. Then I realized—he was with Tarel; he had to be.

Meanwhile, if somehow we managed to get far enough to jump to FTL mode, the scout would have to be our home for as long as it took us to get somewhere. I got up and started to explore it.

She was a lot larger than our family cutter. Built for a patrol crew of six, she actually had two little restrooms; six tiny cabins, each just big enough to get in and out of the narrow bunk; a shower; and a snug little galley. The food storage compartment was a little worrisome, though. It had been stocked for maybe a ten- or twelve-day patrol, and anywhere we decided to go would probably be farther than that. There was an emergency store of dried foods, but I didn't have a good feel for how long stuff like that would last us.

While I was snooping through the galley, I felt a swerve: Deneen had made an evasive move. I jumped up and went back out to the controls area. Tarel came out, too. The monitor screens were on now, and I could see why she was taking evasive maneuvers. The mid-line starboard screen showed a blip that was trying to center on it—lock onto us—and we were sliding to port to keep it off center. There was also a blip on the midline port screen, but it looked a lot smaller, which should mean a lot farther away. On the instrument screen, the hundreds digits *were* blurred now, and the thousands digits said ninety-seven. Ninety-eight.

For just an instant the nearer blip slid into the central ring, but apparently it could only lock on us when it was perfectly centered. At that instant Deneen swerved us sharply to starboard, and the bogey slid out. At the speed we were moving, a swerve like that took us miles off line in a second. If the scout hadn't been encased in its own little quasi-space at the time, we'd have been smeared all over the bulkheads. Or actually, we would have been long before, simply from acceleration.

Tarel and I just stood there, watching. The bogey would get close to the ring, sometimes actually getting into it, while Deneen did her best to keep him from centering. It seemed as if a lot of time was passing, but it wasn't, really. The mileage on the instrument screen passed 300,000—distance from planetary mass, actually. We had a long way to go yet before we dared shift into FTL mode. Twice again the bogey almost centered—once it seemed it must have—and we slipped away. I couldn't help but think that its pilot wasn't trying as hard as he could. He'd hardly dare do any more than be just slightly slow of reflexes though, a tiny bit short on coordination. The whole chase would be recorded on his computer, and if we got away, there'd almost surely be a board of review. I could imagine the Imperial Military Administration on Evdash making an example of her commander and pilot—maybe her whole crew.

That's when I really realized how much others were risking for us. I told myself silently that if we got away, we wouldn't disappoint them.

By 430,000 miles, I'd begun to feel almost optimistic. That's when I noticed that the second blip was getting closer. I didn't know how close it needed to be to have us in range, but it had gotten close enough to identify as a light cruiser, which probably meant it was Imperial. A light cruiser could launch twin-seat chasers when he was near enough, and we couldn't hope to evade them all.

"Any time you want me to take over—" I told her.

She shook her head without speaking, her hands semi-relaxed on the control arm. I'd expected that, and she could pilot as well as I could. So I just stood by, not distracting her anymore. I was ready if needed, or as ready as I could be, and she knew it. She kept evading our nearest pursuer, and we kept getting farther and farther from Evdash, but the cruiser kept getting nearer.

Then the cruiser launched three tiny blips—chasers— and I discovered what it looked like to be really gained on. Their launch position had already been gaining on us, and to that velocity they added their own—not too great at first, but it would increase fast. My glance flicked to the instrument screen—614,000, 615,000, 616,000—and back to the monitor. Deneen's principal attention was still on our original bogey—had to be—as he slipped and swerved around the ring, but mine was on the chasers. They *were* getting closer. And now there were three rings in the midline port screen, each with a little bogey in or near it. As soon as any one of them was near enough to lock on us, that would be it. Their torpedoes would follow us unshakeably, even into FTL if need be.

My eyes had just read 622,000 when Deneen hit the FTL key. I didn't see her do it, but the monitors went blank and so did the for'rd window. *And we hadn't come apart!* The instrument screen read "ALL SYSTEMS FTL-MODE NORMAL, PSEUDOVELOCITY 1." The chasers hadn't launched torpedoes before we jumped; launch would have shown on the monitor. Which meant we were safe from them.

Deneen got up as if she could hardly move, and without looking at me, said, "The old survey cube is in my attaché case." It lay on the deck beside the pilot seat, and she poked it with a foot.

"The old survey cube?" I stared at her. "You want to go to Fanglith?"

"Why not? We don't have anywhere else. Take over. I'm going to take a shower and lie down for a while. We can talk later."

Without waiting for an answer, she went aft to one of the sleeping rooms.

Fanglith! Still, this was not the time to overrule or argue with her. I slid onto the pilot's seat, took the survey cube out of the case, and inserted it in the computer. The computer was standard and the main menu format familiar. At my instruction it gave me the menu for the survey cube, then read off the coordinate equation for Fanglith and wrote it into astrogation. Deneen was right. We could talk about it after she'd unwound a bit, and decide on some other destination, if for no other reason than that we didn't have enough food to get to Fanglith.

Grinder maybe—the place Piet had talked about— where dad and mom were likely to go if they got off Evdash.

PART TWO

THE MEDITERRANEAN

EIGHT

Deneen's nap was a long one—about four hours. Not that I kept track of the time. Now that the pressure was off, it was as if I'd been hit by a sandbag, and for a while I sat around in a sort of daze. I'd lost Jenoor, and Piet, and maybe my parents to the Empire, yet I didn't feel hate or anger or anything with enough juice in it to call grief. I guess desolation would be the word. Anyway, when Deneen came back out and I looked at the chronometer, four hours had passed.

Tarel woke up a little later, and the three of us discussed destinations. We decided to go to Fanglith after all. It wasn't that Deneen argued me into it; she'd have preferred Grinder, too, but the ship's astrogation cube had nothing on a planet named Grinder. Nothing at all. And neither did the one that dad had left us, nor the old survey cube, of course. A nickname, I thought. Grinder was a nickname. And Piet wasn't there to tell us what its real name was. So I ran a computer search for the name Grinder, hoping that *somewhere* in data storage it might be mentioned and cross-referenced to an official name. But there wasn't a single place in all our cubes where "grinder" occurred with a capital G.

There were coordinates for probably all the old colonies, of course, but we didn't know enough about them to make intelligent guesses on which ones the Imperials might leave alone for a while. Or where they might already be. Going to any of them would take time, during which we'd be using up our food supplies, and we could find ourselves arriving somewhere to find an Imperial flotilla sitting there. While Fanglith—Fanglith was probably the last place the Empire would ever get around to. And while Fanglith had lots of dangers, at least they were dangers we knew something about—dangers we were at least somewhat prepared for.

Also, as Deneen pointed out, dad had left us a copy of the old survey cube, as if he'd wanted us to have Fanglith as an option. The medkit contained a broad-spectrum immunoserum, especially important on a world like Fanglith that didn't have significant medical facilities.

It didn't take more than half an hour to talk it all out. Then I went aft to sleep, and found out I had juice enough for grief after all. I don't believe I'd cried since I was ten; now I cried hard enough in five minutes to more than make up for it. Then I slept—for more than six hours, and without a dream, so far as I could tell. When I woke up, I was functional again.

Fifty-seven days was a long trip. The library cubes mom and dad had left in the package helped—especially Tarel. He studied the files on primitive felid worlds that had helped Deneen and me prepare for Fanglith on our first trip, plus the debrief I'd recorded—I'd entitled it *Fanglith*—describing my experiences there.

There was the problem of food, of course. Even Tarel, with his "something out of nothing" metabolism, wasn't in any danger of getting fat. The ship's stocks—ten days of food for six—came out to fifteen days for four, of course. At normal consumption rates, plus there were some dried emergency rations. What made the trip feasible was the chest Deneen and Bubba had dragged aboard—the one we'd supposedly gone to the landing field to deliver. It had extra marine field uniforms and a few other things, but also it had dried field rations. After an hour of reading packages, recording the data on a note cube, and instructing the computer, it came out that we had about thirty days' worth of dried food to go with the scout's regular rations.

Deneen, Tarel, and I lived pretty much on the dried rations, because whoever had put our field rations together had overlooked one thing—canid food. Most of the dry stuff wasn't suitable for Bubba's system, so he got most of the regular food—and even that wasn't really suitable for him—while none of us ate more of anything than we had to.

It could have been worse. The ship's log told us that the life support systems had been inspected and okayed just the day before we'd stolen her, so air and water were no problem. And there was an exercise machine. Also, Deneen and I recorded all we could remember, which was most of it, of the mixture of Norman French and Provençal we'd used on Fanglith. Then Tarel, using the learning program, learned to speak it, too—with our mispronunciations, of course.

One thing that surprised me was how well all of us stood the trip, especially considering how it had started. After my heavy grief surge that first day, the only time I got really depressed was a couple of days later. That's when it hit me really thoroughly that Jenoor was truly gone—that I'd never see her again. After that, I rarely even fantasized that she was with me.

I did fantasize a few good killing sprees though, the first few days. I butchered the Imperial Council all the ways I could think of—but not the marine gunners. Some Evdashian marines in a gun tower, following orders, had poured gunfire into some people they didn't know—strangers a couple of hundred yards away in the semidark. They'd had nothing against us, and chances are they'd wished they hadn't had to. Maybe they'd even tried to shoot a little wild. After all, Deneen and Bubba had escaped without even being wounded, which seemed to me to go beyond luck.

Whatever. The facts were the facts: Jenoor and Piet were dead; Deneen and Tarel and Bubba and I were alive. About mom and dad we could hope.

Deneen didn't talk much the first day or so out; after that, she seemed pretty much her usual self. Tarel did, too, most of the time. His one outsurge seemed to take care of his grief, too, and he'd been rational and decisive when it was needed—at just the time I'd gone momentarily crazy. On the trip he'd been quiet, but no quieter than usual. And although he'd never seen the controls of a spacecraft before, he was soon as familiar with them as Deneen and I were. He did dry runs on flying until he felt at ease with them. And we all familiarized ourselves with the ship's armament.

Bubba was the one who surprised me. Before this trip, his emotions had always seemed really healthy—more so than those of any human I'd ever known. Mostly, he'd been cheerful ever since dad had brought him home to live with us. He'd often been playful, in his way, and somber only rarely. When necessary, he'd been tough—all smarts and action—like when the Norman hunters and their hounds had chased him for hours as a native wolf on Fanglith. And when, days later, we'd had the run-in with the Federation political police in Normandy.

But for the first several days out from Evdash, he kept to himself a lot more than usual, seeming positively moody. I'd *never* seen him that way before. He knew when I first noticed, of course, and had gone into his own cabin and closed the door, so I never asked him about it. I figured if he ever wanted to tell me, he would. After about the third day, though, he got back at least to semi-normal, except that the diet got to him like it did the rest of us.

One of the things we got around to talking about, after a week or so, was what we'd do when we got to Fanglith. The surface was really dangerous there; it seemed as if fighting and wars were their most important activities, with robbery and murder pretty popular too. Actually, Fanglith was considerably more dangerous than Evdash under the Empire, a realization that kind of took me by surprise. On Fanglith it seemed like a case of cultural immaturity. With the Empire it seemed more like cultural degeneracy.

On Fanglith there was also the problem of not blending in with the people there. Oh, for brief periods maybe, or to someone who wasn't really looking, but that was all. Physically we looked about the same, sure, but we thought and acted differently. Without realizing it, we did things they didn't, while we didn't know things that everyone else there knew. We didn't know how to be peasants or nobles, we had no skill with their weapons, we'd be in constant risk of saying or doing something that might outrage or insult them or mark us as fools . . . And, of course, every time we spoke, we were obviously foreigners.

So what could we possibly accomplish there? Our main reason for leaving Evdash, so far as I could see, was to foment revolution against the Glondis Empire. But the more I looked at it, the more impossible that seemed on Fanglith. It was the wrong kind of world, with the wrong kind of history and the most primitive technology. And actually, from what little I knew of it, their governments were worse than the Empire—at least some of them were.

Operating on Fanglith would be up to me, more than to anyone else. I was the oldest, and the only one with much experience on the surface there. And I was male—that was important on their world. I'd have to be the one to land, get provisions, make deals and arrangements.

So naturally, I was feeling pretty overwhelmed by the responsibility, and I told the others just how I felt about it. Deneen just leaned on the little galley table and looked me calmly in the eye.

"Brother mine," she said, "the last time you complained about how impossible things were was on Fanglith. I was a prisoner on a Federation police corvette, but I've heard you and mom and dad talk about it. And Bubba. You were all stuck down there on the surface of the planet with nothing more than hand weapons to work with—hand weapons and some Norman warriors who'd have happily cut all your throats to get hold of your pistols."

Her eyes grabbed mine and wouldn't let them go. "And you pulled that one off."

That was beside the point, I wanted to tell her. That had been then. The situation had been different. I'd been lucky. But all I could answer was: "Dad had as much to do with it as I did."

"Not according to him he didn't." Her gaze withdrew for a minute. "I can see the difficulties you're talking about, and the dangers. But it seems to me that when we get down to it, having a scout ship will make up for a lot. And if things don't shape up for us there, we can take on fresh provisions and try another world somewhere. The fuel slug on this rig is good for years and years if we don't run her too long at high speeds in proximity mode."

She had a point. I'd been letting myself get bogged down in the difficulties. And although dad had played as big a role as I had in the final showdown on Fanglith, all in all, it had been my show. So I said okay, she'd made sense, and we didn't talk much about it the rest of the way.

Meanwhile, Tarel and I let our hair grow, to look more like Fanglithans. Also, we found a drawer with several remotes—small receiver units you can put in your ear for confidential radio reception. They operate on a wireless relay from your belt communicator, and with our hair over our ears, no Fanglithan would know we had them.

Eventually, one day near ship's "midnight," the scout's honker woke us up. We'd set it to let us know when the computer kicked us down out of FTL mode. Ahead of us we could see the system's primary—the sun that Fanglith circled. Seen from where we were, it was a glaring, small white globule against a star-frosted backdrop of deepest black. We were farther out from Fanglith than we'd expected—part of the tiny error inherent in servomechanisms and ancient equations—but still less than a day away in mass-proximity mode.

I had flitter bugs in my stomach. I wasn't sure how much of it was just plain excitement and how much was fear. There'd be enough of both in store for me on Fanglith. I took a deep breath. *Whatever*, I told myself. When we'd taken care of a few preliminaries, we'd be eating real food again, all of us, breathing unrecycled air, and seeing the surface of a planet where surely the Empire hadn't landed.

NINE

The first time we'd arrived, I'd been sixteen and Deneen fourteen, and we'd known almost nothing about Fanglith. So we'd looked it over pretty carefully. You might think we wouldn't need to a second time, but we weren't taking any chances. We made several slow swings around it at 40,000 miles, monitoring for radio signals just in case Imperials *had* landed. We got nothing, and the radio monitoring equipment aboard the *Jav*—we'd named our scout *The Rebel Javelin*—was pretty sensitive. It was certainly a lot more sensitive than most private craft would carry, so we could assume that if we hadn't picked up anything, there was nothing to pick up.

But to make doubly sure, we moved in below both zones of heavy radiation and circled at 150 miles above the surface. We didn't pick up anything from down there, either. Meanwhile, I'd had the computer establishing a reference grid for the planet, and because the scout had a recording broad-band EM scanner, I had it map the surface for us as we flew over it.

All of which used up another day—another day of short and monotonous rations. By then we were ready to put down somewhere, anywhere, to get something fit to eat. So I called a council.

The immediate problem, I pointed out, was that I didn't have anything to buy food with, and what I could think of to trade, they'd have no use for. Except weapons of course—stunners and guns. We had a locker full of them, but they weren't anything we wanted the locals to have. For one thing, they might decide to use them on us.

Which meant I'd have to trade my services for food. The question was, what services?

Deneen eyed me coolly. "Larn," she said, "you're thinking like a planner, which is fine when you have data to plan with, but right now you don't. What you need to do is let me put you down somewhere. Then you circulate and find out what services people want that you can give them."

It sounded simple, the way she said it, but doing it . . . Mainly it bothered me that she'd pointed it out to me in front of Tarel, but she was right. I tended to worry sometimes when I didn't have a plan of action all figured out ahead. And there were—are—times when that just isn't possible. There are times when a person needs to do whatever comes next, and figure that somehow he'll make it come out right.

My mind went back then to something our Norman knight, Arno de Courmeron, had mentioned when we'd been here before. There was a seaport in Provence, on the Mediterranean coast, from which he had planned to ship horses to—somewhere. Sicily. The island of Sicily.

"Okay," I said, "let's see if we can find a seaport named Marseille, in Provence. It's probably as good a town as any to put down near, and maybe while I'm at it, I can get a lead on Arno." I smiled smugly. "Meanwhile, you guys will have to make do with what's left of the dry food while I line up something down below."

Which I'd do for them as fast as I could.

We didn't know whether it was Marseille or not. But it was definitely the biggest Mediterranean seaport west of the high mountains, with a population of maybe, oh, eight or ten thousand, at a guess. The river near it seemed to be the one Arno had called the Rhone—part of the route he'd probably have taken from Normandy. We'd followed it once, farther north.

Here it divided into a number of channels, to flow into the sea through broad, wild, delta marshes. The town we were assuming to be Marseille was the nearest seaport, lying not many miles east of the river, away from the marshes. If it wasn't Marseille, it would do for the time being.

Actually I was enjoying working without a plan. Not that I considered "no plan" a virtue—I looked forward to having one. But it was kind of exhilarating, playing by ear, and it wasn't entirely "no plan"—it was more as if the plan only existed for a step or two in advance, not all the way to the goal.

We'd spied out the terrain from three miles up, with a viewscreen magnification that let us examine things in detail when we wanted to. Especially the road that led from river to town. Where it approached the town, it ran along not far from the sea, with high, rugged hills close behind it to the north. As a road, it was mainly the tracks of animals in the stony, muddy ground, with the cartwheel ruts mostly broken down by hooves. It looked as if it had rained a lot lately.

Just then there wasn't much moving on it. On one stretch, for example, two peasants on foot, with long sharpened sticks, prodded along six of Fanglith's version of cattle. These are big, hoofed animals, with two horns curving out from above their ears. Behind the two peasants, a heavy-bodied man rode on a "horse," an animal resembling a gorn. He seemed to be the men's boss—their "master," as they call them on Fanglith.

A quarter mile ahead of them were three men walking together, carrying stout staffs that could be used for fighting as well as walking. Their clothes were old, dirty, and patched. A hundred yards ahead of them was a two-wheeled cart pulled by a donkey—a small, long-eared animal a little like a horse. The cartwheels looked almost as if they'd been sawed from tree trunks in single pieces.

That was all the traffic on a half-mile piece of road. Not what you'd call heavy use or high speed.

Next, there was the question of where to put me down. From our earlier experience on Fanglith, we'd concluded it was best to keep our ship secret until we needed to exercise some power, because unless we handled things right, people would react to it in one of two ways: either hate and fear, on the assumption that we were what they thought of as devils or demons (I'm still not sure what the difference is); or with greed for our ship and weapons. Either reaction was dangerous to us.

We'd have to come out in the open sooner or later, of course, to develop a political power base and accomplish anything. But for now, I'd land somewhere where the ship wouldn't be seen, and blend in with the population the best I could.

And hopefully get a lead on Arno de Courmeron. Although Arno might not feel altogether friendly to us now, I was pretty sure I could work with him.

Assuming he was still alive. An ambitious knight in this world might die anytime. But Arno would take a lot of killing, and his ambitions had seemed to lie in getting rich, not necessarily in becoming famous as a warrior.

It wasn't hard to decide on a time and place for landing—just before dawn, in a ravine where it opened onto the narrow coastal rim. It was just above the road, and only about two miles from the town walls. The ravine's bottom was rough and sloping, so we wouldn't land the scout. Tarel would lower me the last dozen feet with a winch and sling, while Deneen kept the scout steady.

We thought about landing Bubba with me. When we were around people, he'd be able to monitor for dangerous intentions. But he'd also be conspicuous, and make me conspicuous, especially if he tried to tell me something, so the decision was for a solo landing.

I'd travel light—stunner, blast pistol, communicator, and a pocket recorder I'd record all conversation on. We'd feed the recordings into the scout's computer, running it through the linguistics program to improve our knowledge of local language. Then we could use the learning program to help us learn it.

I'd also wear a crucifix—a local type of religious artifact—around my neck. I'd cut it from a piece of steel in the *Jav*'s tiny workshop. Polished, it looked pretty nice, and it could easily be helpful down below. I'd made three crosses, actually—one for each of us humans. I had a notion that for Bubba to wear one might not be acceptable on Fanglith; their native canids were not at all on Bubba's intelligence level, and were considered simply animals.

This time, I'd wear a remote in my ear. I remembered the trouble I'd gotten into before on Fanglith when Deneen's voice had come out of my communicator. The monks had thought I'd had a demon, and I was lucky not to be burned at a stake.

I stood there in the harness-like sling, wearing a navy jumpsuit. It wasn't much like what people wore on Fanglith, but I didn't plan to stay down long this time, and if I got a chance, I'd get some native clothes before I returned to the *Jav*.

It was moonless and cloudy, and had been showering off and on since evening, which cut down a little on how clearly our infrascope imaged things on the ground. But Bubba assured us that no one was near. Still, as we lowered, we had our windows on one-way opaque— something you couldn't do with our family cutter—so we couldn't be noticed.

Deneen, at the controls, stopped our descent, dimmed our lights nearly out, and keyed the door open. Touching another control, she swung the winch out of its housing above the door and into place in the opening. Tarel hooked its cable to a ring on my sling, and I tugged on it, testing, then stood backward in the door. "Take care, you guys," I said.

"Right," Tarel answered, and reached out. We shook on it.

"You take care, too," Deneen told me over her shoulder. "And don't take too long getting that food."

Bubba stood with his tail slowly waving, his brown eyes fixing me. "Have fun," he told me. It was his standard goodbye, but somehow this time it didn't have its usual jauntiness. *The food on this trip has gotten to him more than any of us*, I thought to myself.

I leaned back and stepped out.

Into another world. Until that moment, Fanglith had
been something we looked out at through the windows
or on the screens. Now I was part of it again, already
separated from the secure space inside the *Jav*. A little
shiver of excitement went through me as I lowered the
fifteen feet to the ground. It had stopped raining, but
the air was cool and moist, and clouds cut off all starlight. Solid ground met my feet before I even saw it. It
was really dark, and the night smelled like—well, it
didn't smell like recycled ship's air. It smelled like wet
dirt and resinous plants.

I pulled the safety pin and turned the harness release, and the sling fell away. Then I gave the cable a
triple tug, signaling Tarel that I was free, and it snaked
back up, leaving me behind. A minute later the vague,
faint light from the door closed off. Another five seconds and the dim form of the *Jav* began to lift; three
seconds after that, I couldn't see it anymore.

Time to get on with it.

I hiked carefully out of the ravine, which was wet and
muddy but stony-rough enough for good footing. It was
so dark that I kept stepping into the little rivulet without seeing it. Five minutes after I'd backed out the
door, I stood on the rough beast trail that served as the
major road to the largest seaport of Provence. I knew
I'd found it when my feet felt the cattle tracks and
stumbled on a wheel rut.

I wasn't worried or even nervous. Somehow my chest
felt big, my body strong, and my self eager.

Because the road was rough and the night so black, I
didn't walk very fast. Only the feel of the tracks beneath my feet kept me from losing it in the darkness.
After half an hour or so, it was definitely starting to get
light; I could actually see a little bit. Minutes later I
passed a hut, then more of them, set back from the
road. This was the part of town that was outside the
walls. About that time I made out the town wall itself,
ahead in the lightening grayness.

The gate, when I reached it, was closed. The wall
was maybe thirty feet high, made of stone blocks, and
had battlements on the top. Huddled against it were

two soggy-looking guys with walking staffs. They looked as if they'd been there most of the night. One eyed me dully, the other curiously.

"Hello," said the curious one. His language was Provençal, as I'd expected it would be here. "Been walking all night?"

"Only since the rain stopped," I said.

"How'd you keep dry?"

"Tent," I lied. "But I didn't like who I shared it with."

He shrugged.

"When do they open the gate?" I asked.

"Sunrise. Best they can guess on a morning like this. Come a long way?"

"Pretty far."

"You ain't no Norman, but you been in Normandy, I'll wager, from your talk."

I could get myself in trouble if I kept answering questions, so I just nodded.

"English?" he asked. "I've heard the English are tall, and I never seen clothes like yours before."

Instead of answering, I asked a question of my own. "Ever hear of a Norman named Arno of Courmeron? I'd like to find him. I've heard he brings war horses here, to ship to Sicily."

He shrugged. "Not many Normans take the sea route. Most go over the Cenis Pass and south through Italy. Brigands and barons are more to their liking than storms and Saracen pirates."

I nodded, remembering what I'd heard of Saracens. They were a military people whom the Normans had warred with on Sicily. It was the Saracens whom Arno had fought in the battle that had won him his knighthood, at a place called Misilmeri.

"But Normans have shipped horses out of Marseille a time or two," the man went on. "It's faster than overland. No doubt they'd do more of it if horses were better sailors. They get sicker'n a pregnant woman at the slightest seas, and are likely to go down and break a leg."

Marseille, he'd said. We'd hit it right. "Are you a sailor?" I asked.

"Aye." He gestured at his companion. "We both are, though Marco here finds it hard to get hired anymore. Lost a thumb in a bight, and don't neither row nor haul ropes so well as he did. Though better'n you'd maybe think."

I hadn't understood every word he'd said, but enough. The other man removed his right hand from his armpit, where he'd been keeping it warm, and displayed the scarred nub, red and ugly, where once a thumb had been.

"How can I get some food?" I asked. "Quite a lot of food."

The talkative sailor snorted, and eyed me even more curiously. "How much is a lot? All you can eat and drink you can buy at an inn, if you've got a few coppers. And the market is in the middle of town. While if it's a shipload you want . . ."

"I have no coppers," I told him. "I'll have to see what I can do to get some."

"What *do* you do?" he asked. "Clearly you're no farmer, nor no sailor, I'll wager. You're no knight nor sergeant, nor mercenary neither, going about without weapons." His eyes traveled up and down me. "A monk, I'd say, except your clothes ain't monkish. And what else is there?" He shook his head. "It's sure you're no merchant."

"Mercenary's closest," I told him, and an idea struck me. "I'm a bodyguard. If a merchant wants his person kept safe, he'll do well to hire me."

"Is that so?" An eyebrow had raised. "Jesu knows you're a big one, and maybe strong, though I might say you don't look the type. Not a scar to be seen." He paused. "Nor any weapon at all, unless you carry one of them little daggers hid in your clothes, and they be mainly useless in a fight."

I didn't answer, just squatted down beside them. I'd talked too much already. I had no business claiming to be a fighting man on this world; someone might easily call my bluff. And unless I was willing to use my stunner or pistol, which was undesirable, I could be dead in a hurry. Hand-foot art was nothing to face a trained swordsman with, and the odds wouldn't be good against a skilled knife fighter either.

It was most of an hour before the gate opened, and by that time it looked as if the weather might clear. The clouds seemed thin again, and in places blue showed through. I didn't even say goodbye to the two sailors, just walked inside and followed the muddy road, which became a muddy street.

Marseille smelled bad. I'm sure that not all the water in the street was rain. It seemed as if these people didn't have much idea of sanitation, and I was glad we'd used the broad spectrum immunoserum in the medkit.

There weren't many people on the street yet, but most that I did see seemed lively enough and not unhappy. One young guy, a year or two younger than me by his looks, was striding along whistling, his step springy. His clothes were red and yellow beneath their grime.

"Hello, young sir," I said. "Can I ask you a question?"

He stopped and looked me over. I stood about a head taller than him. "Ask away," he answered.

"I'm looking for a merchant who will hire me. I do calculations very quickly." It seemed to me that that was a safer thing to advertise than martial skills.

The young guy looked interested. "Calculations?" he said. "Well, that can be useful. My own master has a Saracen slave to do calculations for him. His abacus is different from ours, and he's very quick."

Our conversation wasn't as neat and direct as I'm telling it here. His pronunciations were a bit different from those I'd heard before on Fanglith, and he used words that were new to me, while the Norman French I mixed with my Provençal gave him a certain amount of trouble. So a couple of times we had to stop and sort out meanings with each other.

Anyway, an idea began to develop. "Very quick, you say," I said, referring to the Saracen slave. "I am quicker. I calculate more quickly than anyone in Marseille!"

His eyebrows arched. "You think so?"

"I know it." I took the communicator off my belt, a military model with a microcomputer built in. "Give me a problem."

"Add seven to itself nine times."

I didn't need to use the micro for that. "Nine sevens added to seven equals seventy."

He looked impressed, but also uncertain. It occurred to me that he couldn't do arithmetic himself, so he couldn't tell whether I was right or not. I cocked an eye at him. "Is your master's slave faster than that?"

"I think not. Your answer was virtually instantaneous."

"Who is the fastest calculator in Marseille?"

"A merchant and shipowner named Isaac ben Abraham, a Jew from Valencia. He uses an abacus of beads upon rods, like the Saracen, which is much swifter than the boards and disks that others use."

"Does he wager?" I asked.

His face went instantly thoughtful. "Would you bet against him?" he asked back.

"If we're going to talk about things like this, we should know each other's names. Mine is Larn."

"Mine is Reyno. Would you? Bet against him?"

"I have nothing to bet," I answered. "But if you do, or if others wish to bet, for a percentage of their winnings I would contest against this—Isaac?"

"Isaac ben Abraham. Let me take you to my master, Carolus the Stonecutter. He sometimes wagers, but he will wish first to see the horse run."

"Of course," I said. "Take me to him." Meanwhile I was recording our conversation. It would be useful to speak Provençal better, including speaking it without a mixture of Norman French.

He nodded, and we began to walk briskly in the direction he'd been going. "I could stand to win a bet," he said. "I am in love with Margareta, the youngest daughter of Henrico the mason, and she with me. We wish to marry. But first I must have money, and soon, before her father promises her to someone else. She is already fifteen, though small for her age," he went on. "In her family the women mature late."

Already fifteen. Jenoor had been sixteen, would have

been seventeen soon now. Again I had that empty feeling. Where would we be if she and Piet had escaped with us? Together on some more or less civilized world, probably Grinder. Compared to Fanglith, Grinder would seem like home.

I spent the quarter-mile walk to Reyno's master's feeling sorry for myself, hardly aware that Reyno was whistling again. The stonecutter's place was two stories high, and set back from the street about thirty feet. The front yard was partly filled with blocks of rough-cut stones, some of them partly recut, and the ground was littered with chips and shards. A short stocky man, wearing a rough leather apron and holding a hammer and chisel, was examining one of the blocks as if looking for the right place to attack it. Reyno tossed him a cheery "good morning" and led me past; the man was not Carolus.

As you might expect, the building was made of stone, its blocks cut to roughly the same size. The stout plank door was open and we went in. There was more work space inside, with blocks lying around on the dirt floor. The windows were large, probably for light, and had no glass; the shutters I'd noticed, which opened back against the outside walls, were apparently all there was to close them with.

Carolus the stonecutter was a tall man for Fanglith, or at least for the places I'd been—only a few inches shorter than me. Even with a bulging middle, he looked extremely strong. He scowled at us as we came in.

"You're late," he snapped to Reyno.

"Yes sir. I met this young gentleman and brought him with me. His name is Larn. He has an interesting proposition—one that could be profitable."

The stonecutter's dark little eyes moved to me and stayed for a few seconds before he said anything more. My jumpsuit looked a lot different from clothes in Provence or Normandy, or any I'd seen at any rate. For a shirt, they generally wear a thing resembling a loose jacket that covers the upper legs. They call it a tunic. Instead of pants, most of the men wear a sort of leggings, with a kind of undershorts—more of a diaper, actually—to cover their genitals. None of it really fits. Also, the shoes don't have separate soles, and they don't press shut around the foot. Instead, they have a leather thong you draw them snug with and then tie.

"Where are you from?" Carolus asked me.

So there it was. I was going to have to tell him something, and it had to be a lie—hopefully, one that wouldn't trip me up. Remembering my one-night lecture on the world of Fanglith from Brother Oliver, more than two years earlier, I answered "India." India was a place that everyone had heard of and apparently no one had been. Things that were said about it sounded pretty imaginative.

His eyes had paused at my crucifix. "You're Christian."

"Yes. Although I've not been thoroughly instructed in it."

He shrugged. I'd already learned that most Christians hadn't been. "What is this interesting proposition?" he wanted to know.

"I'm a master calculator," I said. "Reyno tells me that the swiftest calculator in Marseille is a man named Isaac ben Abraham. I am faster at difficult calculations than he can possibly be, and perhaps at simple ones too. It seems to me we could have a contest, he and I, and there could be wagers. Whoever bet on me would win. In reward, I would get part of their winnings."

Carolus looked thoughtful. "You have not seen the Jew at his abacus; he is lightning swift. He is a man late in middle years, who was calculating long before you were born."

This kind of conversation would lead nowhere. "You have a slave who does your calculations," I said. "Is he fast?"

"Faster than most. But not so fast as the Jew."

"Let's see how much faster I am than your slave."

For just a moment Carolus stood examining me. Then he turned toward a staircase that led upstairs through a raised trapdoor. "Faid!" he bellowed. "Down here!"

A few seconds later a slender, dark-complected man came down the stairs. He might have been thirty or thirty-five. "Yes, my lord?"

"I have need of your calculations."

"Yes, my lord." Faid walked over to a table beneath one of the windows. Carolus, Reyno, and I followed. There Faid sat down, and with one hand drew a sort of open-topped small box to him, a box with rows of beads on what seemed to be thin wooden rods. He looked questioningly at Carolus.

"Do a difficult problem," Carolus said to him, "but do not say from what roots, or what the answer is."

For just a moment Faid looked puzzled, then shrugged. His fingers moved quickly, the beads clicking for a few seconds. "It is done."

Carolus turned to me. "Where is your abacus?" he asked.

I took out my communicator, which was also a microcomputer, and switched it on. "Here," I answered.

He turned to Faid. "State your roots," he said.

"Twenty-eight fourfold."

"One hundred twelve," I answered. I didn't need my computer for that.

Carolus's eyebrows raised slightly and he turned to Faid. "Is that right?" he asked.

"Exactly right." The Saracen looked at me with considerable interest. "And what are the portions if you divide 144 into 16 equal parts?" His fingers raced as he asked it.

"Nine each," I said. "I need no abacus for that." Our math teachers in lower school had drilled us thoroughly. It looked as if this was going to be easy.

Faid looked up at Carolus. "He is right." Then he turned to me. "What sort of question would cause you to use your abacus?"

"Oh, the square root of some large number. Do you know how to do square roots?"

Faid nodded. "In the main they are problems for geometers. I can do them, but it takes time."

"Fine," I said. "Calculate a large square; that'll be easier. Then tell me what the square is and I'll give you its roots."

"Stand away then," he answered, "so you cannot see what roots I use."

We moved a few steps away and I turned my back to him. After a short while he said: "The square is 1,369."

I tapped 1,369 into the computer and asked for the square root. "The root is 37," I said, and turned to look at him. It had taken me about two seconds, which was about half as long as Faid stared at me before he said anything again.

"That is correct." He sounded impressed, or maybe awed would be more like it. "You must be Indian."

Carolus pursed his lips, then made a decision. "Faid, mention this to no one. None of it. How fast he is, that he comes from India, none of it. And you, Reyno: Keep that glib mouth shut, or I'll see you tongueless." Then he turned to me. "What is your name again?"

"Larn."

"Larn," he said, "we have things to talk about."

TEN

Carolus sent Reyno to Isaac ben Abraham, inviting him to contest with "a youth who is truly marvelous at calculations." Ben Abraham answered in writing, which Faid read to his master; reading was something else the Saracen could do and Carolus couldn't. After commenting that it was unimportant to him whether someone else could calculate faster or not, ben Abraham said it would amuse him to take me on. He offered to bet fifty gold bezants or an equivalent in Pisan solidi.

Carolus the stonecutter was a careful man who would bet only what he could afford to lose, even when it seemed almost certain that he wouldn't. And he felt very uncomfortable at the thought of betting fifty bezants. He sent back word that he would bet only twenty. Reyno had almost nothing of his own to bet, but borrowed two bezants from his master. Carolus was grumpy about lending it, and I suspect he only did it to keep Reyno from trying to borrow elsewhere and being questioned. He felt uneasy about word of the contest getting out.

Ben Abraham, smelling Carolus's uncertainty, decided he could probably beat me, and got Carolus up to thirty against his own sixty. Then, in amusement, he agreed to cover Reyno's small bet at odds of three to one. All of this was arranged through Reyno as courier.

Carolus was to pay me a sixth, or ten bezants, if I won. I wasn't sure what he'd try to do if I lost, but I couldn't see any chance of that happening.

The contest was to take place in the office of Isaac ben Abraham, shortly after the hour called "sext"—local midday, as far as I could tell. After eating an early lunch, we walked there through spring sunshine. I was impressed by ben Abraham's offices. They were clean, and there were decorative woven cloths called tapestries on some of the walls.

I was even more impressed with Isaac ben Abraham. He was the biggest man I'd seen yet on Fanglith, and the tallest except for a Norman knight named Brislieu. Besides which, he looked as if, under the fat, he'd be very strong physically. His face went with an age of about fifty or fifty-five, but his long black hair had only scattered threads of gray. He also had a bigger, thicker beard than I'd ever imagined, and wore the richest clothes, topped by a long, fur-trimmed, brown velvet cape. All in all, when he spoke in his rich bass voice, people were likely to pay attention.

And it was obvious that he washed, he and the man who ushered us into his office. I'd never seen a clean Fanglithan before. I hadn't realized there were any.

He had his servant pour wine for us. It was weak and kind of watery—intended for flavor, not to get anyone tight. After Carolus introduced us, ben Abraham looked me over with eyes that were shiny black. "Larn," he said, as if tasting the name. "What is your age?"

"I am a few days short of nineteen."

"And you are already very fast?"

"Very," I answered.

"By the design of your crucifix, I take it you follow the Church of Rome, yet it appears that you bathe. How is that?"

I had no idea what a safe answer might be, but I had to say something. "I was told to by the Abbot of St. Stephen at Isere. For a rash I get sometimes." I crossed myself when I'd said it, the way I'd learned to do at the monastery, and changed the subject. "I'm ready to contest when it is time."

I'd no sooner said it than the cathedral bells began to ring. A cathedral is a large church—a building in which the Christians carry out important religious activities. Cathedrals apparently always have a bell tower. The people of Fanglith don't have clocks. They read the hour by the shadow on an etched metal plate set in the sun. They also measure intervals of time by the flow of sand through a narrow opening between adjacent glass hemispheres. But most people simply go by the ringing of bells in the city's cathedral. These are rung several times a day to tell the people when it's time to pray.

As soon as the bells had stopped ringing, Carolus and Reyno lowered their heads and began to pray out loud. I didn't know the prayers, but it was expected of me so I did the best I could: I recited a poem, "The Greening of Dancer's Desert," in Evdashian:

> 'Twas on the planet Dancer
> In the System Farness Meth,
> There spread a windswept desert
> Named the Emptiness of Death.
> The director, Kalven Denken,
> Wearied by its furnace breath,
> Swore to plant its desolation,
> End the Emptiness of Death

He never dreamed what it would cost,
Nor the kind of coin. In faith,
Had he known, he'd not have sworn
To plant the Emptiness of Death. . . .

I kept going until the others stopped, and when we were done, Carolus scowled at me suspiciously. Isaac ben Abraham looked on with interest, and again with that hint of amusement.

"What heretical tongue was that?" Carolus demanded.

It smelled like trouble for sure. My answer was as much a surprise to me as to him, and based on what Arno of Courmeron had said at the monastery two years earlier. "That was Aramaic," I told him. "The language of our Lord Jesu Christ."

I could only hope Carolus didn't speak Aramaic. He frowned. "It sounded like Saracen to me," he said suspiciously.

It was Isaac ben Abraham who answered. "It does indeed. We Jews speak Aramaic in our churches and homes, in the reading of the Talmud. Also, we speak it in trade with Jews of other lands. From his dialect, obviously Larn learned it in the Holy Land, from Syrian monks, whose tongues are not colored by any vernacular." He looked at me with respect. "Truly, I am impressed."

I was more than impressed. I was relieved, but also a little worried. I couldn't imagine what reason Isaac ben Abraham might have had for lying me out of trouble.

After that, the contest was an anticlimax for me. We were to calculate in rounds—the best of nine would win. In each round, ben Abraham would pose a problem and we'd both calculate the answer. Then I'd pose one. If we tied a round, each of us winning a half, then we were supposed to replay the round until one of us won both halves.

But of course I won right away. I didn't know what to expect from Isaac ben Abraham then, or his household guards. I only hoped I wouldn't have to use my stunner. But what he did was pay Carolus and Reyno what they'd won, weighing out the coins to satisfy Carolus that they hadn't been shaved. Reyno was practically dancing, and Carolus's usually sour face was actually smiling as he paid me my ten gold bezants.

Then ben Abraham had wine poured again. "And what will you do with your winnings, young Larn?" he asked.

"I'm not sure how much I can buy with ten bezants," I told him. "I'd like to buy food—fresh meat, cheese, fish, and flour. And dried fruit, if I can get any. And rent a donkey to take it to friends I know, who are hungry."

Carolus looked at me as if I was crazy, but didn't say anything. Ben Abraham looked at me as if he'd like to know what I was really all about. Reyno looked at me as if he didn't really see me; his thoughts were on the girl he might be able to marry now.

By evening I had a donkey loaded with freshly butchered beef, a huge round cheese, dried fish, dates, olives, and other foods I'd bought in the market. Plus two daggers, two short swords, and a set of cheap local clothes for all three of us. The short swords were way the most expensive: a bezant each. Except for a dagger that I'd fastened to my belt, all of it was loaded in two big baskets slung across the donkey's back. They almost hid the donkey.

And I also owned the donkey! I hoped I could bring him back to the market and sell him for what I paid for him. But if I simply had to let him loose, that would be okay too, because I still had two of my gold pieces left.

ELEVEN

I left the city gate just before it closed at sundown, and followed the road westward, leading my donkey by his rope halter. Off to my left was the sea, beautiful in sunlight, and a beach with no one on it. After a little while I turned off on a trail that wound its way down to it.

The beach seemed like the nearest decent landing place, except for the road itself. After unloading the baskets onto the sand, I tied the donkey to a bush a little way above the beach—far enough that the scout shouldn't scare him out of his wits. Then, when it was dark, I called Deneen to come get me. When they landed, Bubba trotted down the ramp and off into the brush above the beach without a word. He needed to get out and stretch his legs and hunt. Knowing Bubba, I had no doubt he'd catch fresh meat by dawn, when he was to meet us. And no way would he bother my donkey, or anyone's livestock. Well—not my donkey, anyway. But he was bound to be pretty desperate for a proper meal.

After Tarel and I got my purchases loaded into the scout, we took off, and Deneen parked us twenty-one miles above Marseille. There I loaded the contents of my recorder into the computer, and while Deneen and Tarel started putting the food away, I had the linguistics program analyze the language contents against the Provençal and Norman it already knew. It didn't take long—a few seconds. Then I had the computer copy it into the learning program. When that was done, I sat down in the copilot's seat, put on a learning skullcap, and proceeded to upgrade my knowledge of Provençal, running through all we knew of it now until I had it thoroughly.

That done, I took off the skullcap, got up, and went back to the little galley. Deneen was bloody to the elbows. "Next time," she said, looking up at me grimly, "see if you can get the meat cut up into pieces that'll fit into storage. This place doesn't have the facilities for cutting up forty-pound hunks of beef—especially tough beef!"

I could see what she meant. They were trying to work on a counter fourteen inches wide. And not only were they bloody, and the counter bloody, but blood was dripping onto the floor and had smeared the wall behind the counter. She and Tarel had taken off their shoes, and their feet were smeared red. So far, they'd gotten about a fourth of the beef cut and wrapped for putting away.

"Sorry," I said.

She held up one of the belt knives we'd had on Evdash. "This is the biggest thing we have to work with," she added, a little less hostile now. "It would help if you bring a butcher knife next time, even if you do bring the meat in smaller pieces. And we need rags to wipe blood with. We're trying not to use paper toweling; we're almost out of it."

She gestured at the large cleaning drum, where I could see the clothes I'd bought. "I put them in there on *sanitize*, in case they've got any of those mean little critters you got infested with our last trip here." She grinned then, sheepishly. "Oh, and let me thank you for bringing all these tasties, brother mine. You really did do good work getting them, and I honestly appreciate it. It's just that the meat needs a few improvements in preprocessing."

"Can I help in here?" I asked.

"There's not room for three at once. No, just stand there and admire us, and tell us what you have in mind to do next."

So I did. Before dawn I'd go back to my donkey. Then I'd return to Marseille and see if I could have a long talk with Isaac ben Abraham; I had the notion I could learn even more from him than I had from Brother Oliver two and a half years before. Certainly he could expand our knowledge of Provençal a lot. And if it was unusual to transport horses by sea, then, as a ship-owner, ben Abraham might know of Arno. I had no idea how many shipowners there were in Marseille, or even if Arno had gotten this far with his horse herd. It was a long dangerous distance from Normandy.

"Then," I finished, "we may have enough information to plan intelligently."

"I'd like to go with you next time," Tarel put in. "I'd like to get a firsthand feel for what it's like down there."

I looked at that and felt uncomfortable with it, but I couldn't come up with any strong reason why he shouldn't. He was as old as I'd been the first time I'd landed alone on Fanglith, and he already knew quite a lot of the language. "All right by me," I answered. "It'll probably be safer with two of us. Tell you what: I'll help Deneen. You wash up and spend some time on the learning program, upgrading your Provençal. Then, after we try on our new clothes, we'd better get some sleep. We need to get down there before daylight."

Deneen set the scout's honker, and it woke us up an hour ahead of estimated daybreak. Then, twenty-one miles above Marseille, we ate a quick breakfast while watching for the first sign of dawn to touch the horizon, which, from our altitude, was four hundred miles east. That would give us roughly twenty minutes to get down and on the beach and let Deneen get away while it was still full night on the surface. When the first touch of dawn showed, far to the east, we hurriedly finished eating and stowed our dishes in the cleaner. Then Deneen dropped the twenty-one miles to the beach. As we slowed for landing, the infrascope showed what had to be Bubba lying a few dozen yards from the donkey—far enough, and no doubt downwind, not to upset it seriously. Except for those two, there was nothing large and warmblooded anywhere near.

When we landed and Tarel and I stepped down the ramp, Bubba was at its foot. "Catch anything worth eating?" I asked him.

He grinned—something he hadn't been doing a lot of. "Even rodents good after long time on ship's food," he woofed, then trotted up into the cutter.

Even without any overcast, we couldn't see far in the moonless night. The cutter was lost in darkness only seconds after the door closed.

Nothing had happened to my donkey while I was gone, but a lot had happened to the bush I'd tied him to. He'd eaten most of the tough little leaves and a lot of the smaller twigs. I untied his halter rope and we started up the slope from the beach. Looking off to my right, it seemed as if there was already a hint of gray dawn where the land met the eastern sky. By the time we got to the road, there was a distinct wash of gray along the horizon, and even with lots of stars still bright above us, we could see a little better.

It was pretty much daylight when we reached the city gate, and we squatted there with a few others, backs to the wall. Minutes later we watched sunlight touch the hilltops to the northwest, and heard the heavy gate bar being drawn back. We stood up, getting out of the way, heard the hinges groan, then the gates were pushed open by the gate guards.

It's not surprising that so many Fanglithans are burly and strong for their size. Just about everything seems to be done by muscle power, and lots of simple things, like opening the massive, timbered gates, are heavy labor. Of course, not all Fanglithans are husky and strong, by any means. Their genetics dictates that lots of them will have slim builds, and I suspect that most of them weren't properly nourished as children. That's probably why they're mostly short by our standards; at least it's a better explanation than genetics. Their parent stock hadn't been any different from our own, or not much different, anyway. They'd been mind-wiped political prisoners dumped on Fanglith eighteen thousand or so years ago by the mad emperor Karkzhuk.

Another thing about Fanglithans—a surprising number have lost their teeth. They don't seem to have any idea of dental care, and that probably interferes with proper eating. I suspect that quite a few of them have chronic physical ailments that would be easily cured in high-tech societies, or wouldn't have happened in the first place.

Like I said though, a lot of them are husky and strong-looking, even if short, and that included the gate guards who watched us enter. But they saw nothing troublesome in Tarel and me, even as big as we were by their standards. We were dressed now in native clothes, and the shortswords and daggers on our belts weren't unusual.

We went first to the marketplace, where I sold my donkey back to the man I'd bought it from. He only offered me half what I'd paid him for it, and as a matter of form and principle, I dickered him up to two-thirds. He wasn't more than about five feet tall, but it didn't seem to bother him at all that Tarel and I, five-ten and six-one, were really big by Fanglithan standards—or at least by standards in Provence and Normandy.

From the marketplace we went straight to Isaac ben Abraham's. The armed servant at the door recognized me, but had us wait in the courtyard while he sent someone to notify his master. The man was back in a minute, and escorted us to ben Abraham's office.

The merchant's eyes, alert and wise, watched us in. "You are back quickly," he said, then chuckled. Ben Abraham's version of a chuckle was more of a deep rumble. "If your friend is another rapid calculator," he added, "I am not in the mood for more contests. What may I do for you?"

I'd thought a bit, in my bunk before I slept, of how I would answer that question—how I'd open the conversation to get us the kind of information we needed. "My lord," I said, "you are a learned man, while in this land I am ignorant of much I should know, as you no doubt noticed. Yesterday you saved me from possible trouble, with what you said about my 'Aramaic,' which I believe you knew was not Aramaic at all."

"Nor any other language I have ever heard," he answered. "Not Greek nor Italian nor Spanish nor Arabic. Nor Armenian nor Swabian, as far as that's concerned. Certainly not Hebrew, and definitely not Aramaic." He paused, his gaze sharpening. "Your calculations were fast beyond belief. Are you Indian?"

"No, I'm not Indian, although I told Carolus the stonecutter that I was. Carolus doesn't care for things that feel mysterious to him, and I needed to tell him something he could accept. In fact, I'm from a land called Evdash, and so far as I know, no one in this part of the world has heard of it except from me.

"And that brings me to another matter. I have been in Provence before, and also in Normandy, two and a half years ago. At that time I had as a friend and ally a Norman knight named Arno de Courmeron. I would like to find him again. When we parted, I had provided him with a herd of war horses, and he intended to drive them south to Marseille . . ."

At that point, Isaac ben Abraham's bushy eyebrows arched. I decided he must know Arno, or at least have heard of him, unless he was reacting to what I'd said about providing Arno with a herd of war horses.

". . . from where," I continued, "he intended to take them to Sicily by ship. Do you know anything about him?"

He nodded. "This Arno has come through twice—the first time, incredibly, with only two mercenaries to help him. It seemed impossible that three men could have brought forty war horses hundreds of dangerous miles from Normandy, with brigands and barons hungry for plunder all along the way."

Forty! Unless that was a rough approximation, he'd actually increased his herd after we'd left him. "When was the last time?" I asked.

"Late last summer. He had three knights and sergeants with him that time, and three villeins. And again, forty horses. All mares this time—all of the war horse breed."

"Did any stories follow him?" I wondered if he'd made a name for himself with the stunner and blast pistol we'd left him.

"None that I've heard. He came to me asking for transport. I'd hauled Norman war horses before, for William of Caen, and your Arno had heard of me. I built their stalls so the horses cannot fall in a storm and break their legs."

"What did you think of him?"

"Of Arno de Courmeron? A very hard man, like every other Norman I've met. And very young for what he was doing. By all reports, at his age—at any age—most Normans of noble birth think only of fighting and plotting. It is that or the clergy. A Norman knight turned merchant was new to me.

"What is your interest in him?" ben Abraham asked then. "Or in any Norman? You do not seem warlike."

I didn't try to think an answer, just let the words come. "My own land, Evdash, has been conquered by the evil Glondis Empire—an empire that could someday come even to Christendom and try to enslave it. I hope to build a kingdom here that is wise and just, and powerful, that can defeat Glondis when the time comes. It seems to me that the Normans could help, and Arno de Courmeron is the Norman I can best work with."

Ben Abraham's face had gone unreadable. He nodded. "There is something about you that is different," he said. "I have no idea what it is. You have a power that is not force, and perhaps you can do what you say. But I will tell you something that perhaps you do not realize.

"I have talked with more than a few Normans—even with the steward of Robert Guiscard, whom the Bishop of Rome now has anointed Duke of Sicily as well as Apulia. And I deal with many people from almost every part of the known world. I am always interested in people, and what they have to say, and my home and table are not unknown. So they talk to me—merchants, ship's captains, traveling nobles. And sometimes I travel, for trade. I once spent two weeks in the court of the Saracen Lord of Palermo; many wise men are his guests, and hold long discourse there. I have talked with the secretary of the Bishop of Rome, and shared wine with the Lombard mayor of Amalfi. I have dined with merchant princes in Byzantium, and discussed commerce with the steward of Philip the Fair, the Frankish king, in his castle at Paris.

"All of these have had much experience with Normans, and I would like to describe for you the impression I have gained from them. The Normans are more than adventurous: They have an extreme restlessness, and a recklessness that often leads them to victory, although sometimes it takes them to their own destruction. They have a thirst for power that seems beyond quenching. There is no people in the known world who exceeds them in their love of fighting—not even the bloody Vikings, from whom the Normans drew their founders and their name. They have a courage that is frequently foolhardy, and a craftiness that leads often into treacheries both outrageous and bloody.

"And I have heard it said that those who go to Italy are the worst of them all.

"Their overlord in Italy, Robert of Apulia, is even called Guiscard, 'the Cunning,' and wears the name with pride."

I wouldn't understand all of ben Abraham's words until I'd run them through the linguistics program aboard the scout, but I understood enough to make my stomach knot.

"You may wish to enlist the help of the Normans," ben Abraham went on, "but the Normans help mainly themselves. To whatever they can take."

I nodded, feeling his black eyes on me, remembering the Norman Baron, Roland de Falaise, his utter lack of honesty, his attempt to have me clubbed to death by trickery. Even Arno had tried treachery against me, twice. Though he'd also saved my life, not to mention helping us rescue Deneen from the political police and capture the Federation corvette. Which the Normans, with the recklessness ben Abraham had just mentioned, had then blown apart, along with thirty of their own knights.

Yet ben Abraham made the Normans seem even more dangerous than I remembered them, mainly by showing them to me as a culture, not as a few dozen warriors. And by letting me see them through someone's eyes besides my own.

But I had to start somewhere, and Arno seemed like a good somewhere.

"I thank you for your warning," I told ben Abraham. "I have experienced some of what you described. It is why I wish to find Arno; I know him well enough that I believe I can work through him." *I hope*, I added to myself.

"I would not dissuade you," ben Abraham said. "Only, make sure you know what you're dealing with. Your own ambitions are not less than any of theirs, and I sense in you a strength of your own that I suspect can be formidable, though not brutal. Yours is an ambition of a kind that dukes with armies have undertaken and failed with, but every kingdom was begun by someone, and often against great odds."

It was really embarrassing to hear him say it. It made me feel like a huge fraud—I was only Larn kel Deroop—but this was no time to correct his impression of me.

"Thank you," I said, and moved the conversation on to other things—mainly the geography, peoples, and princes of the Mediterranean. There wasn't any question that ben Abraham was the smartest man I'd met on Fanglith—the best informed and least given to statements that sounded like runaway imagination and superstition.

And a born teacher who'd obviously rather instruct a couple of young strangers like Tarel and me than attend to business. A couple of times his secretary looked in at us, as if he had questions that needed answering, but ben Abraham frowned him back from the door.

I recorded all of it. I'd feed it to the computer that night and receive it back through the learning program, the words analyzed and defined. I have a darned good memory, and good logic circuits of my own. But for linguistics analysis, the computer was parsecs ahead of me, and the learning program would help me remember it.

Finally it was lunchtime, and Tarel and I ate with ben Abraham as his guests. Then I arranged passage for myself to Reggio di Calabria, in Italy, on one of ben Abraham's ships, which was leaving in four days. Reggio was just across the Strait of Messina from the Sicilian port where Arno had taken his horse herd.

When I'd paid my fare, I had just one gold piece left, plus the silver I'd gotten when I sold my donkey that morning.

Ben Abraham walked us to the courtyard, and as we shook hands, I asked him one last question. "My lord," I said, "yesterday you told Carolus the stonecutter an untruth, to shield my own. Why?"

His face was serious when he answered. "I am a Jew," he said. "And in the lands of Christendom, any non-Christian is always in at least some small risk of his life for being what he is. It seemed to me that you might be in serious risk of yours unless I spoke for you."

Our eyes held for a moment before I thanked him for his courtesies and help. As Tarel and I walked away, it seemed to me that I was alive only through the risks, large and small, of strangers—certainly on Evdash, and perhaps now, here in Marseille. And by Father Drogo and Pierre the tanner in Normandy, as far as that was concerned—men who had no reason beyond their own ethics to have helped me.

TWELVE

When we left Isaac ben Abraham, there still were hours to wait before calling Deneen back down. It seemed to me we might as well spend it learning something, so Tarel and I walked down to the waterfront to see what we could see.

The ships weren't much; they looked even smaller up close than they had in large magnification from a few miles above. The ones we looked at had a mast, though on some of them it was lying in the bottom of the ship, or in a few cases, on the deck or the dock or the beach. Most of them weren't decked over, though; all they had as decks amounted to flooring in the bottom of the ship. Others were partially decked over, fore and aft, with the midships open, and a few were decked over from stem to stern.

We talked to some sailors about ships and the places they'd been—sailors who spoke Provençal. Their talk of places was a bit of this and that, and a lot of it sounded— umm, more or less imaginative. I got the impression that part of the time they were lying on purpose, as if they were trying to see how much we'd believe. We (mainly me—Tarel didn't say very much) also questioned them about the names of different ships' parts and gear. Mostly the men on different ships used the same terms, so I felt they were honest with us on that. I didn't have Evdashian equivalents for most of their terms, but I recorded brief descriptions of the parts in

Evdashian—enough to serve as memory tags to go with the Provençal words.

Then we walked the streets of Marseille, asking questions of artisans and shopkeepers. By late afternoon we were more than ready to eat dinner and leave. The inn we stopped at looked better than others we'd seen, but it wouldn't begin to pass a health department inspection on Evdash; they'd board it up and burn it down. It was even worse than the dining hall in Baron Roland's castle in Normandy. The food was edible—a vegetable stew, a chunk of roast beef, coarse, dark, smelly bread, and smellier cheese. It was the dirt and grease that bothered us most, and again I was thankful for the immunoserum we'd taken.

Some of the customers there didn't look very savory, either. But we were bigger than any of them, and we wore shortswords, so no one bothered us. If they had, I'd have tried first to bluff our way out of it, using our stunners only if we couldn't avoid it. Hand-foot art wasn't promising. Being as big as we were, we'd hardly be attacked with less than swords, and it seemed to me that using our own swords would be suicidal. We had no training, no technique.

In a sense, our swords were a lie, because we weren't the swordsmen they implied. But in another sense, they told a truth in a way these people could accept: We were armed and deadly, our weapons more dangerous than swords in anyone's hands. I just didn't want to use them.

We left the city a little before the gates closed at sundown. There was also a small gate by the main west gate, no wider than an ordinary door, where we could have been let out after the big gate was closed and barred. But neither of us had any desire to see what Marseille was like after dark. Together we backtracked the same route we'd walked that morning, ending on the beach, where we took off our shoes and leggings and waded until it was starting to get dark. It was starting to cloud up, too, the thin sickle of moon low in the west adding little or no light to the evening, even when there wasn't any cloud in its way. I'd call Deneen down as soon as it was full night, then feed my recording to the computer when we were aboard.

We'd have three days to use the learning program, and to relax on the surface in some place remote from people. Somewhere we could set the scout down and not be seen. An awful lot of Fanglith was like that.

And that's what we did the next morning—or rather, what Deneen did. At daybreak she headed north to find the place we'd first landed, in the high mountains. But the ground in that district was buried deep in snow, so she headed westward to islands the infrascanner had charted when we'd been surveying for signs of Imperial forces.

The island we picked was beautiful—sandy beaches, old volcanic mountains green with forest, and narrow valleys that ran down to the ocean. From the air, there was no sign of people at all, or of large animals that might be dangerous.

The day was as beautiful, and as peaceful, as the island.

We landed where a small stream ran into a little inlet, and Deneen got out and walked on the solid surface of a planet for the first time since that night on Evdash when she'd run up the ramp in a fury of gunfire some sixty days earlier. The sky was a towering blue vault, and there were none of the bad smells of Marseille. Nor any threat—at least nothing evident and immediate. A volcano could erupt, of course, or a comet could strike the planet, but the odds were minute. There were no swordsmen or bowmen around, and no reason to expect, say, an Imperial corvette.

We did find the remains of a small stone hut, not a hundred feet from where we'd landed, its walls so tumbled that we didn't recognize it until we almost stumbled over it. A large and ancient tree had grown up within the square of fallen walls, hiding it from the air.

Even so, after an initial walk on the shore of the inlet, we set a watch schedule. One of us would stay in the ship. The radio monitor was set to detect any traffic on communication bands, and it would trigger the honker if it picked up anything.

I started out by insisting that the ship be kept closed, in case there was something dangerous we'd missed on our overflight scans. But Bubba hadn't picked up anything telepathically, either, so I backed down on that. We could even have activated an energy shield around the scout, but it would have been a needless drain on the fuel slugs.

I assigned myself the first watch, and after a half hour on the learning program, spent the time reading a long article in one of dad's library cubes, about naval tactics on primitive felid worlds. None of the worlds discussed had been as primitive as Fanglith, but it was something interesting to do.

Then Tarel replaced me on watch. They'd hiked inland, so Deneen and I went for a walk on the beach. (Bubba was hunting. He preferred his dinner fresh-caught.) It was beautiful, with a light surf breaking, washing up on the sand, the forest lustrous green in the sun, the sky a deeper blue than I seemed to remember over the Entrilias Sea and Lizard Island.

We didn't talk much for a while, just walked. I should have been enjoying it, but walking on the beach made me think of Jenoor. I let myself slide into a silent swamp of "if only," and "we should have . . ."

I was aware enough, though, to know that Deneen had something on her mind, too. But I'm not much for asking personal questions unless I've got a good reason to, and besides, I was busy feeling sorry for myself. After a little bit it was Deneen who broke the silence.

"A scething for your thoughts," she said.

I shook my head. "No point in both of us being depressed."

She nodded, and we kept walking, right about where the larger waves reached. The biggest washed over our feet and wiped out our tracks behind us. "You know what?" she asked after a while.

"No. What?"

"Tarel told me he loves me and wants to marry me."

"When was that!?"

"Today. While we were hiking up the stream."

"What did you tell him?"

"I told him maybe someday. I do like Tarel, a lot, but I definitely don't love him. And even if I did, the level of medical services on Fanglith has got to be near zero, we aren't set up to take care of babies on the *Jav*, and we don't have any anti-conception drugs."

I nodded. That was my little sister—look at the angles and avoid regrets. What would we have done if Jenoor had gotten pregnant? But we hadn't planned then to go to a planet as primitive as Fanglith. We'd expected to be on Grinder, wherever that was.

"How'd he take it?"

"He said he'd already seen the problems, but thought I ought to know what was going on with him."

I walked along a little troubled. It wasn't surprising that Tarel was interested in Deneen, and he was a good guy. I hoped this wouldn't get to be a problem for anyone. We definitely didn't need complications on a planet like Fanglith.

She broke that train of thoughts, too. "Do you know what's going on with Bubba?" she asked.

"No. What?"

"I don't know either. But something is. Now and then he gets absolutely glum, and that's not like him."

"I figured the lousy food's been getting to him," I said. "It had to be tougher on a carnivore than on us. He ought to be getting over it now."

"It's more than the food. He's got something on his mind."

"He's worried about Lady," I suggested. "And the pups."

"No, we talked about that, he and I. He feels they'll do okay wherever they are. And you know Bubba; he just files things like that. If you can't do something about something, don't worry about it, and he's the kind that can really make that work."

Why are you bringing up these things? I wondered. *I just want to enjoy this place for a couple of days.* But I knew that wasn't fair. I hadn't been enjoying it; I'd been wallowing around feeling pathetic. I was the captain now, I reminded myself. Everyone's problems were mine, at least to a degree, and I needed to take responsibility for my crew and how they were doing.

We didn't talk any more about Tarel's proposal, if you could call it that. He didn't seem inclined to make a problem out of it. But she'd opened my eyes a bit by telling me.

Tarel had been attentive to Deneen, helping when it was her turn to fix meals or wash dishes. He really was a good guy, had been ever since we'd known him. Courteous and considerate, aware and intelligent . . . Even reasonably good-looking. And as I said before, surprisingly strong—one of those people who seems to have been born strong. I couldn't help but wonder what Deneen might have said if he wasn't so darned *serious* about things. He just very seldom laughed or even smiled very widely.

As for Bubba, we didn't see much of him till just before we were ready to leave. He seemed cheerful enough when he got back, but he was different from the way he'd been at home on Evdash. There wasn't the sense of openness I'd always felt from him before. It was as if he was withholding himself a little, as if there was something he was keeping to himself. Sometimes it was really noticeable, particularly now that I was paying attention.

Our vacation lasted three days and two nights. The third night we spent parked above Marseille again. At dawn of the fourth day, a raw, breezy, overcast morning, I was waiting at the town gate.

Two hours later I was on one of Isaac ben Abraham's ships, heading east through a choppy sea, a following wind pushing us along. And briskly, considering how small our triangular sail was, and how blunt the ship's broad bow.

Somehow, I felt glummer than Bubba at his glummest, as serious as Tarel. And a little seasick from the ship's pitch and roll, although I got over that pretty quickly. Tomorrow maybe it'll clear up, I thought, and we'll have sunshine. Maybe I'll feel better then.

THIRTEEN

The ship had been one of the larger in Marseille, all
of sixty feet long. Loaded as she was, her gunwales
amidships were only about four feet above the water.
The full length was decked. Below deck there were
dozens of bales of what they call "wool" on Fanglith—
the curly and remarkably thick hair of an animal called
"sheep." One of the other passengers told me the fur is
cut off the sheep's entire body, right down to the skin,
and grows back to be recut the next year. The hairs are
so tangled together that when they cut them off, they
hang together in a mat.

Below deck were also thousands of ingots of copper,
silver, and lead—especially lead—which were mainly
what made the ship ride so low in the water. Besides
the cargo of wool and ingots, there were nine passengers, all men. We slept on the bales of wool below deck
and ate the same food as the ship's crew.

Before long I was sharing my clothes again with
minute biting insects, called lice and fleas, that seem to
be ever-present pests on Fanglith.

The next day *was* nicer—clear, though still chilly—
the wind continuing from the west. For a while, a
school of very large fish swam alongside us, more or
less in formation. Their smooth-looking gray bodies
moved along in a series of arcs, curving clear of the
water and then back in. The sailors called them porpoises.

In late afternoon we saw a headland to the southeast,
a high ridge. One of the passengers told me it was the

north end of a large island named Corsica, which the Saracens had once held but had been driven from years before. Before dark we'd rounded it and were heading south, more slowly now, with the wind and the island on our right. With the wind from the side we not only went slower, we also rolled heavily, and for a while I felt a little seasick again.

At dawn the next day we were out of sight of land once more. The wind had eased quite a lot, but was still from the west, and our progress was slower yet. I spent a lot of the day asking questions of the other passengers, secretly recording our talks, but I got tired of that after a while and went below deck to kill time napping.

I was wakened by loud, excited talk. A pirate ship had been spotted, and I followed other passengers up onto the deck to see what it looked like. Head on, I couldn't see how long it was, but even seeing it from a distance it seemed to be more slender, and probably rode less deeply in the water. It had a sail, triangular like ours, and I thought I could make out oars hurrying it along. Our captain had turned us to run ahead of the light wind, but after watching for a while it was obvious that the pirate ship was gaining on us.

I was standing by the rail beside a merchant passenger who'd been to sea a lot. "How can you tell they're pirates?" I asked him.

He looked at me as if I was dense. "Because they're using oars. Only warships and pirates use oars. And because, by their lines, they're Saracens. Plus, they changed course toward us as soon as they saw us."

"What happens if they catch us?" I asked.

"They board us." He drew a shortsword and tested its blade grimly with a thumb. "And it's not if, it's when. Our only chance is that some warship, Pisan or Genoese, will show up. Don't hold your breath."

"What happens when they catch us?"

"We fight until either they kill us all or we surrender. Any of us taken alive will be held for ransom or made slaves. If you have no one to ransom you, you'll do well to die fighting."

"How much is the ransom?"

He looked me over, appraising my clothes. "More than you have," he said sourly, and turned away to watch the pirate ship again.

I watched, too—long enough to estimate that we had less than an hour, maybe half an hour, before they caught us. The sun was already down, the light beginning to fade a bit. If we could stay ahead of them long enough, I thought, maybe we could hide in the darkness. But no. I scanned the sky and there was the moon, half full now, pale in the early evening. The way they were closing the gap, they'd be close enough to see us by moonlight if they hadn't actually caught us before dark.

Of course, I could always use my blast pistol. I couldn't imagine them trying to board us after I'd fired a few charges into them. But that would make me a lot more conspicuous than I was ready to be—or rather, the wrong kind of conspicuous. Which didn't leave much for me to do but call in my one-ship space fleet, the biggest in the system.

I went down the stern ladder below deck again, among the ingots. Three of the passengers were down there, sitting near the ladder, talking quietly. I passed them and sat down amidships. They were watching me now, the strange foreigner with all the dumb questions, so when I put the remote in my ear, I made it look as if I was scratching. Fanglithans do a lot of that. Then I took my communicator off the belt inside my cape, palming it, and when I took it out, I pretended to raise my crucifix with the same hand and kiss it.

"*Jav*, this is Larn," I murmured in Evdashian. "*Jav*, this is Larn. Come in please. Over."

"Larn, this is the *Javelin*." It was Deneen's voice in my ear, also in Evdashian. "There seems to be a bogey chasing you. He's gaining on you. Over."

"Right," I answered. "They're pirates. I don't want to shoot them up myself if I can help it; I'm not ready for that kind of publicity. So here's what I want you to do. If we can stay ahead of them till it's pretty much dark, I'd like you guys to sink them with your heavy blaster. Got that?"

"Sure. If you can stay ahead of them till it's pretty much dark, we're to sink them with our number one blaster. What if they catch you while it's still fairly light? Are you going to take care of them yourself then, or do we step in?"

Apparently the three passengers watching me could hear me faintly. Two of them crossed themselves and began to pray. They probably assumed that praying was what I was doing, and decided it was a good idea.

"I'm not sure yet," I answered. "I'll have to play it by ear. I'm going back up on deck in a minute to watch, but meanwhile, as it stands now, I don't want you to shoot them up till it's too dark for anyone down here to see what's doing the shooting. It's all right if they see *something* up there, but not what the something is. Got that?"

"Got it. Why don't you just call and tell us when to start?"

An idea had been just out of sight, nudging my mind. Now I saw it. "Good idea. I'll call you in Provençal. And listen. . . ."

When I finished explaining what I had in mind, I put my communicator back inside my cape and went up on deck. The other three had watched me the whole time, so I crossed myself before I left, and nodded at them soberly as I went to the ladder.

The pirate ship had gained quite a bit on us, and the evening seemed hardly any darker than when I'd gone below. It didn't look as if we'd stay ahead of them long enough. Besides which, there was no safety or hope ahead of us that I could see, and it occurred to me that our captain might decide to turn back and fight—get it over with.

So I went to him. He was manning the heavy steering oar himself, his eyes sternward toward the pirates. "Captain," I said, "I've been praying to the Angel Deneen. She told me that if we stay ahead of the Saracens till darkness, they'll be destroyed with fire from heaven."

His eyes narrowed. I wasn't sure what he was thinking. "Can we?" I asked. "Stay ahead of them till dark?"

"It is in the hands of God," he said after a few seconds.

"Good," I told him. "We must leave it there, in the hands of God, and not defy him by turning to fight, for he will surely save us."

The captain scowled without saying anything more to me, as if he thought I was crazy. I leaned against the rail to watch the pirates gaining on us.

After a few minutes it seemed to me they weren't gaining on us as fast as they had been. I suppose their oarsmen were getting tired. And the light was noticeably less, though it was still more like daylight than night. Maybe it *would* get dark before they caught us.

"Larn."

It was the remote I'd left in my ear.

"There are more than forty pirates, not counting the guys who are rowing. And they look really tough. If you change your mind about when, we're ready to put them out of commission."

I didn't take out my communicator and answer her; it wasn't the time or place for that. She'd have to assume I got it. But I nodded anyway, in case they had me in the viewer under magnification.

There were eleven in our crew, and ten passengers including myself, just about all of us on deck now. Several had shortswords already in hand, but I doubt that any one of them would really qualify as a warrior. Gradually the distance shrank between the pirates and ourselves, and gradually it got darker. It began to look as if it might get dark soon enough after all. And looking upward I could see the scout; it had come down to maybe four or five hundred yards and was barely visible against the darkening sky. You had to look for it—know it was up there—to see it.

The pirate ship was only about two hundred feet behind us. I stepped away from the rail a little and took out my palmed communicator, raising it as if I was lifting up my crucifix. Then I bellowed out as loudly as I could: "Don't be afraid! The Angel Deneen will save us! She has promised!"

Just about everyone on the ship looked at me. None

of them looked actually scornful; stories about divine intervention were common on Fanglith. But none of them looked very convinced, either. And the pirate ship came on. After another couple of minutes I looked up again. I could sort of make out the *Jav;* she was maybe two hundred yards up now, and the pirates not more than eighty or a hundred feet behind. I switched on my communicator. "Angel Deneen!" I shouted. "Save us from the Saracens!"

A heavy-caliber blaster thudded once, and a hissing charge exploded into the pirate ship. We could hear them yelling back there. Then a spotlight speared down from above, drawing every eye, and someone up there—Tarel, I learned later—fired four more single rounds about a second apart. The pirate ship started to burn in the thickening dusk as we pulled away from her, but she apparently sank in a hurry, because the flames disappeared quickly, as if drowned.

FOURTEEN

Moise:

Even though the slavemaster had slowed the beat somewhat, I was so tired I thought I would die of it. But he was pacing the walkway between us, and I still feared his whip more than death. Besides, I always felt that way when we were chasing some merchant ship, and hadn't died yet. A man can stand more than he thinks.

Ahead on the merchantman, I heard someone call out loudly. We were that close. Soon we would ship our oars and rest while the Saracens boarded her, but until then I had to keep on.

Cool as the evening was, sweat trickled into my eyes, and dripped from my nose and chin to fall on my bare thighs. I gasped for breath. Again I heard a shout from ahead, nearer now—and then the world exploded! My bench was torn loose, thrown back, and I fell on the feet and legs of the oarsman behind me, a Tuscan named Guittone. I had no idea what had happened. As I struggled to disentangle myself from Guittone's legs, there was another terrible sound, and more, and I felt water rising rapidly around me. Men were screaming, some of them calling to Allah to be merciful. None of them knew—none of them could have known—what had struck us, any more than I did then.

The ship sank quickly—indeed, had broken in two— the halves pulling apart, with one swinging to the left and one to the right. The half with the mast had turned onto her side. I was floating free of it, chained to my broken bench. Around me, many of my captors—ex-captors now—were clinging to wreckage or swimming toward one of the halves, and it seemed well to move away from them, although there was no place to swim to except into the near-night. The water was winter-cold. I managed to get my broken bench beneath me, then kicked and paddled away, careful not to overturn again. Minutes later I could not see any of them any longer, although distantly I could hear injured men calling for help.

Tarel:
I hadn't liked shooting into the pirate ship, but it was necessary. There wasn't much question about what the pirates had in mind, but it bothered me to shoot at people who couldn't defend themselves against us. There wasn't even anything they could *try* to do.

On the target screen I could see their ship almost as clearly as if it were daylight. It surprised me to see it break in two. I suppose it was partly because it was going along pretty fast, for such a primitive ship. The blaster bolts must have torn enough out of the hull that it acted like a scoop, and the pressure broke it where the explosions had weakened it.

Deneen turned off the spotlight, but I could still see with the target screen. Guys were swimming to the halves of the hull, which were still afloat, one full of water to the gunwales, the other on its side. Deneen felt the way I did—wanted to go down and rescue people—but it would be suicide to take pirates into the *Javelin* with us.

What she did instead was lift to about two hundred yards again, and we sat there watching, unwilling to just leave. Then I noticed that one guy was paddling away from the wreckage, which seemed peculiar. It occurred to me that he might have been a prisoner or something—maybe one of the oarsmen. They might have been slaves; there'd been a guy with a whip making sure they kept rowing.

"Deneen!" I started, and before I could get any more out, she said, "I see him." She's like that sometimes, as if she knows what you're thinking. We watched him paddle and kick until he was about a hundred yards from the others. Then he slowed down, as if he felt safer now, or maybe tired, and Deneen started to lower us toward him.

At twenty feet or so she hit the control for the door. It opened and I went over to it. We were behind the guy and he hadn't even seen us. It turned out he'd noticed the light on the water in front of him, from the open door, but of course, it never occurred to him what it might be. Meanwhile Deneen lowered us to five feet.

He wasn't more than a dozen feet from me, so I spoke to him in Provençal. "Let me help you."

He turned, jerking as if he'd been stung, and the board he was on turned over, dumping him off. For a moment, when he surfaced, he just stared toward us as if he didn't see anything there. Then his eyes bugged out and his mouth sagged open.

"We'll take you out of the water if you'll let us," I told him.

He started talking in some language I couldn't understand, not as if he were talking to me, but more as if he were talking to himself. I'd never heard anyone pray before—hadn't even heard of praying until I'd gotten the concept from the computer when I was learning Provençal. Prayers are pretty important on Fanglith. Meanwhile, Deneen kept the *Jav* settling downward until we weren't more than twenty inches above the waves, which weren't very big. I reached out toward him. He shook off the shock of seeing us then, and started paddling the ten feet or so to me. I guess I didn't look as fierce or mean as the people who'd had him last.

I looked around for something I could reach out with that he could grab hold of. When I didn't see anything, I lay down on the deck, grabbed the edge of the door-way with my left hand, and reached out with my right. When he got to me, we grabbed each others' wrists and I pulled.

There was a problem: He was chained to the broken bench he was on. I hoisted him partway in, then took hold of the chain and pulled the board in too. He just lay there on the deck then, looking around. I could imagine what it was like for him. The scout was so different, so completely unlike anything he'd ever seen or imagined or dreamed of, that he must have thought he was dead or crazy. In fact, he told me later that that was just how he felt. And Bubba's big wolf face was looking at him about thirty inches from his own.

Deneen:

I wanted to follow the merchant ship and see what was happening, but Moise's feet were still sticking out the door. He was also bleeding on the deck—not heavily, but he *was* injured. I told Tarel to get him in. Tarel took hold of him under the arms and pulled, and I closed the door. Then I lifted to a hundred yards and moved to a position above the merchantman.

It had changed its course from east to southeast, the direction it had been going before they'd spotted the pirates. It looked to me as if everyone aboard it was on deck now. I called Larn and he answered right away, his voice soft and not too far from laughing.

"It worked like a charm," he told me in Evdashian. "They think I'm really something." Then, in Provençal, he called: "Thank you, Angel Deneen! Thank you for answering my request! You have saved us from the Saracen!"

"That's all right, brother mine." I said it in Evdashian, in case he'd switched on his speaker—which it turned out he had. "Do you need anything more just now?"

"No," he said, in Evdashian himself again. "I'll let you know if anything more happens."

I didn't tell him about our new passenger. I didn't have enough information yet to make it worthwhile, and didn't want to worry him. I just put the spotlight on the midships deck for a moment, centering on Larn—one last sign from the heavens. Then I switched it off and parked there, invisible from below. In Evdashian I told Tarel to take our passenger into the head, sluice him off in the shower, and do whatever seemed necessary for his wounds, so far as he could. I also told Bubba to stay with them in case the guy turned out to be dangerous after all. (Not that I needed to; Bubba would know, and he'd do whatever was needed.) Then Tarel could put our—guest? prisoner?—in one of the suits of navy fatigues we had on board, and feed him, and we'd see what we could learn about him.

Meanwhile, I made sure my stunner was set on medium-low. If I had to use it, I didn't want to endanger Tarel or Bubba. But for some reason, I had the distinct feeling that I wouldn't have to use it—that we had a new friend and ally on board, not an enemy.

FIFTEEN

The rest of the trip took four days. Four days that started out miserably for everyone else aboard ship, because they all came down with diarrhea that night—every one of them—and had it for two or three days. The ship didn't have any latrines of course, only buckets and the sea, and at times there was no time to wait for a bucket. I offered my thanks from a distance to the inventor of the immunoserum.

Lice and fleas, on the other hand, had no respect at all for immunoserum, or even for people who could call down angels and lightning from the sky, and foreigners seemed to taste as good as native Fanglithans to them. On Fanglith, though, people hardly thought of them as an affliction; in fact, they hardly thought of them at all. Everyone I'd seen seemed to have them, and apparently all the time. Lice and fleas were like breathing and eating—a part of life.

Maybe Fanglithans would even miss their lice if they lost them; I'm not sure. I wouldn't. *Itch!* True, I was starting to get used to them, but life on Fanglith would have been a lot nicer without them.

Anyway, not getting diarrhea fitted my image as someone special—someone protected by an angel. Where before some of the people on board had disliked me as a dumbbell full of foolish questions, now everyone was at least polite, including the captain. Some of them were in absolute awe of me, and at meals I even got larger portions than the others. But no one tried to hang around with me.

The day after the pirate incident, Deneen told me about the guy they'd rescued. He'd been a galley slave, forced to help row the pirate ship, and was about the same age as she and Tarel were. His name was Moise ben Israel, and like Isaac ben Abraham, Moise was a Jew, a member of a different religion and culture from Christians. His family had been moving from a city called Genoa to one called Amalfi, where Jews were not so badly treated. When the Saracens attacked the ship, his whole family had drowned or been killed.

Moise could read and write, spoke several languages, and knew a lot about how things were done on Fanglith. He seemed to be adjusting well to Deneen and Tarel and the cutter.

And Bubba approved of him—said he was a good guy. One thing Bubba didn't miss on was what people were like.

The next to last day was stormy—the wind behind us, the sky and sea two tones of gray. Big waves would loom above our stern, some of them fifteen feet high or higher. They'd raise us up as they caught us, then we'd seem to slide down their backside as they passed. And there the next one would be, heaving itself above us from behind. To me it was exhilarating.

The captain had two men on the steering oar. As he explained it to me, it was important that we stay headed downwind. If we broached—came about sideways to the waves—we could easily turn over. He didn't seem worried, though, so I figured the danger wasn't great.

Some of the people prayed quite a bit though, including several of the crew, and they looked at me a lot, as if they hoped I'd pull off another miracle. The only miracle I could think of was to have Deneen pick me up if we foundered, and when the storm got a bit worse, I called her. They were keeping an eye on us, she told me, and if we foundered, Bubba could easily identify me among the people in the water.

While I was murmuring to her, of course, people were watching hopefully, soon after that, the wind started easing up. The waves stayed pretty big for a while, but it felt as if the danger had passed. Judging from the sideways glances people gave me, I was getting the credit for it, which was fine with me. It was just the kind of notoriety I wanted.

The last day dawned to seas that were a lot smaller, and they got smaller yet through the day. In mid-afternoon we saw land ahead. It looked like a continuous shoreline at first, but as we got closer I could see an opening that the captain told me was the Strait of Messina.

About then I noticed that some of the crew were starting to look a little nervous, and I asked one of them if something was wrong.

"Charybdis," he said.

"What is—Charybdis?"

He used a word that didn't mean anything to me, but his explanation, complete with hand motions (the Provençals are great for using their hands to help them talk), made it clear: Charybdis is a whirlpool. In the Strait of Messina. And it could, he told me, swallow a ship.

I asked the captain about that, and he nodded. "It could. But many ships go through there every year, and only now and then does the whirlpool take one of them. Perhaps when there is a storm out of the north, or the ship has a careless master." He shrugged. "Or maybe with someone on board whom God has decided to strike down—perhaps a heretic. Some say there is a monster in it that takes a ship when she is hungry. But there are more monsters told about than exist, and I do not believe there is one in the whirlpool."

He crossed himself though, after he said it.

When we passed through the strait, I kept watching for the whirlpool, but didn't see it. What I did see on both sides was rough, mountainous country without much forest, and to the southwest, on the Sicilian side, an incredible mountain in the distance. It was broad, climbing gradually up and up, with miles and miles of snow. The captain told me its name was Aetna.

It was starting to get dark when we landed in Reggio

di Calabria, a town ruled by Normans. I was almost out of money, and the captain agreed to let me sleep on the ship that night. It brought the ship luck to have me aboard, he said; it would bring it still more to grant a boon to a holy man.

It took me a minute to realize that by holy man he meant me. And from what I understood of the concepts of *holy*, I felt a little embarrassed. I'd tricked him, and everyone else on board, and didn't feel good about it.

I had the ship almost to myself. The other passengers had left. The mate and another sailor sat on guard by the gangplank while two others, their relief, slept nearby on wool bales dragged up on deck. A lopsided moon shone down.

They'd dragged up more than enough bales for themselves, and as I lay down across a couple of extras, scratching and waiting for sleep, I thought about what I'd done. So I'd used trickery. It had been necessary; they'd never accept me for what I was. They wouldn't believe. Or if they did, they wouldn't understand. And if the word got around, I might get executed as a demon; that had almost happened at the Monastery of St. Stephen of Isere, my first time on Fanglith.

What I'd done on this ship had helped the people on it—saved them from being killed or enslaved by the pirates—while what I hoped to do would keep them from being enslaved by the Empire.

Because if the Glondis Empire lasted long enough, it would come to Fanglith someday and subjugate it.

And that uncovered the unasked questions that had had me in the glums off and on lately. Did I actually believe we could turn this planet into a rebel world? And if the Empire came to Fanglith, would the Fanglithans be any worse off then they already were? Or might they actually be better off?

But enough of the old legend was obviously true that I could assume the rest was, too. The human population of Fanglith had started out mind-wiped and naked, without as much as a knife or even a memory—a few thousand political prisoners dumped here 18,000 years ago by the Mad Emperor, Karkzhuk. And with that miserable start, it was impressive that they'd advanced this far. There was no reason to think they wouldn't someday be truly civilized, but if the Glondis Empire took Fanglith over, they'd make a slave labor pool out of it.

Of course, the big question was whether we could accomplish anything here. What was needed was some kind of superman—someone out of an adventure thriller—not Larn Rostik kel Deroop.

I shook off the crud of self-devaluation and looked up at the stars. Evdash was up there somewhere, I thought to myself, and then I thought of Jenoor, killed by the Empire, and started deliberately to build up a good hate to toughen my mind for the job we had here. But working up a hate was just a dodge, and I knew it. It didn't change the way things were; it was just a way of not looking at them. I needed to get my attention out of myself, so I took out my communicator; I'd talk with Deneen.

I didn't use the remote. The guards would hear her voice, but that was the kind of thing they expected of me now. I was established as someone who communicated with the angels.

Deneen:
Moise was something else, and finding him could almost make me believe in fate. Virtually everything about us was new to him, including knowing what the stars really were, and the galaxy, and Fanglith itself. You'd never imagine how the Fanglithans had envisioned and explained their world and the universe. Yet he'd adjusted so quickly to us and to what we'd shown him, with so little confusion and not even a headache, that both Tarel and I were really impressed. Moise was not only very bright, he was very adaptable.

I wonder if mental adaptability might not be the key to maximum success in this universe.

You might think we'd have gotten bored, parked fifteen miles above the surface with "nothing much to do." Actually, we were as busy as we could be, including Moise, because after talking with him a while, I'd decided he'd make a good consultant, and perhaps a contact man on the surface. I wasn't sure about that yet.

So Tarel and I had taken turns questioning him—picking his brain—and educating him. Recording all of it, of course, then running it through linguistic analysis and taking turns using the learning program. We were expanding our knowledge of the language and of Fanglith both.

In turn, we educated him. Over the next four days we described to him what the universe and galaxy were really like, gave him a course in the basic principles of technology, and let him know a little about ourselves. Not everything. But that we were refugees from a far world, and that we wanted to make a place for ourselves on Fanglith without attracting hostile attention from the people here.

We'd had to talk Provençal, of course—the only language we knew that he could understand. Fortunately, Moise was from a seaport called Genoa, where the language, Piedmontese, was pretty much like Provençal. He could understand us, and we understood him, without a lot of trouble. He told us he also spoke Hebrew, Aramaic, and quite a bit of Greek. And Arabic, the language of the Saracens. It had been important in Tarragona, the place where they'd lived before going to Genoa. The pirates had spoken Arabic, too. He'd learned quite a bit of Arabic poetry where he'd lived in Tarragona; he'd thought they were the best poems of all. And the poetry had built his Arabic vocabulary well above the street vocabulary of the children he'd played with.

I'd become aware on our first trip to Fanglith that there was a bad communication scene on this world, but now I began to realize how bad. Because all of those languages, plus a bunch of others, were spoken in just the region around the Mediterranean. Who knew how many different languages there might be on Fanglith? It seemed a safe bet that there were hundreds of them.

Because Arabic was important around much of the Mediterranean, it seemed to me that it might be useful to us. So between times, I had Moise say Arabic words into the recorder, discussing in Piedmontese what they meant. Then I'd load them into the computer. But for the time being we'd stick with Provençal/Piedmontese. Moise said we should be able to make ourselves understood with it, more or less, in Tuscany and Venice, which were important regions of Italy.

Moise was unusually well educated, I realized—even compared with most of the "nobility" of the time. But it was interesting how little he knew of geography—even the geography of the Mediterranean. He knew a lot about a lot of places and peoples, but a map he tried to sketch for us, in our first session, was so crude and incomplete that, comparing it with the one our ship had made, we couldn't figure out where it was supposed to be. And he had no idea where it was on our map.

It turned out that on Fanglith they hadn't developed map-making as a technical skill. They hardly even had the concept of an overall geographical view—of the planet's surface as something you could sketch on a coordinate system. If they could get where they wanted to go from where they already were, that was enough for them.

Briefly we took him out to 5,000 miles—briefly because that was in one of Fanglith's heavy radiation belts, and because we couldn't see Larn's ship from there. Instead of being scared or awed or anything like that, Moise was positively enraptured. Later, I had the computer print out a map of the whole Mediterranean region for him, and the country north of it all the way to the northern sea. From the way he'd reacted, you'd think I'd given him something of fabulous value, which I guess maybe I had.

When the pirates had attacked the ship his family was on, his mother and sister had jumped into the sea so they wouldn't be sold as slaves. Neither one of them could swim. His father had ordered Moise to lie on his face, then died fighting. Moise, because he was young, and for Fanglith big, had been chained to a rowing bench to replace a slave too sick to row anymore. The sick slave had then been thrown into the sea as a lesson to the others not to get sick.

Moise had never exercised much before, and he told us with a laugh about his first couple of days at the oar. The skin had rubbed off his hands, and in general his body had gotten so tired he'd thought he was dying. Then there'd been a couple of days when the wind had been right, and they hadn't had to row. That's when his muscles, from legs to shoulders and arms, had gotten so stiff and sore he didn't think he'd ever be able to move again.

But he had. Because the next day, when they were ordered to row again, he'd seen the whip used. He'd rowed then in spite of his soreness. Three weeks of slave food and rowing changed him from kind of pudgy to lean and sinewy. In the months since then he'd added a lot of muscle.

He was lucky, he told us, to have had the captain he'd had. He'd heard that some pirate captains underfed their slaves. His had fed them enough to keep them strong for rowing. He'd even given them dates and raisins, along with dried and salted meat, occasional stew, and what Moise called *massah*—some kind of bread.

Most of the time we stayed at fifteen miles, keeping the viewscreen locked on Larn's ship, and Bubba kept some telepathic attention on what was going on down there. I checked in with Larn once a day just to stay in touch. After we'd sunk the pirate ship, he'd only called once while he was at sea. My brother isn't the kind who needs his hand held.

But after they got to the port of Reggio, he called again, sounding kind of bummed out. It seemed as if he was wondering what he was down there for. I could see his problem; it was ours too—Tarel's and mine.

"Larn," I said, "you're worrying about no workable plan again."

He didn't say anything back right away.

"Can I make a suggestion?" I asked.

"Okay. Sure."

"We've got an intention. Right?"

"I guess so. Yes."

"So what is it, then? The intention."

It took him a minute—well, ten or fifteen seconds—before he answered, I suppose because what he was looking at didn't seem do-able to him. "Make this a rebel world," he said at last.

I was playing it by ear myself now, and what I said next surprised me. "Take it back another step," I told him. "Our real intention is to rid the Empire of tyrannical rule. Right?"

There was another lag, and when he answered, his voice was thoughtful. "Right. That's right."

"So how about this, then: You're down there doing things, making decisions step by step to suit the situation—the best you can and with no need to hurry. And if you keep that intention in mind, to rid the Empire of tyrannical rule, your decisions will move us in that direction.

"Does that make any sense to you?"

"Yeah, I guess so. Yeah."

"Good. And we're not in a hurry! We can't make a rebel world out of Fanglith overnight. As far as that's concerned, maybe it's not even possible. Take things a step at a time, learn, and wait for the bright idea that you *can* build a plan on. And if things don't look good in a year or two, maybe we'll decide to go somewhere else, to some other planet. We don't *have* to make it on Fanglith."

I shut up then, to give him a chance. After a minute though, when he hadn't said anything more, I spoke again. "Brother mine, are you there?"

I heard him chuckle then, the welcomest sound I'd heard in a long time. "Yeah, I'm here. Thanks, sis. You're the greatest. This is Larn, over and out."

"This is the *Jav*, over and out."

I switched off the mike. *Maybe not the greatest*, I thought, *but I am pretty good, if I do say so myself*.

Tarel and Moise were already sleeping. Only Bubba was awake with me, looking at me and grinning, his tongue hanging out. I winked at him, then put on the learning program skullcap and began my first lesson in Arabic.

Moise:

These people who rescued me were clearly not children of Abraham. Nor were they Christian, nor of Islam. Yet if they were heathen, they seemed nonetheless people of honor and nobility. And surely they had shown me kindness and many wonders. Even their huge wolf-like dog spoke with them in his own language, which they understood, and they answered him in theirs. Deneen says they will start to teach me their language tomorrow.

Although they have knowledge and power incredibly beyond my own, they treat me almost like one of them. True, at first they locked me in my room at night, but that was a reasonable precaution. And they showed me no other distrust, though they knew nothing about me except what I told them. They have told me their dog reads the thoughts of men, and has told them I am honorable, worthy of their trust. Perhaps he does read thoughts. I will test him when I learn to understand his speech.

Being with them, I feel an excitement like none I have imagined before. And even though they are goyim, if they ask me to help them in their endeavors, as I expect they will, I will surely agree. For I have no family, nor anyone else in all this world.

PART THREE

CAPTURED

SIXTEEN

Larn:

A few hours later I woke up, just barely, and feeling kind of chilly, went below and fell right asleep again. The next thing I knew, someone had grabbed me and jerked my right arm up behind my back. A second person was taking the blast pistol, stunner, and communicator off my belt. Someone else, on deck, was holding a flickering torch down through the hatch; now he backed away.

"Not to struggle." The guy talking was the one who'd taken my weapons. "I wish not to harm you."

The words were Evdashian! Broken Evdashian! Then whoever was holding me jerked me to my feet, harder than he needed to. He was *strong*, with hands like very large clamps.

I was absolutely wide awake now, but confused. How could the Imperials have found me? And wouldn't the political police have spoken in Standard? Besides, someone whose language was Standard wouldn't speak Evdashian with that accent. It occurred to me then that maybe they'd been here ahead of us this time. Maybe they had native monitors on Fanglith now, who'd picked up my communicator traffic.

But I couldn't really believe that; it seemed impossible that this was happening.

The guy who had me in the hammerlock pushed me toward the ladder. There was just enough light that I could see the one with my weapons start up the ladder.

The man following me had to release his hammer lock to climb the steep steps after me, but at the top, the guy with my weapons was waiting in the dark with my stunner pointed at me.

The sailor on watch was standing well back from the gangplank, obviously afraid of the guys who'd captured me. His relief man was sitting awake on a wool bale, staring, unmoving. The moon, about three-quarters full, was lighting the scene from about thirty or forty degrees above the western horizon. Considering the geometry of the planet, moon, and sun here, that made it about midnight.

Then the man behind me reached the deck and clamped the hammerlock on me again.

The one with my weapons definitely seemed to be the boss. I could see now that he wore a conical Norman helmet, and I was willing to bet he had a hauberk on beneath his cloak. A knight's outfit. But he was familiar with civilized weapons, because he turned and put both the sailors to sleep with my stunner. I hoped it was to sleep; if he'd reset it upward from the medium setting I usually kept it on, at this range they were probably dead. He hadn't needed to shoot them at all; they hadn't been about to do anything.

Meanwhile the guy behind me never paused, just kept walking across the deck and down the gangplank, pushing me ahead of him. The guy with the torch had started off ahead; the one with my weapons came along behind now. A little way along the wharf we came to several horses, watched by a fourth man. The guy in charge stepped in front of me and turned, stunner steady. Now, in the moonlight and torchlight, I could see his face.

"Brislieu, let go his arm." This time he spoke in Norman French. My arm was released.

"Arno!" I said. This was harder for me to believe than my first idea about Imperials. How had he learned to talk Evdashian? No wonder I hadn't recognized his voice! Then I recalled: The last day we'd been with him, he'd spent a couple of hours plugged into the learning program, absorbing Evdashian—just before the

Federation corvette had blown up; a little before we'd left Fanglith. It was surprising he could speak it at all; that had been two and a half years earlier, and he'd never had a chance to use it, even once.

"I'd come here looking for you!" I told him. "But how did you find me? How did you even know I was back on Fanglith?"

He laughed softly. "Your French has gotten worse," he said, again in Norman French. "You've been speaking too much Provençal. We'll talk of how I found you, and of other things, when we're out of town." He gestured toward one of the horses. "That one is yours; get on. We have some twenty miles to ride. And do not try to escape. You'll be more comfortable sitting in the saddle than tied over it on your belly, and the scenery will be better that way."

I put a foot in the stirrup and swung up onto the horse—one of the heavy war horses that the Normans call *destriers*. Arno had swung into the saddle without letting the stunner move away from me. Then we rode off down the dirt street, the horses' iron-shod hooves thudding softly in the quiet night. I hadn't ridden since Normandy; the horse's smell and the roll of its gait felt good to me. At one point we encountered a street patrol, but they didn't pay any attention to us. I suppose they recognized Arno and Brislieu as Norman knights, and Normans were the masters here.

The wall around Reggio was higher and thicker than the one at Marseille. One of the gate guards opened a narrow gate for us, and before long we were in the moonlit countryside. Here Brislieu took the lead and Arno rode beside me, their squires sharing a horse behind us. After a few moments I repeated my earlier question:

"How did you find me?"

Arno chuckled. "Those who gain fame are easy to find. I had come to Reggio to arrange to ship horses to Palermo, and in an inn I heard a ship's captain tell a marvelous story, about a holy man who talked to his crucifix. Or actually to an angel, through his crucifix.

And either the crucifix or the angel talked back to him; I forget just how he told it."

Arno laughed again. "The angel sent down lightning from the sky, which struck and sank a corsair. And moments later the eye of GOD shown down as a shaft of golden light, to fall unerringly on the holy man. Then, later, when a plague of grippe sickened all others aboard, this holy man, who was named the Blessed Larn, was not touched by it.

"Later still, when a storm threatened to send one and all to their deaths, this Larn, who was from India incidentally, called on the angel again. *Angel Deneen*, he called her. And the water smoothed around them like a silver mirror, though at a little distance the waves heaved and tossed more savagely than before."

I could see Arno's grin in the moonlight. "Even allowing for exaggeration," he continued, "I might have wondered if it was you, even if he had not named you. And indeed I did not catch your name clearly when first he said it, for not only was he speaking Provençal, but his mouth was full at the time. But your sister's name left no doubt."

He chuckled again. He'd changed since I'd seen him last; his mood was lighter. "Lightning from the sky. That was something you didn't show us before. Or was that the shipmaster's imagination?"

"He stretched things a little," I said, "but it was pretty much true."

He looked me over now as we rode. "You've grown," he said. "You were tall already; now you're as tall as Brislieu. Or very nearly. What brought you back to—our world?"

It was hard for him to say "our world," as if he'd never quite accepted that there were others. In spite of everything he'd seen.

I didn't answer right away—didn't know just how to start, although I'd thought before about what I'd say to Arno when I found him. The country air was a little chilly, an early spring night in a warm climate. Moonlight lay a shimmering path across the strait to our right; to our left it lit the rugged hills, and filled the ravines with inky shadow.

"What brought us to Fanglith?" I answered him in Evdashian, slowly and carefully, so that hopefully he'd understand. It seemed best that Brislieu and the others not know what I was saying. "Tyranny and death. The rulers who had driven us from our first home, our first world, have become even more tyrannical."

I paused to let him get that much of it, then continued. "It has named itself the Glondis Empire, and begun to conquer more worlds—including the world where we'd made our new home." I peered at Arno, trying to see his shadowed eyes. "Eventually I expect they'll come here to conquer yours."

He answered in Evdashian, thoughtfully. "Then why come you here, if they will someday follow?"

He still held my stunner in his hand, pointed at me.

"Not to hide," I told him. "We would find no satisfaction in hiding."

"Then why?"

What to tell him? The truth, I decided—the truth in its simplest terms. "We left our home world under gunfire," I told him, still in slow and careful Evdashian. "We were being shot at by powerful weapons. Three of us were killed—shot down as we ran to the sky boat. One was my wife; the Glondis Empire does not hesitate to kill women. We had planned to go to a certain world where we would be welcomed, to help build a rebellion. But our leader, the one of us who knew how to go there, was also killed.

"Your world was the one world we knew the way to, where we felt the Imperial sky navy had not gone yet, because you are so very far away here; much farther than other worlds with people on them."

I had no idea what Arno might be thinking. Maybe that I was crazy—possessed by a demon, as the abbot of St. Stephen's had thought that summer day. But Arno had seen our family cutter and ridden on it several times, which should make a lot of other strange and unlikely claims seem at least marginally possible.

"So we came here with more intentions than plans,"

I went on. "We will try to set ourselves up as support-
ers of some able and powerful man, and help him
establish a kingdom on this world—a kingdom that is
too strong for any power here to defeat—then help him
form an empire that is not evil like the Glondis. And
help him manage it; help him make this world so strong
that if, or when, the Glondis Empire comes here, they
will not be able to enslave you."

As I said it, it seemed to me that we could never
make Fanglith that strong. It was too primitive!

"You came here in a sky boat again?" Arno asked
very matter-of-factly.

"Yes. There's no other way."

"And you have a supply of the weapons you had
before?"

"A small supply." Suddenly I felt a light surge of
excitement. I was onto something after all. "And if
we're successful in setting up a kingdom here, we can
go back to our own part of the sky and find a world
where more such weapons can be gotten, and bring
them."

*And experienced rebels with assorted skills, to help
build a technical base here*, I told myself. *That might
possibly work; it just might*.

We kept riding through the night, his eyes on me,
and I knew he had to be digesting what I'd said. Maybe
planning something, too. What had Isaac ben Abraham
said about the Normans? "They have an extreme restlessness, a recklessness. . . ." Something like that. And
also something about "treacheries bloody and outrageous."

Then Arno quit pointing the stunner at me, clipping
it on his belt without saying anything.

"Where are we going?" I asked, in Norman now.

"To the castle of Roger of Hauteville, at Mileto, some
twenty miles south of here."

"Will I meet Roger?"

"Roger and his elder brother Guiscard, the duke, are
on Sicily, where they captured Palermo three months
ago. Palermo is Sicily's greatest city—one of the world's
greatest—and beautiful beyond words. I fought there. I

led a squadron. Then the duke dubbed Roger the Count of Sicily. Roger will rule the island for him, though Guiscard, as duke, will keep Palermo as his own.

"Roger has said he will keep his castle at Mileto, where we are going now. It is no stronghold such as Normans build here, but its walls are thick, and he has no lack of men to defend it. And he controls the country far around.

"He has given me my own fief outside Palermo, where I am having a castle built of stone, atop a rocky hill. I have my own liege knights and sergeants there now, looking to it."

Arno had obviously come a long way in less than three years. He was peering at me as if trying to see what I thought of all this, but the moon was on the wrong side; my face was shadowed. "It is good land," he went on. "Much of it is lowland, nearly flat, with a mountain stream that carries water the year round. But there is no great marsh, and therefore, it is said, no fever. And because the lower slopes are northerly, the pasturage grows thicker and stays green longer."

"So you're going to remain a warrior after all," I said, "instead of becoming a merchant."

"Not so. I have become a baron, but I am also a merchant who raises destriers for our knights and sergeants. That's why I am here in Calabria just now, instead of on my own fief. I've been grazing my breeding herd on the count's land here until I should have my own. In town today I arranged to have them shipped to Palermo. Late tomorrow a ship will come to the wharf at Mileto, and we will load them."

"But most merchants are free men, isn't that so?" I asked. "While a baron is a vassal, owing military service to his liege lord."

For some seconds there was only the dull plodding of hooves on dirt, the occasional click of an iron shoe on stone. Then Arno answered. "No man is truly free. A merchant makes agreements with buyers and others, and owes them goods or services. He pays in money or goods for protection, and more often than not he owes the moneylender."

We rode a way farther without saying anything, Arno's eyes ahead. Finally, he looked at me again. "As a younger son I have no inheritance," he told me, "and my eldest brother is not a man of influence. For me, the road to wealth can best begin by swearing fealty to a great lord, preferably a conqueror, and making myself of special value to him. Also, both Guiscard and Roger are granting fiefs that have little to do with land. One great noble will build Guiscard a fleet with which to conquer Greece or possibly Africa. In my own case, in lieu of military service, I may pay Roger in destriers if I wish.

"I caught Roger's eye on the battlefield at Misilmeri, nearly four years since, and happily, he had not forgotten me when I returned a year later with my first herd. Italian horses are not suited to our Norman tactics; they lack the weight and strength. So the destriers I brought were almost beyond price. My second herd was mostly brood mares, with only three great stallions. With them I . . ."

Deneen's voice spoke unexpectedly from the communicator at Arno's belt. He was so surprised he jerked, then reined in his horse. I stopped mine, too. I hadn't remembered to switch it to remote reception after I'd used it the last time on the ship.

"Larn, this is *Javelin*," she was saying. "Larn, this is *Javelin*. Over."

"I should answer her," I said.

He reached to his belt and took off the communicator, peering at it. "How is it used? I've forgotten."

"It's a different model from the one I had before. This one is military. Here," I added, reaching.

He scowled, holding it away from me. "Tell me," he said, "for I will not put it in your power."

"All right," I countered, "hold it in your hand and let me touch the magic places."

"Larn, what's the situation down there?" Deneen's voice went on. Obviously, she thought I had it on remote and that no one else was hearing her. She sounded somewhere between exasperated and worried. "Bubba says you're out in the countryside. I seem to have you located on the viewer—I presume it's you—with four other men on the road that goes south along the coast. Come in please, if you can. Over."

While she was saying that, Arno held the communicator out for me to touch. I opened the transmit switch and raised the volume a bit. "Okay, Arno," I told him. "Talk to her."

"Hello," he said in Evdashian. "I am Arno of Courmeron."

"What? Who are you? I can't understand you."

She could understand him all right. She wanted him to give me the communicator. But from his expression, he wasn't about to.

"You understand me so good as you must. I am Arno of Courmeron."

She did something with the switch, and the communicator made clicking noises, sharp and rapid. "Larn, can you hear me?" she said. "What's going on there? Whose voice was that? Over."

He wasn't very happy with that either, but he held it out where I could talk into it.

"Hi, Deneen." I was speaking Evdashian too, slowly, so that Arno could more or less follow what I said. "That was Arno of Courmeron. And I didn't find him; he found me. He'd heard about me in an eating place, and surprised me when I was sleeping; he and three other Normans. He's got my stunner and blast pistol and communicator.

"Don't worry, though. Everything is all right so far. He and I are talking about things we might do together. Right now we're going to where he's staying."

Arno was watching me intently. I'd need to throw in some words he didn't know so he wouldn't understand what I had to say next. "I'll activate the remote if the opportunity presents. You palpitate the switch additionally after I enunciate the appellation of our telepathic quadruped."

I paused. It was desirable that Arno *did* understand what I said next, so this time I spoke simply. "Arno is holding me prisoner, sort of. He doesn't fully trust me and I don't fully trust him, but I think he and I can work something out together. Meanwhile, you follow us from above. You can use magic to know whether I've been harmed or not." Magic Arno accepted, more or less, while technology was foreign to him. I paused now for emphasis. "If I'm harmed," I continued, "you know what to do. And take good care of Bubba."

As soon as I said "Bubba"—the "appellation of our telepathic quadruped"—the speaker not only gave another series of clicks, but a loud squeal. I don't know how she did the squeal part.

"Here," I said to Arno. "I need to fix it."

He hesitated, then moved his horse closer so I could look the communicator over. Reaching, I switched it to remote. "There," I said. "That may fix it, or it may make it worse.

"Deneen," I added, "my communicator is acting up again. Same old problem—clicking noises. I've adjusted the gummox. If you can hear me, transmit again and let's see if it's working now. Over."

Both Arno and I looked at the communicator as if watching would help it work. Of course it didn't make a sound that he could hear. "Deneen," I said, "we do not receive you. Transmit again please. Over."

Her voice murmured in the privacy of my ear canal. "Well, brother mine, was that quiet enough for you? Cough if your remote is working. Over."

I coughed, cleared my throat, then looked at Arno, and he at me. "The amulet refuses to talk for now," I said in Norman, shaking my head. "I've had trouble with it before. It will work for a while, and then for no apparent reason it quits."

Of course Arno, being a Norman, was suspicious. I could read it in his face, even by moonlight.

I shrugged. "It will probably work all right later. Will it be all right for me to put it to rest? No use running down the power cell." The last two words were in Evdashian, of course. "That which gives it power," I added in Norman.

To him it was all magic. I could almost smell his distrust as he nodded. "Do what you must," he said, "as long as I keep the amulet."

"If you insist," I answered, and reaching again, switched off the transmitter. The remote would continue to function.

As we started down the road, the remote murmured again. "Larn, I'm getting ready to give him a demonstration. You might want to prepare him so he won't think he's being attacked."

I had this natural urge to answer, but didn't. "Arno," I told him, "if I know Deneen, we can expect her to do something to prove her power to you. I'm sure she won't harm anyone, because we'd like to be your allies. But it may be pretty noisy, so be ready."

He nodded, saying nothing. It wasn't more than half a minute later that a spotlight caught us. Brislieu, taken by surprise, stopped his horse and drew his sword, glancing upward for a moment. Arno was too smart to look at the lamp even briefly; it would make his pupils contract. He looked only at the illuminated area of the ground. Their squires halted behind us; I don't know what they made of all this.

Then the light switched off.

Nothing more happened for a long minute. I sat holding the reins tight, waiting. If what I suspected happened next, my horse might easily start bucking; the average saddle gorn at home would have. Then the light came on again. This time it wasn't an intense and narrow beam, but spread to flood a grove of trees planted in rows not far from the road. I tensed, almost sensing Tarel at the weapons controls.

The dull "thud thud thud" of the heavy blaster punctuated the night, a series of twelve or fifteen shots in maybe six seconds. Energy bolts hissed, trees burst, fragments of wood whirred and plunked around. The horses, well trained, jerked and danced but settled down quickly. Then it was quiet, and the floodlight showed shattered stubs where the nearest trees had been, two hundred feet away.

After a moment it switched off again; only the dark was left. I wondered if any locals had seen what had happened, and what they'd make of it if they had.

The light came back on, its beam narrower again, to

shine on a steep, rocky slope about a quarter mile away. Our eyes went to it. The blaster thudded again—one, two, three, four—the bolts slamming one after another into the bedrock. Shards flew, and above the target point a large slab broke loose to slide crashing to the foot of the slope.

Then once more it was dark.

"I think she's done now," I said quietly in Norman. "We have much more powerful weapons this time than before. And we are harder. We have seen our friends killed, and we are looking for allies."

As I said it I had a kind of feeling I'd never had before, a sort of dry emptiness that marked some kind of change in me. It wasn't especially bad, but it wasn't good either. There was a certain flavor of regret to it, but not a heavy sadness or anything like that. And with it came a sense of strength as well. I didn't think I'd ever be awed by Normans again. Impressed by them maybe, but not awed.

"Let us go on," Arno said, also in Norman. "We have miles to ride yet." His voice was quiet. He sounded more than just impressed; he sounded as if he had things to think about.

SEVENTEEN

A Norman sergeant, wearing helmet and hauberk, let us into Count Roger's castle at Mileto. I'd never been in a Norman-built stone castle, so I couldn't compare this with one of them. But it was a lot different from the timber castles that were usual in Normandy. The stone defensive wall was so thick that the small gate we went through was like an inky tunnel.

The grounds inside were like a big country estate with a wall around it. Arno told me it had been built for a Byzantine governor. There were no lights, not even a lamp by a door, and the moon was all but down, hidden by a hill. But even by simple starlight, the buildings were graceful, more beautiful than any I'd seen before on Fanglith.

I couldn't tell how many buildings there were. Quite a few. Some had wings, and courtyards of their own. There were gardens with privacy walls, and trees for fruit and shade. I could smell something in flower. But the walls had corner towers, one much larger than the others, to remind me that war was a way of life on Fanglith.

Arno had told me that Judith of Evreux, Roger's wife, really loved the place. I could understand that, especially if her father's castle in Normandy was like the castles I'd seen there. Arno didn't say so, but I got the idea that he liked this better, too.

We headed for the big stone tower. After Arno had warned the squires to say nothing about what had happened that night, they took the horses away to rub them down and feed them. Arno, Brislieu, and I went into the tower. Our "bedroom" was the large dark hall, lit by a single lamp—a bowl of oil with a cloth wick and a flickering small flame. I could make out other men sleeping—knights and sergeants no doubt. After each of us had gathered together his own little heap of the dry hay piled in a corner, Arno and Brislieu stripped off their hauberks. Then we wrapped ourselves in our cloaks and lay down to sleep.

They didn't smell nearly as bad as the Norman knights I'd been among in Normandy, or the monks in Provence, as far as that was concerned. What dominated my nostrils was the hay—a clean, pleasant smell. I wondered if they'd learned about baths in this new country they'd conquered.

*   *   *

Arno:

It had been a long enough day, riding in to Reggio, arranging for a ship with a horse hold, finding and capturing the star man, and riding back to Mileto. But my mind was roiling like a kettle over a fire, too full of thoughts just then for sleep.

The star man! He was ignorant, carried no sword, spoke inadequately, had only a vague idea what to say or do. Even with his sorcerous weapons, which on two occasions I'd deprived him of, and with his sister overhead in their sky boat, he should have been dead long before this. Instead, since the first hour I'd known him, he'd gone from one dangerous situation to another, slipping through each as if, in truth, he *was* guided by some angel, or the Holy Spirit Himself.

I remembered my old training master, Walter Ironfist, telling us that the only lasting luck was the luck you made for yourself. And while I accepted that, the knowledge did not seem particularly useful. But in the case of this Larn, certainly his luck was beyond mere chance.

I could wish I'd never met him; yet I had. I seemed drawn to him, and despite myself I liked him. And if he, in some way, created luck, one might do well to share a project with him.

Once I'd seen Sicily and come to know it a bit, seen how wealthy Saracen princes lived, and Jewish and Byzantine merchants, I too wanted wealth. And it seemed to me that I could best become wealthy by being a merchant. Fighting, living in the saddle, sleeping among the rocks with one's hauberk on, saddle for pillow, hand on sword hilt and one eye open—it all has a certain flavor. Yet while I admit to relishing it, it was a life I would willingly sacrifice for wealth.

Obtaining wealth, however, takes more than sacrifice, else there'd be far fewer poor. But I am nothing if not smart—smart even for a Norman. I knew I could learn to be a merchant. I could even see how to begin, for here was a great demand for war horses, while in Normandy there was a good supply. Even the Frankish animals were adequate, and at a lesser distance. And like every Norman knight, I knew destriers; knew them well. All I needed was money to buy them with, and the luck and will and toughness to get them here from the north.

The money to start with, I obtained from the Battle of Misilmeri, where we'd killed Saracens by the thousands—killed them till those who yet lived surrendered to us. We'd been reeling from exhaustion by then, hardly able to stay upright in the saddle. Our arms ached, seemingly beyond our power to raise for another blow.

Nonetheless we'd dismounted. The more experienced among us summoned the energy to begin searching the dead, and as the rest of us watched, our exhaustion was forgotten. Those of us recently from Normandy could hardly believe the coins and gems the Saracen knights carried in their purses to ransom themselves with if captured. We cut pieces from their robes, made bags of them, and emptied their purses into the bags. And the rings of gold and silver, many set with precious stones! How many fingers were cut free of how many dead hands that day! We sergeants and knights chose the richest-looking bodies for our efforts, then left the poorer to the Lombard mercenaries and went to the quarters assigned to us.

And while, by Saracen standards, or Byzantine, or Jewish, we were not wealthy, any one of us was wealthier in gold, silver, and gems than almost anyone in Normandy.

I knew then how I could buy horses.

But that was not the end of it. For Roger had seen my strength and prowess in the battle—indeed, had heard of me from skirmishes earlier—and I was knighted. Beyond that, his brother Guiscard levied an unbelievable ransom on our prisoners, knowing it would be paid. And when in fact it was paid, Guiscard, royal in fact and power if not in title, distributed it among his army. I began to see myself not only with a great horse herd, but also sleeping on a soft bed, on silk sheets, with slaves and servants to tend my needs.

When I was able to obtain an audience with Roger, and tell him my plan to raise horses, he approved at once. For in every skirmish we were likely to have destriers killed or maimed, and their like were hard to come by in the south. And our Norman style of fighting depended on their size and strength and ferocity as much as on our heavier mail, our stouter swords. With our ranks closed and our great war horses between our thighs, we Normans are the greatest fighting men of all, not even excepting Varangians or Swabians, for all their fierceness and great frames.

If I could help solve the problem of enough good horses, Roger told me, then he would absolve me of the fealty I'd sworn him and let me go my way. I felt myself fortunate in having had such a noble lord, and in fact I was.

Then, on my way back to Normandy, I'd met the star man beside the road that comes down from the Cenis Pass into the valleys of Savoie. I could barely understand his speech, which was Provençal poorly spoken. He had seemed unarmed and as innocent as a girl— almost too innocent to survive beneath heaven. But then I learned what powers he held, glimpsed what force I might gain from him, and suddenly the life of a merchant seemed small and trivial. While wealth, it seems, was after all only part of what I wanted. Now I could see a kingdom, even an empire, waiting to be grasped by getting his weapons and skyboat into my hands. I had but to wait—bide patiently and strike when the time was right.

But the time was never right. And at last it had seemed to me that my best chance was to deal honorably with the star folk—Larn and his father and the great wolf that seemed to think and speak like a man. And finally I had it in my hands—the great warship of the sky, taken from their enemies by might of Norman arms, and by the star folk's own cunning and daring, which even a Norman could admire.

And then that great fool, Roland de Falaise, destroyed the warship, and with it all our knights and sergeants except Brislieu, whom I had sent on an errand. I know it was Roland who did it; no other could have been so perverse. The warship had burst in the air with a force unbelievable.

With that, my dream of empire had been in tatters. It seemed then that my only chance was to take the skyboat from the star folk. But my attempt was without cunning or force, ineffective, and my offer of fealty to them if they would take me with them to their world was both ill-advised and rejected. I was back to horses again, and to my earlier dream of being a merchant.

In time I almost convinced myself again that it was all I truly wished. And indeed I made much progress. Then I had eaten supper in the Greek inn near the cathedral, overheard the captain's tale, and found the star man once more.

And there it was again: The dream, the possibility, of empire! If I could gain their skyboat and their weapons, and use them cleverly . . .

Larn:

As late as it was, I didn't feel sleepy at first. For one thing, my thighs and rear end weren't used to riding horseback. And for another, I was chilly. But mainly I had stuff on my mind.

It seemed to me that as smart as Arno was, he wasn't in a position to be my number-one man on Fanglith. He wasn't the native leader I needed. The kind of man I should be looking for was someone already established in power. His Count Roger maybe, or even better, the duke, Robert Guiscard. Those guys already had armies, and ruled pieces of real estate that apparently were pretty big and important for a planet like Fanglith, where communication and transportation were so primitive. Give them communicators and air support and let their enemies see a demonstration by a turret blaster, and they wouldn't have to fight to conquer.

I shifted on my grass pile, trying to get more comfortable. Arno, I told myself, would be my front man, my introduction to Roger or Robert.

"It sounds as if you're getting it all sorted out."

Deneen's voice in my ear startled me, and I heard her laugh. "We're sitting about a hundred yards above you with the windows opaqued. There are so few people awake down there that Bubba can follow your thoughts. He's been giving us a running summary.

"I've been thinking about possible rescue plans," she went on. "If you'd like, I can put Tarel down on the roof of the building you're in; there's a trapdoor in it. He could take a stunner and have a remote in his ear, and Bubba and I could guide him in finding you."

I looked at that. "Bubba, can you read Arno's thoughts?" I asked with my mind. "It would help to know more about what he's thinking."

There was a long pause, a minute or longer. Bubba's form of speech was hard to understand over a communicator, and I could picture him giving his answer to Deneen.

"Arno's still awake," she said at last, "but Bubba hasn't been paying much attention to him. He's not used to Norman French, or to the nonverbal mix in Arno's thoughts. The general tone doesn't feel threatening, but if you want, he'll monitor and see what he gets."

I knew that Bubba does better with people whose thought style he's used to. "Fine," I said. "If Arno's still awake, Bubba can monitor him for a while, and if he learns anything I ought to know about, tell me.

"Meanwhile, let's leave things the way they are—at least for now. I'll play things by ear, and you can bail me out later if necessary. I'm pretty sure Arno plans to take me to Sicily with him, and that's where I need to go anyway. That's where Robert and Roger are."

That's about all that needed saying just then. We "talked" a minute longer just for company, but I knew it was hard work for Bubba, so we ended off. Then I got myself as comfortable as I could and waited, scratching, for sleep. It seemed to me that, in spite of the lice and fleas, I'd rather be down here than up there: it was more interesting.

Now *there* was a different viewpoint for me! I was learning to relax and enjoy the situation. Give me a little time and maybe I'd make a good adventurer after all!

EIGHTEEN

The next day wasn't all that enjoyable though. For one thing, I felt as if I should have slept a few more hours. And the weather had changed; it was beginning to be windy again, but out of the south this time—a warm wind gritty with sand. The *sirocco*, they called it, out of Africa. By the time we'd climbed into our saddles to help fetch Arno's horses, it was a stiff breeze, damp and almost hot. We chewed grit, breathed grit, and got grit in our eyes. Nobody there seemed very happy about it.

It could last for days, they told me, though it might be gone tomorrow. If it ever came to a vote, I'd vote for gone tomorrow.

The country behind Mileto was rough, with draws and little canyons, and Arno's herd was scattered in several loose bands with some young locals keeping track of them. There were three stallions, thirty-seven big mares, and thirty-three foals—a lot of horses. It took us till afternoon to get them all down out of the hills and penned near the wharf. There Arno selected sixty to take to Palermo this trip. That was all the ship would hold—the biggest horse ship available in Reggio.

Then we went back to the tower—the *donjon*, they called it—and actually bathed! The Normans were quite cheerful about it—not only Arno, but Brislieu and their squires. They even had soap, and what the soap lacked in quality, the Normans made up for with scrubbing.

It was the first time I'd had my clothes off since before I'd boarded the ship at Marseille. There were red blotches—bug bites—all over my body; it was pretty impressive. They didn't bother me the way they had at first though. And the Normans didn't have the blotches. It was as if the body quit reacting much to them after a while.

When we'd gotten rid of the grit temporarily, we had a meal. Then Arno and I sat alone in the shelter of a garden wall to talk. I'd thought he might present me to Roger's wife, but he didn't. I decided that one, he didn't know how to explain me; and two, he didn't want them to know what sort of resource I was.

What we did do was talk about the kind of kingdom or empire he'd run, if he had one. First of all, he said, he would establish his sovereignty over the Greeks—the Byzantines. Then he'd bring the cleverest artisans and weapons makers of Byzantium to his court, which would be at Palermo. At the same time, he'd send me back to the heavens to get more of our powerful weapons, an idea that fitted in with my own.

Also, he would not, he said, allow the barons to build castles; it encouraged them to defy the king. He'd let each subject people rule themselves by their own laws and leaders, after swearing fealty to him as their sovereign. Guiscard had begun to do this, and was finding that it greatly reduced revolts and other unrests.

And again following Guiscard's example, he would appoint Jews and Greeks to administer the offices of government. They had the knowledge, could read and write and compute; and besides, he said, Normans had no genius for the job.

I decided that Arno had the makings of a good ruler. "But look," I told him, "today you won't even trust me to hold the speaking amulet in my hand. Yet later, you're going to trust me to leave this world in the skyboat?"

"Of course," he said. "Things will be different then."

"Different how?"

He didn't answer for a moment, as if deciding whether or not to tell me. "First, I shall require your oath," he said at last, "and then I shall marry your sister. She and our children should be assurance enough that your oath will be kept."

I guess my expression must have told him what kind of jolt that was, because he added: "Do not be concerned. I shall always treat her honorably and respect her ways, requiring only that she be baptized. Admittedly I have scarcely spoken to the lady, but I have often thought about her, remembering what she looked like, and how brave she proved in the teeth of your enemies in Normandy. Thus not only have I yearned for her in seeming hopelessness, but I admire her greatly."

I didn't say anything; it seemed best not to. And I guess Arno decided he'd said too much, because after a quiet minute or so, he excused himself and left. I don't suppose it ever occurred to him that Deneen might have other ideas, might tell him to go jump in the whirlpool Charybdis. At the very least.

The ship from Reggio didn't arrive that afternoon, and I could see why: a south wind was a head wind. It wasn't practical to sail south in the gritty teeth of the sirocco. We'd see what tomorrow brought. Meanwhile the servants would have to feed the horses hay.

That evening we ate with the other knights and sergeants and their squires in the donjon—twenty-one of us in all. I was the only one who didn't wear a hauberk at the table. It was a strange tradition. But at least no one wore their helmet.

When Roger was at home, Arno told me, Roger and his family customarily ate dinner with the troops. At other times his family ate separately, which apparently was different from Norman custom. In any case, the food was a lot better and more varied than it had been at Roland's castle in Normandy.

Also, there was wine instead of sour beer, and when the eating had slowed down a little, there was storytelling. One of the knights, Rollo, wanted me to tell about India, but I could see that getting awkward. I wasn't sure I could lie fast enough, or convincingly enough, or keep my lies consistent. So I told him I could speak of it only in my own language. Rollo decided that was an insult, and challenged me to fight—he'd drunk at least three or four big cups of wine, while I'd been getting through the evening on just one.

I wanted to avoid a fight if at all possible, for two reasons. Make that three reasons. Even if the fight started without weapons, I wasn't sure it would stay that way. Second, I didn't want them to know about hand-foot art; it was my secret weapon. And third, I don't like to fight. But Arno handled the situation; he got up and said it was unseemly to ask a holy monk to fight. And when the marshal of the house troops agreed with him, Rollo didn't push it.

Meanwhile it had gotten dark outside, and the lighting was poor, of course—a dozen of the crude oil lamps. Some of the troops went to their sleeping places and lay down; I decided that was a good idea and followed their example. After an hour I was still awake, still listening. The stories were interesting, and I was following the Norman with only a little trouble now and then where I lacked a key word or concept. The lamps had burned low or out, all that was left of the hearth fire was embers, and the last three or four men finally gave it up for the night.

I remember thinking that I wished Deneen would call. Minutes later I was asleep.

The reason she hadn't called was too much mental activity in the hall, which made it impossible for Bubba to read my thoughts. I'd been asleep long enough that the lamps and hearth fire were entirely dark when the remote spoke in my ear.

"Larn! Larn! Wake up. I've got something important to tell you."

Something important to tell me!? The thought that hit me was that they'd detected an Imperial cruiser.

"Not that bad," she said. "A complication, not a catastrophe."

"What complication?" I thought to them.

"I was doing a routine check of ship's systems a while

ago, and the fuel slugs have serious peripheral crystallization."

I thought I knew what could have caused it, or at least contributed to it: prolonged and constant operation in mass-proximity mode. I knew for sure what would happen if it wasn't reversed: It would get worse. And the further crystallization advances, the faster it advances, until beyond some critical point, you can't activate FTL mode anymore. If that happened to us, we could be stuck on Fanglith forever.

"A shutdown should reverse it," I thought back at her.

"According to the systems manual," she answered, "it will have to be about a six- to ten-day all-systems shutdown. The only alternative is to head outbound and go into FTL. Eight or ten hours at FTL would decrystallize it, but that's too iffy."

Even a day at FTL sounded better to me than a six-to ten-day shutdown. "What's iffy about it?" I asked.

"We'd need to get out about 700,000 miles before I'd try FTL. Fanglith's a little more massive than Evdash. That's 700,000 miles in mass proximity mode, with crystallization accelerating all the way. The computer says it's marginal whether we could go FTL when we got out there. The crystallization might have gone too far. So I plan to go back to the island we visited. It's the safest place I know of on Fanglith, and we'll get along okay there. After six days, if the reversal isn't complete, maybe then I'll take her out and go FTL to finish it.

"Now what I need to know is, do you want me to pick you up and take you with us? I don't like leaving you with no one to bail you out if things come apart down there."

To my surprise, I wasn't even tempted. "No," I told her, "I'm pretty safe here, for Fanglith. I doubt if anyone around here is interested in messing with Arno, and he doesn't want anything to happen to me. And as far as the ship ride to Palermo is concerned, we'll be following the Norman-controlled coast all the way. I don't think we have anything to worry about; just get that crystallization reversed.

"Anything else to report?" I added.

"No, that's it. I'll say goodbye now and we'll be on the island before daylight. I'll be in touch again in six or eight days. Ten at most." She stopped then for a moment, a stop that I knew was just a pause.

"Larn?"

"Yeah?"

"I just want you to know that besides being my brother, you're also my best friend."

Well I'll be darned, I thought. "Thanks, sister mine. That goes both ways." And I meant it.

With that she cut off, and I could picture her accelerating westward toward the island coordinates. I lay there savoring our conversation for a minute or two before I went back to sleep.

PART FOUR

THE VARANGIANS

NINETEEN

The sirocco began to die down late the next morning.
The locals said we were lucky, that usually it lasted
longer. Just before dusk the ship arrived from Reggio,
probably the biggest ship I'd seen close up on Fanglith,
with a taller, heavier mast than usual and a square sail
instead of the usual triangular one. Tomorrow, Arno
said, we would leave.

The next morning we met with the captain in a steel-
gray dawn. The wind was out of the north now, and
chilly instead of gritty. It would be best to lie at the
dock a while, he said. The wind would make the Strait
of Messina hard to navigate northbound. But Arno was a
Norman and the captain wasn't. We would start this
morning, Arno insisted, and if we had too much trouble, we could put in at Reggio or Messina. Roger had
his own docks in both ports, which we could use without fee; Arno had a letter of authorization.

The captain shrugged and agreed. He was Greek,
and his French quite broken, but I got the idea that it
wasn't a big deal to him either way—sail or lie at the
dock. We started loading the horses.

Most of the deck could be taken up in sections, like a
mosaic of hatch covers. Each horse stall in the hold was
just wide enough for a destrier, with a sort of leather
sling so the horse couldn't fall in rough weather and
maybe break a leg. The horses were loaded in—you
could almost say they were inserted in their stalls—
with a block and tackle fastened to a boom. That seemed

to be the reason, or a reason, for the taller, heavier mast: It served as part of the boom rig for loading the horses.

When all sixty horses had been loaded, we cast off—Arno, Brislieu, and three sergeants, along with their squires, myself, and the ship's crew. The crew kept giving me sideways looks and plenty of room; Arno had spread the word that I was a holy monk from India. I didn't know whether he had some purpose in this or if it was his sense of humor.

The breeze was brisk, but nothing like a storm. The captain took us around the point of land just west of Mileto and we entered the wide, lower end of the long, funnel-shaped strait. The wind picked up a bit then, and he tacked northwestward across it. An hour later, though the clouds were breaking up, it was blowing considerably harder, and the ship was pitching pretty badly. Arno agreed that we should turn southwest and make for a little bay north of Taormina, the harbor of Taormina still being held by Saracens. But before long they decided that Catania was a better choice. It was considerably farther, but safer; we wouldn't have to sail across the wind.

Then, around mid-afternoon, the wind began to slack off markedly, and Arno had us turned north again. I was beginning to get a better idea of how hard it could be, with sailing rigs as crude as ours, to travel by sea with nothing more than wind power. I'd be willing to bet that sport sailors back on Evdash had a lot fewer problems with wind direction than the Fanglithans did.

At any rate, after five hours at sea we were quite a lot farther from Palermo than when we started. The swell continued pretty high, lifting our bow, then the entire ship, letting it slide down the back side, but we weren't taking spray across the deck anymore. The captain had the crew remove some of the hatches so the horses could have sunshine and fresh air.

As we zigzagged clumsily northward, we saw a sail riding the wind southward toward us—a square sail like our own. The captain told us it was almost surely not Mediterranean; Mediterranean vessels carried triangular sails. Ours was an exception, designed for hauling destriers.

Before long we could make out her hull, which was slender. My first thought was pirates, and that was Arno's thought too. But the captain said a corsair would have a triangular sail; this looked like a ship of Norse pilgrims on its way home from the Holy Land.

The word "Norse" triggered Arno's interest. The Norse, he told me, had founded Normandy, and some of his ancestors had been from Norse kingdoms. Also, the Varangian mercenary regiments in the Byzantine armies were Norse, and were famous fighting men. He asked the captain if we could sail near enough for a close look at their ship, and after a moment's hesitation, the captain agreed. He changed our tack so that we'd pass close to her.

The Norse ship moved fast by Fanglithan standards, riding high in the water, and soon we got a good look at her. Her lines were as smooth as the pirate's had been, and more slender. A "long ship," our captain said; he'd never seen one before, but he knew of them. Most Norse ships were broader, he told us, to carry cargo. We passed her at a distance of no more than two hundred feet, and there seemed to be fifty men or more on board her, most of them watching us. One of them had climbed her mast to the spar, presumably to get a better look.

Then we were past, and our attention left her. No one was even aware when she began to put about; she was mostly through her turn when our steersman noticed and called out. By that time her sail was down and she had oars in the water, her oarsmen pulling hard. Over the next few minutes, the Normans and I watched her draw up on us. It took skill to row in a swell like that. Our captain changed our course northwestward, angling toward the Sicilian coast, but it was obvious that she'd catch us. With the primitive Fanglithan sail rigs, oars worked a lot better in a headwind.

And Deneen was hundreds of miles away with all systems shut down, which meant no radio.

When the long ship had drawn near, I could see one

of her men in the bow with a grapple in his hand, rope
attached. I could imagine the technique: When they
were close enough, he'd throw it and hook us. Brislieu
had strung his bow, but Arno warned him sharply not
to shoot. The Norse, he said, might all have bows,
many to our few. Instead he drew his—my—blast pistol.

"Let them draw alongside," he muttered. "Do not
cut their lines." He gestured with the blaster. "This
will put the fear of God into them. They'll let us go as if
we carried the Devil himself, and we'll have their grapples for our own."

The Norseman began swinging his grapple around his
head, then released it, its line snaking behind it across
the water. It fell onto our deck, narrowly missing me,
caught the gunwale, and bit deep and hard into the
wood. Then other Norsemen threw grapples, and strong
arms drew the ropes taut. They shipped their oars
then, the oarsmen lending their tough hands to the
ropes. I could see them plainly now—well-tanned,
bearded men, mostly with brown or blond hair. At
about fifteen feet, Arno leveled the pistol at the Norsemen in the bow and pressed the firing stud.

And nothing happened! It flashed through my mind
that the safety was on; the double safety on this heavy
military model was different from that on the police
model he'd had before.

"Let me have it!" I shouted at him.

But instead, one of the Norsemen let him have it—
slung a throwing axe spinning toward us. It slammed
hard against Arno's helmet—fortunately end on—sending
him sprawling unconscious.

The pistol went sliding along the deck, but what I
dove after was the stunner on Arno's belt. At close
quarters, it would stop the Norsemen as well as the
blaster would, and it was closer to hand. Arno's body
was lying on the stunner, though, and by the time I got
my hands on it, the Norsemen were boarding us. Brislieu
and the sergeants and squires, in true, reckless Norman style, had drawn their swords, and for maybe half
a minute I could hear their furious fight. If I'd gotten
to my feet, or even to my knees, I'd probably have

been killed for my trouble, so I shoved the stunner and communicator into my shirt and lay beside the unconscious Arno, playing dead. Blood was spreading across the deck planks—Norman blood, I thought—and the brief noise of fighting had stopped.

Pilgrims from the Holy Land!

Then brown hands with pale hair curling on their backs turned Arno over and took off first his sword belt, then his helmet, collet, and hauberk. Unfamiliar voices were speaking a language I'd never heard before—a language with a sort of tonality—almost a singsong quality. There was quite a bit of laughter. Someone grabbed me then and started to turn me over, and abruptly I scrambled to my feet. I didn't want them to take my stunner and communicator.

One of them drew his sword, and I raised my cross, holding it out at him in my left hand. My right hand drew my stunner, aiming from beneath my cape. As he hesitated, I started chanting my school fight song good and loud, as if it were a prayer, moving my cross up and down between us to hold their attention on it. Then I pushed the firing stud, and the blond swordsman just sort of sank to his knees and toppled over on his face.

Talk about a reaction! For four or five seconds no one said a thing. After that, they all started talking at once, while I slipped the stunner back inside my shirt. I was still holding my cross up. Then the Norseman who seemed to be the leader bellowed something and they all shut up. With his eyes slitted at me, he said something else in a quiet voice and someone grabbed me around the arms from behind so hard I thought my rib cage would break. Another put his knife tip to my throat. I held very, very still.

Their leader was a broad, thick-shouldered warrior whose red hair and beard were marked with white. He turned to our captain and said something that had to be Greek—it sounded pretty much like what our captain and crew talked among themselves, though I could tell it was accented. Our captain answered. The Norseman looked at his fallen warrior, then at me, and said something more in Greek, and again our captain answered. They talked back and forth for a minute or so, then the Norseman pursed his lips and frowned, said something to the man who had hold of me, and I was let go.

I sucked in a big breath of air and looked around. Except for Arno, every one of the Normans was dead, lying in their own blood—including the squires, none of them more than fifteen years old. I could see three dead Norsemen too, while another was sitting on a hatch cover having a gashed arm bandaged. He was bloody from shoulder to feet—must have lost at least a quart of it—but instead of looking pale and weak, he looked angry and mean. I'm not sure how I looked; probably green.

We were broadside to the swell now, rolling heavily from side to side. Some of the Norsemen were down in our hold, looking at the horses and talking enthusiastically. I learned later that the Norseman who'd climbed their mast had seen our rich cargo of horses. That was what inspired them to turn and attack us.

The Norse leader shouted orders, and the men in the hold started coming back on deck. Some of them laid the dead bodies out on the deck boards—Normans and Norsemen both. When they were done, the Norse leader stood over the corpses. He called again, sharply, and two more of his men came out of the hold. Then all the Norsemen took off their helmets and stood quietly. Their leader wore an ornate gold cross on a chain around his neck, and he held it up with his right hand, then raised his eyes to it and started chanting in his own language. It occurred to me that he was praying.

He prayed for about half a minute, then let the cross fall against his hauberk. Another brief order, and some of his men grabbed the dead under the arms and knees and threw them over the side. He turned to look at me, gave another order, and one of his men grabbed my arm and pointed to their ship, gesturing forcefully. His grip was like a steel pincer, his hands as fiercely strong as Arno's. The two ships had been tied snugly against each other, side by side, and were rolling and wallowing, their gunwales at almost the same level; apparently, they wanted me to cross to theirs, so I did. Two of the Norsemen lifted Arno and carried him across.

Within minutes the ships were separated. The Norse had left a small prize crew of their warriors on the horse ship, with her Greek captain and his men. Both ships had turned before the wind now, and we were sailing southward together about two hundred feet apart, with the long ship in the lead, her sail raised again.

I wasn't feeling too pessimistic. If the Norsemen had been going to kill Arno and me, they probably would have done it already. And I had the communicator. In six or eight days Deneen would be back, and if worst came to worst, when the time came, I could jump over the side at night and let her fish me out.

It occurred to me then to turn off the remote in my right ear. Deneen wasn't around to talk to me, and even just turned on, it was a constant tiny drain on the communicator's power cell. When I needed it, later on, I didn't want a rundown powercell.

TWENTY

Arno didn't wake up for half an hour, and when he did, he was confused. We sat on the bottom decking of the open Norse ship, talking quietly, his speech vague and mumbly at first as he gradually remembered what had happened. After a while, the Norse leader came over to us with one of the Greek sailors from the horse ship.

The Norseman said something in Greek, and the Greek repeated it in Norman French. His Norman was good—a lot better than his captain's had been—and obviously the Norseman had brought him aboard to interpret.

"He wants you to stand up," the Greek said.

It was me the Norse leader was looking at, so I got up.

The Norseman spoke to me again, the Greek translating. "I am told you are a holy monk."

"That's right."

The Norseman eyed the cross that hung from my neck. "Do you follow the church of Miklagard, or that of Rome?"

Somehow the question felt dangerous, so I sidestepped. "India. I am a Christian of India."

"Umh." He thought about that, frowning, then said something more to the Greek and walked away.

"What did he tell you?" I asked.

"He had planned to sell all of us, and the ship and horses, to Saracen merchants in Spain. But he says he cannot sell a Christian holy man, certainly not to the Saracens, so he will have to take you with him to his homeland."

Well, I thought, mark one up to being a holy monk. "He asked if I followed the way of Miklagard," I said. "Where or what is Miklagard?"

"These men are Varangians. Miklagard is their name for Byzantium."

Varangians? "What are Varangians?" I asked.

He shrugged. "They are barbarian mercenaries who come from the North. Some come on ships like this, across the Mediterranean. But mostly they come, or used to, across the Black Sea from the Rhos land. They pay no heed to kings, but bond themselves by oaths to whatever leaders they choose. Most of these men have been fighting for the Emperor, and are returning now to their homelands with the gold they have earned."

The Emperor. That would be the Byzantine emperor, I decided.

"And they plan to sell you?" I said. "Does that mean you'll be a slave?"

"Yes. But I am a skilled sailor. I will probably not be chained to a rowing bench or sent to the mines."

He didn't seem all that upset. Resigned was more like it.

Meanwhile Arno had gotten to his feet and stood by, taking it all in. Now he called out in what seemed to be the Norse language! It surprised heck out of me; I hadn't known he knew it. The captain, who was standing about thirty feet away in the bow, turned and stared at him, then said something back in Norse. Haltingly, Arno answered, and the captain came over with an interested expression. They talked for a couple of minutes, Arno often pausing as if groping for words. The captain reached out, squeezed Arno's arms and shoulders with big hands as if testing his muscles. Then he laughed, nodding, said something more, and drew Arno by an arm to the center of the long ship while calling in Norse to its crew.

Most of them moved toward the middle of the long ship, with Arno in the center, and there seemed to be some sort of brief meeting. Everyone was grinning or even laughing, then serious for a few moments, then cheering. A keg was passed around, which must have held five gallons, and they all drank, some from big mugs. Those who drank from the spout held the keg above their faces as if it didn't weigh a thing, but when it got to me, it still must have weighed twenty-five pounds or more.

Our Greek had come over to where I was sitting. He had no more idea what was going on than I did. After a few minutes, Arno came back. My eyes must have been out on stalks by then.

"What was *that* all about?" I asked. "What did you say to him? How did you know their language?"

Arno chuckled. With the wind behind us now, no one was rowing, so we moved to adjacent rowing stools. "I never told you the history of my people," he said. "The first Normans were Norse pirates called Vikings. Most were from the kingdom of Denmark, though Hrolf, our first duke, was from Norway. They had been harrying the coast of France from ships much like this one, and the Franks were unable to deal with their ferocity. The Vikings would sail up a river to some town or monastery and capture and loot it, putting the people to the sword, then setting the place on fire before they left."

Arno chuckled again. It bothered me that he could laugh about it.

"So Charles the Simple, the Frankish king, offered Hrolf the duchy now called Normandy," Arno went on, "if he would stop his raiding. Hrolf was a great Viking lord, a sea king with many men sworn to him. And Hrolf, whom the Franks called Rollo and who later took the Christian name Robert, would be the duke. All the king required, besides the end of his raiding, was that Hrolf allow himself to be baptized, for the Norse were not Christians then. And Hrolf was also to recognize the king as his sovereign, but owing him only one man's military service for forty days a year. Which, the story goes, the king in turn promised not to demand of him, though I doubt that even Charles would promise that.

"Denmark was crowded in those days, and many Danes, as well as certain other Norse, came to Normandy then to take land. The Franks who were there before them became their villeins. Many of the Danes who went there were *drengr*—unmarried men—and becoming baptized, took Frankish wives. Also they ceased their seafaring and learned to fight on horseback—like the Franks, but more skillfully. And they still had the bold, fierce, Viking nature, which we Normans keep to this day."

Although I followed all of that easily enough, there was one point of confusion. "But the Greek said that these are Varangians. How does that fit with Vikings? And apparently they not only speak a language of their own, but Greek."

"Varangians are the same people as the Vikings. Varangians are Norse who went to Byzantium to fight for the Emperor, and the language of Byzantium is Greek. Byzantium is wealthy beyond belief, and its Emperor pays richly for warriors of skill and valor. Many Norse go to Byzantium, and return to their homelands wealthy by Northern standards."

"And the Normans can also speak Norse?" I asked.

Arno shook his head. "Almost none do. I'm the only one I know who speaks as much of it as I, although there may be a few others. When I was born, my great-grandsire was an old man—seventy. As a small boy, I was intrigued by him, for he could find his way around the castle as if he still had the eyes which had been taken from him by a sword stroke, fighting river pirates on the Seine.

"In summer, he liked me to sit in the sun with him, when I was small, and we would talk. He taught me the Norse language, which as he spoke it then was mixed with more than a little of our good Norman French. And he told me many stories in Norse, of old days and old ways. I did not fully understand them then, of course, but I remembered; I heard them often enough that sometimes I told them to him."

Arno smiled, shaking his head. "I loved that old man, although I will tell you that he never entirely forgot the old gods. Indeed, I believe our priest suspected as much, for he often told my mother I should not be allowed with great-grandsire. He dared not accuse him of paganism though, for he had no evidence. And in name, my great-grandsire was still the baron there, though in his blindness, first my grandsire and then my father bore the responsibility.

"Great-grandsire—his name was Knut—had been born in Denmark, but Harald Bluetooth, who in those days was king there, had become Christian. And demanding that all Danes be baptized, and had begun to burn the shrines of the false gods, replacing them with churches.

"So my great-grandsire's father, disapproving of Christian ways, took his wife and children and left the country, going up to Norway, which was pagan still. It was there my great-grandsire grew up, worshiping the old gods, and when he was fifteen, went a-viking. In time, the band he was with took service with Ethelred of England, and fought Sveinn Forkbeard, who'd since become Denmark's king.

"But the band broke up when its leader, Gisli Ketilsson, was baptized and demanded that his followers do the same. Then my great-grandsire went home to Norway, where he found Olaf Tryggvesson king, and the people being baptized left and right. The shrines of the false gods were being burned, there'd been fighting, and in one fight, my great-grandsire's father had been sent to his grave.

"So he went with a Viking band to Normandy, where they took service with Duke Richard in quieting rebellious freeholders who were protesting certain changes from old Danish law to feudal law, which they considered a Frankish heresy. And the duke, not aware that great-grandsire was pagan, knighted him, his valor and the force and cunning of his sword making up for indifferent horsemanship."

Arno chuckled. "And in Normandy he was baptized at last, having seen, if not the truth of God, at least the daughter of William of Courmeron, who would not give her in marriage to a heathen. When William died without living sons, great-grandsire received the fief from the duke. From heathen Viking to Christian baron in a ten-year! By then he'd learned to ride with all but the best of them, though he swore he'd been fortunate to survive some of those wild early hunting rides through the forest.

"Then, when I was six, I was sent to serve at the castle of Hugh of Falaise, Roland's father, a man far nobler than his son would ever be. At certain holidays, we pages and squires would go home. Great-grandsire had entered his dotage, and somehow could no longer speak French, but only Norse, which, since grandsire's death, no one else there could speak except myself. Even from his Norse the French words all had fled, so that I had trouble understanding him at first. But because I could at least somewhat understand him, I spent much of my time with him when I was home. Until, when I was twelve, I was called to weep beside his bier."

I'd never thought of Arno weeping, even as a kid. He wasn't chuckling now; he wasn't even smiling.

"They said he'd regained both his French and his full wits on his last day, and, calling for the priest, had been absolved of all his sins, which I doubt not were less numerous and fulsome than those of many men who'd been Christian from the womb."

Arno shook his head as if throwing off a sense of loss. "I had not heard the Norse language again until today, and indeed could speak it only with difficulty at first."

"What did you talk about?" I asked.

"The leader's name is Gunnlag Snorrason, and he has accepted my oath. I am now one of his men. He was a Varangian himself once, and had fought against Normans in Apulia. Others of his men had fought Normans in Greece, or fought beside Norman mercenaries against the Patzinaks. The Varangians know the strength of Norman arms, and when they found that I could speak their tongue, albeit haltingly, they were pleased to have me. In fact, it clearly amused them to have a Norman in their ranks. To them I am a sport, like a Saracen bishop in God's church."

He chuckled, grinning ruefully. "Gunnlag Snorrason is no son of Tancred—no Roger de Hauteville, no Robert Guiscard or William Fer de Bras—and this vessel is all there is of his domain. But it is far far better than the cinnabar mines of Spain, where it is told the slaves live short and sickly lives and there is always a demand for more to replace the dying. And I can like these Varangians, for if they have learned to admire Normans in battle, Normans have learned that Varangian strength and valor is hardly second to our own. Were it not for Varangians, Guiscard might well rule not from Palermo but from Byzantium itself, and not a dukedom but an empire."

Later, Arno's cheerful mood turned somber, and that evening before we slept, he let me see what was bothering him.

"Larn," he said.

"Yes?"

"Why didn't your sister drive the Varangians away?

With her mighty weapons, she could have sent them to the bottom."

I lied to him. "I don't know why. She has other things to do than hang around taking care of me. And until today, you've had my speaking amulet. I haven't been able to keep in touch with her."

"Can you call her now?"

"I tried. She didn't answer." I took my communicator off my belt, switched it on, and murmured into it. "Deneen, this is Larn. Deneen, this is Larn. Come in, please. Over."

As I spoke, I had this feeling that she was going to surprise me and answer, but she didn't. Shrugging, I switched it off and put it back on my belt. "It seems to be working," I told him. "I just don't get an answer. But it only works over a few hundred miles. She's probably farther away than that."

He pursed his lips thoughtfully. I wished I was like Bubba and could read thoughts.

TWENTY-ONE

Late that night I woke up. I'd been dreaming of Jenoor, and in my dream she'd been alive, talking to me. I couldn't remember much about it, except she'd been telling me she was all right. I also remembered that in the dream it seemed as if she'd come to me in dreams before.

It had been such a joyous dream; now it was gone. I lay there for a minute, trying to remember more of it, but couldn't. Even what I did remember was slipping away, and a slow wave of despair washed through me. Getting up, I looked around. To the right of the long ship I could see a low coastline not many miles away beneath a full moon.

One of the Varangians had wakened at my movement and was watching me. I ignored him and went aft to where the water casks were lashed, for a drink, being careful not to step on anyone. I thought about talking to the steersman, getting into the Norse language the way I had Provençal, by gestures and pointing. I decided that wouldn't work too well with him handling the steering oar, so I went back and lay down again, where I dreamed some more about Jenoor.

But the next time I woke up, the sun was rising behind us, which told me we'd changed direction from south to westerly. The wind had shifted, too, coming out of the northeast. The square sail billowed roundly, and we were moving right along.

The most surprising change was that we were towing the horse ship now! Its own sail was full like ours, but the line was taut; we were adding to her speed, though it slowed us down. I called to the Greek—his name was Michael—and asked if he knew what that was about.

"We are entering waters where Saracen pirates and warships are more likely to be met," he said. "Our captain"—he meant the Varangian captain now—"wants to pass through them as swiftly as possible without separating from the other." He gestured toward the horse ship some hundred feet behind us.

And he really did want to get through fast. First we ate breakfast, which was the same as supper had been the day before: dates, smoked meat, and a hard, flat, crusty thing that the Norse called *flatbraud*, all washed down with watered wine. As soon as we'd finished, men were assigned to the rowing stools. Sliding the oars through the oar holes, they began to row in rhythm. It had to be in rhythm, or they'd have been banging oars together. An overweight Varangian with a hand missing set the rhythm of their stroke by striking a drum.

No question about it—we were going faster now.

I began to see a long, hard day ahead. Not all the

oars were in use; only about half the Varangians were rowing. It didn't take too much imagination to see what would happen after they'd rowed a while: The rest of us would replace them. I looked at my hands. There wasn't a callus on either of them. Then I looked around for something I could make a sun visor with. I wasn't nearly as tanned as the Varangians, and I didn't want my face to slough off at the end of a day on a rowing stool.

Sure enough, row I did. One shift would row for an hour—the one-handed bosun had an hourglass—then the other would take over. At midday we all quit rowing to eat lunch, which was the same as breakfast, followed by a longish rest, during which most of us slept. Then the rowing began again. Before my first shift I cut cloth pads from my cape to protect my hands, and I'm sure it helped, but even so, before the day was done, my palms were raw and oozing. The only good thing I could say about it, if you could call it good, was that I'd sort of gotten used to the pain. At the end of the first shift, I leaned over the gunwale and scooped up a bucket of salt water from the sea. After each shift I soaked my hands in it, though it stung. I wasn't sure the immunoserum would keep my blisters from getting infected, and a saltwater soak was the only treatment I could think of.

To start with, I told the captain I'd never rowed before, and asked for some coaching. Instead of a coach, he gave me the rearmost starboard oar, with no one on the next two stools in front of me. I saw why quickly enough. The long ship was rolling more than a little, and for the first couple of minutes I kept missing the water every few strokes, fanning the air. Then I got grooved in and it went pretty decently. After a while, I was even digging the water about the same each stroke.

My hands weren't my only problem. By the end of my first shift, my legs and back and arms were really tired. I kind of semi-recovered on the off-shifts, but by the end of the day I was more exhausted than I'd ever been before. When Michael gave me the good word that the captain wasn't going to make us row at night, I was too tired to be ecstatic, just awfully grateful.

On our first off-shift, Arno came over to me. "I've heard what you did to Jon Eriksson," he said. "Apparently it was you who took my weapons of power."

I resisted the impulse to remind him who "the weapons of power" actually belonged to. "Just the stunner," I said. "And I'm keeping it. The blaster went flying when the ax hit you. It's probably on the other ship with your horses."

He gestured at his belt, with its sword, dagger, and recharge magazine attached. "These were returned to me," he said, "and even my purse of gold. But this"—he indicated the magazine—"is empty. Who would have taken its contents except you? And why would you have taken them if you did not have the blaster?"

"Arno," I told him wearily, "I may have lied to you a time or two, but not this time." With an effort, I got to my feet. "Come on," I said, and headed for the stern. Arno followed, puzzled. I beckoned to Michael to come along too, and went to where Gunnlag stood with the steering oar under one brawny arm. "Gunnlag," I said, "when you attacked our ship, Arno had a marvelous device from India which I had given him. I saw it fly from his hand when he was struck by the ax, but it did not go into the sea. It was of metal, and about this long"—I showed him with my hands—"with a short handle at one end. Would you find out if any of your men have it? It would have been just lying there, and they could not have known that it was his. I'd like him to have it again if possible."

I said all that in short sentences, Michael interpreting. When I was done, Gunnlag nodded. "I will ask at midday, when we stop rowing to eat."

"And there was something else," I added. "Some small objects that were kept in this." I touched the magazine on Arno's belt. "He thought I had taken them for safekeeping, but I had not. Perhaps someone else has them."

In response, Gunnlag bellowed a name, and one of the Varangians came over. They talked briefly in Norse.

"It was Torkil here who took the strange objects from Arno's purse," Gunnlag said to me through the Greek. "They seemed useless to him, so he threw them aside, but not into the sea, he thinks. Perhaps they are on the other craft."

I thanked him then and returned to the bow. Arno followed, looking at least as unhappy as before. "You have humiliated me," he said grimly when we'd sat down.

"How did I do that?"

"By taking up my cause with Gunnlag. It was mine to do."

I stared at him. "Is that how things are done among the Varangians? Or is that a Norman way? Or perhaps only your own feeling about it? Gunnlag didn't seem to think there was anything wrong with what I did."

That stopped him. "Besides," I went on, "you didn't believe me when I told you I didn't have them. I thought if they turned up from someone else, that would settle it. As far as that's concerned, you'd practically accused me of stealing them from you, when actually you'd stolen them from me. Now Gunnlag is your witness that I said I gave them to you. It seems to me you don't have much to complain about."

He sat frowning, not really looking at me. I guess he was thinking. Then he nodded curtly and moved a few feet away where he sat facing aft. I lay back and closed my eyes until our shift went on again.

He felt a lot better at midday break, when one of the Varangians came up with the blast pistol. I was glad it had a so-called "shelf safety"—the second safety that Arno hadn't known about. Otherwise the Varangian, poking around in curiosity, might easily have shot a hole in the bottom of the ship, or killed some shipmate. I showed Arno how to disengage it, and advised him to leave it on when he was just wearing it around.

In turn, Arno was halfway friendly toward me again. During our other off-shifts, with Michael's help, I talked with a few of the Norsemen, including Gunnlag Snorrason. The captain was from a Norse kingdom called

Sweden, and at sixteen had gone to the Rhos land, where the warrior band he belonged to took service with a great prince named Jarisleif from time to time. Apparently the Rhos princes fought one another a lot. Jarisleif himself was descended from a Swede, as were most of the princes there.

Between hostilities, the Varangians occasionally raided Slav villages, selling their captives as slaves to the Greeks. Gunnlag laughed after he told me that. It had seemed, he said, as if the Greeks had all the gold in the world. So when his chief had a falling out with Jarisleif, their band had gone south in boats, down a great river to the Black Sea.

It had been a dangerous trip. The southernmost end of the river flowed through grasslands held by the Patzinaks—dark fierce horse barbarians who grazed their herds there. Reaching the Black Sea, the Varangians had rowed to Miklagard to take service with the Greek Emperor. Miklagard had proved everything men said of it.

Gunnlag cocked an eye at me then. "Surely you have been to Miklagard. How could one come here from India and not visit Miklagard?"

"Through the sky," I told him. "Through the sky." And he believed me, or that's how it looked, anyway, because after probing me with his eyes for a moment, he nodded.

He'd fought for the Emperor for eight years, Gunnlag told me, then had shipped home to Sweden. With the gold he took with him, he'd had this ship built on a great lake called Vänern, then rode it down the river Göta to the Northern Sea. In his youth, the old man who'd built it had built ships for the last of the Vikings. This one was built much like them, for ease of rowing, but a bit broader and deeper of keel for long sea voyages. By having his passengers row when the winds were not favorable, the trips went faster and there was less quarreling on board.

This had been Gunnlag's third voyage carrying pilgrims to the Holy Land. But when they had stopped at Crete, they'd been told by an admiral of the Byzantine

Emperor that pilgrims landing in the Holy Land recently had been sold into slavery there. The Emperor was gathering a new army to punish the Saracens for it, and surely those who took part would be rewarded not only with gold in this life but with Heaven afterward.

Most of the Swedes had planned to go to Miklagard anyway, after first visiting the holy city of Jorsala where the Christ had died. Instead, following this bad news, they went directly to Miklagard, where most of them entered service in a Varangian regiment. Gunnlag had recrewed his ship with Varangian veterans wishing to return to the lands of their birth. Now, aboard ship, there were not only men from Sweden, but from Denmark, Norway, and even distant Iceland, all speaking dialects of Norse. There were even two who'd been born in the Rhos land and had never seen the home of their fathers, though they could speak their tongue.

That night, lying chilled in the bottom of the long ship, I couldn't help wondering if the Fanglithans would ever become civilized. But then I remembered Brother Oliver and the monks, and Isaac ben Abraham. And back in Normandy, Father Drogo and Pierre the tanner, each of them a man of peace. Maybe dominance by warlike cultures was just a phase, one that Fanglith would have to live through.

Then what phase was the Federation-turned-Empire in? Was tyranny just a phase? If it was, it had been recurring for a long time. And meanwhile, I told myself, what I needed was warriors. The Glondis Empire made slaves of peaceful people.

TWENTY-TWO

The next morning I was so stiff and sore I couldn't believe it. Me, who'd always been so good at athletics, who'd been one of the stronger kids in school! I could hardly close my hands or pick up food with them. About my only consolation was that I wasn't the only one. Michael and Arno weren't moving around too well either. I don't suppose Arno's sword-callused right hand was peeled raw like mine, but I wasn't so sure about his left.

One of the Varangians grinned at us and said something in Norse. Arno had been practicing the language, and seemed to be doing pretty well, so I asked him what the man had said.

"He said the oar does that to you, when you're not used to it. And that the best cure for the oar is the oar. Yesterday one of them told me they were all sore the second day out of Miklagard."

I examined my hands—an oozing mess. I got another bucket of salt water to soak them, then just sort of flexed and unflexed them to limber them up before using the oar again.

The first minute was the worst, as far as pain was concerned.

As I rowed, I thought of the young slave oarsman that Deneen and Tarel had rescued. He must be pretty tough, I decided. I hoped he didn't cause any problems on their wilderness island. In Deneen's description, though, Moise had sounded all right. And Bubba had approved of him; that was the best assurance I could ask for.

By mid-morning my muscles weren't nearly as sore, although I was tired again, and even my hands felt better. As I had the day before, I soaked them in salt water for a while after each shift. We were finishing off our lunch when one of the Varangians saw sails to the southwest. They were triangular—two at first, and quickly two more. If we kept our present course, we'd just about run into them.

Gunnlag began shouting orders. Then, pulling on his steering oar, he put us into a long turn toward the north. The other rowing shift moved quickly to their oars. Of my shift, some began lowering the spar and sail, while others hauled furiously on the tow rope, taking in the slack that formed before the horse ship's steersman could match our turn. Arno ran to the stern of the long ship, his expression a mixture of chagrin and determination.

I saw Michael questioning a Varangian, and went over to him. "What is it?" I asked.

"The captain believes the sails are a Saracen fleet, and I think he is right. If that is so, we will have to abandon the prize ship and flee, else we will be taken."

Abandon the horse ship, *and Arno's herd!* Meanwhile, Gunnlag was determined to pick up his men aboard her. By that time I could see seven or eight sails, and surely they had seen ours. I grabbed the braided leather rope and helped pull; under the circumstances, I almost forgot how sore my hands were.

When we'd completed our turn, the oarsmen slowed until we'd pulled the prize ship's bow against our stern. As soon as they bumped, Arno vaulted across, and I thought I knew why: He wanted to find the spare charge cylinders for the blast pistol. Meanwhile the Varangian prize crew was scrambling aboard the long ship, but not the Greek crew; they were staying! Whether by choice or Varangian order, I didn't know. When the last Varangian was aboard, one of them raised his sword to cut the rope—and Arno wasn't back aboard yet! I grabbed the Varangian's sword arm and began yelling.

"Arno!" I yelled. "For God's sake, get back here! They're going to cut the rope!"

The Varangian stared, bug-eyed and indignant, for just a second, then aimed a punch at my head with his free hand, but I ducked it. Gunnlag shouted at him, then across at Arno in Norse, and the man I had hold of stopped trying to shake me loose. A moment later Arno came out of the hold and leaped aboard. Another Varangian cleft the rope.

"They were not there!" he said. "Someone must have thrown them overboard, else I'd have found them." His eyes were blazing. "If I had them, I could drive back the entire Saracen fleet. Then I'd take over this ship and make them row us to Palermo as my prize!"

I didn't argue with him. For one thing, there wasn't time. By then the mast was lying in the long ship's bottom with the spar and sails, and Gunnlag ordered all oars manned. It was plain how things were shaping up. Maybe twenty sails were visible now, and I had no reason to think there weren't more. Five others had dropped their sails and veered toward us—five of those nearest the front. Obviously they were being rowed, which meant they were either warships or pirates. And I presumed that pirates didn't travel in large fleets.

One of the Varangians was handing oars to my shift, and we added our strength to the rowing. The graceful long ship surged, almost seeming to fly on the water. It occurred to me how relative things are—how much they depend on your local frame of reference. Even in mass proximity mode the *Javelin* could travel in minutes a distance as far as from Fanglith to her moon, and we thought of mass proximity mode as slow. Here we were traveling—what? Not more than than ten miles an hour, I thought, and it seemed fast.

After a few minutes, Gunnlag's big voice called again, and the bosun slowed our pace a few strokes a minute. We might have to stay ahead of our pursuers for hours, I realized, and it wouldn't do to use ourselves up at the start. I glanced up to see what I could see, which under the circumstances wasn't much. They'd struck their masts too. I returned my full attention to rowing; I had to keep the stroke and not miss the water with my oar.

Meanwhile we had spare men. There hadn't been oars for all of my shift, and now we had the prize crew aboard as well. So after a while some of us were replaced at our oars to rest, including all three of us non-Varangians. Ordinarily, the Varangians didn't mind rowing, and considering that this was a matter of escape or die, they probably wanted the best oarsmen on the oars. Which didn't include Michael and me, or even Arno.

I took half a minute to try contacting Deneen, on the off chance she was somehow powered up and tuned in, but got no answer. Then I followed Arno back to Gunnlag Snorrason in the stern, with Michael behind me. Most of the Saracen fleet was out of sight again; apparently they'd continued on their original northwesterly course. Judging from the sun, we seemed to have veered all the way around to somewhat east of north.

Only three of our original five pursuers could be seen. I suppose the other two had turned aside to capture the horse ship. But the remaining three, I told myself, ought to be more than enough, considering that Arno had no replacement charges for his blaster. And their bows had a lot longer range than my stunner; it was only effective up close.

Arno was talking to Gunnlag in Norse—he'd gotten pretty good at it—and of course I couldn't understand. So I questioned Michael. From what he said, I got the impression that a warship was more of a troop carrier loaded with infantry than it was a fighting ship. Lots of naval battles on Fanglith amounted to boarding the enemy with your troops and fighting it out with swords. Any one of our pursuers would have two or three times as many fighting men as we had, maybe more.

No, he said, the Saracens were not the fighters the Varangians were. Mostly they were men of smaller frame, less brawny and not so savage, wearing lighter mail and wielding lighter weapons. That much was well known.

But they were brave and skilled, and when they caught us they'd be fresh, because slaves did their rowing.

Could slaves row as hard as the Varangians? I asked. Michael thought not—Byzantine slaves couldn't anyway. But the *dromans*, the big Saracen warships, had as many as fifty great oars each, each pulled by two men, with the whip to inspire any who didn't pull hard enough.

After a while we sat down at the oars again for about an hour. The next time I was relieved, the Saracens had gained quite a bit. The Varangians who weren't rowing were arguing with each other and with Gunnlag. Michael explained that some of them wanted to stand and fight while others thought we ought to keep running.

It seems that Arno had told them earlier that the Normans held most of Sicily now—probably including the part we were headed for. Even if they didn't, a strong party of determined warriors might make their way to Norman territory. And Roger, the Count of Sicily, who was notoriously generous, would be glad to hire Varangians in his army, or help them continue home as Christian pilgrims.

Those who wanted to run figured we might reach Sicily, and that if we were about to get caught, *then* we could stand and fight. Those who wanted to make a stand now figured we didn't have a chance to reach Sicily, and they wanted to fight before they got any more tired from rowing. They assumed they were going to get killed anyway, and they wanted to kill as many Saracens as they could while they were at it.

Michael told me the Varangians were famous for never surrendering. According to him, the most dangerous thing you could do was trap Varangians.

Finally, Gunnlag had heard enough, and bellowed one short command. The argument thinned down to a few "last words" by some of his men to some of the others, then stopped. We kept going.

Arno went up to the bow. I followed and sat down next to him. "What decided the argument?" I asked.

He looked at me and grinned, reminding me of the Arno I'd seen before a few times—happy-go-lucky.

"I told Gunnlag that if we stopped, the Saracens would come up on us all at once. But if we kept running, they'd probably come up on us one at a time. And that one at a time I could use the device you gave me to sink them or drive them away."

He took it out of its holster and looked at it thoughtfully, slipping the silent safeties off and on. "It isn't accurate at a distance, and without the recharge cylinders"—he used the Evdashian words for them, of course—"I must make each shot count, which means we must be close, within reach of their arrows. If they come at us all at once, we'll be under heavy fire, and these"—he gestured around to indicate the Varangians—"would stop rowing to fight. We would surely be taken then.

"Not that I explained all that to Gunnlag. Best he thinks of this as thaumaturgy instead of the handwork of some weapons artificer."

That took me by surprise. I'd assumed that Arno himself still thought of it as magic.

"It was then he made up his mind," Arno finished.

He looked me over. "In your way, you are brave. And you are one of those who are still alive after the danger or chase or fight are past. You proved that in Savoie and Normandy, more than once. Nonetheless, if it comes to it and they close with us, I'll see that one of the Varangians covers you against arrows with a shield. Then, just before the ships touch, you rise up with your stunner and sweep its force along their rail. Some of us will cut the ropes."

He grinned again. "We will arrive at Palermo yet, you and I."

Before Gunnlag ordered us back to the oars, I tried the communicator once more, just in case. And once more got no answer. When I sat down to row again, we could see Sicilian hills in a faint line along the horizon.

At the end of our next shift, the hills were a lot closer, but the Saracen dromans were too. At the end of the shift after that, the nearest two dromans were almost even with each other, and I could imagine them treating it as a race, with us as the prize.

The bosun quickened our pace, and I wasn't sure I could make it through my next shift. Arno wasn't rowing now; he was with Gunnlag in the stern. He must have had quite a bit of experience with the blast pistol we'd left with him before; I hoped he'd gotten good with it. When at last I was relieved, I could see more than the Sicilian hills, which weren't so high here. I could even make out the shore, we were that close. Maybe three miles, I thought, and turned and went aft.

Behind us, the Saracens were so near, I could easily see the oars of the nearest two. They'd gotten strung out at last. There was the nearest, then maybe a couple of hundred yards back the second. The third was probably a half mile farther still.

I couldn't tell whether we were going to reach the shore ahead of them or not. Or what we'd do if we did. Looking down into the long ship's bottom and then over the side at the water, it seemed to me she couldn't draw more than four feet of water. But for seaworthiness, she had a keel. And for all I knew, the keel could be deep enough that we'd hit bottom in water over our heads. Or there might be a reef offshore, or a shoal, and we'd pile up on it a quarter or half mile out.

I supposed the Varangians could swim, but not with hauberks on, or swords at their belts. And in Normandy, I'd discovered the hard way that a blaster, or at least some blasters, wouldn't fire after being submerged in water. Did the dromans have small boats aboard? Would they launch them to attack us as we swam, or to follow us ashore? Did the Normans control this part of the island? If they didn't, were there Saracen troops in the vicinity? Were those hills wild? How far could we travel without being discovered?

I went aft to wait with Arno.

The first droman was close enough now that I could see the white of her bow wave, and make out men at her rail. Five would get you ten, I thought, that they had bows strung and ready. The cadence of their rowing was no faster than ours, but their two-man oars gave longer strokes, and their ship, if not as graceful as the long ship, had lines well built for speed.

At maybe a hundred yards they shot a few trial arrows, which fell close astern of us. The Varangians not rowing stood in the walkway with shields, ready to protect their oarsmen. One also stood by Gunnlag to protect him while he steered. At this point, Arno and I crouched with only our heads above the gunwales. A minute later the Saracens fired a small volley, and the first arrow struck the stern; we heard it thud.

Arno raised up enough to level the blaster, holding it with both hands, wrists braced on the gunwale. Then he fired, and I saw a flash at the bow of the droman, but I couldn't see if he'd blasted a piece out of the bulwark or actually hit a bowman. A bowman, I decided; I could hear men yelling, and it didn't sound like battle cries. By the flash, his next bolt hit the bow a little above waterline. The hole would have been a good foot wide, I'd think, and hopefully low enough to be taking water. But the droman came on, and a flight of arrows rose visibly from her, so Arno fired two more bolts into the massed archers in the bow.

This time we heard unmistakable screaming. He must have killed a couple of them, messily, and the droman began to veer off. That's when he lucked out. I mean, it may have been what he was trying to do, but he had to be lucky to do it: As she began to veer, he fired again and apparently hit the mast, because the mast and sail fell across the aft oarsmen.

Even with luck though, it had been great shooting at that distance, with a pistol. I needn't have worried about Arno's marksmanship.

By that time, Saracen arrows were falling in and around our stern. Our own oarsmen didn't miss a beat, but neither did those on the second droman. I don't know what their captain thought was happening on the first ship, but it didn't change his mind about anything. At about eighty or ninety yards, a volley of arrows lifted from her bow, and Arno sent two bolts into the mass of archers, then several at her bow.

The last time he touched the stud, nothing happened: her charge was exhausted. I kept my head down as the arrows started to fall—enough of them that I was surprised none of us was hit, though several stuck in Varangian shields and a number had thudded, vibrating, into the wood of the long ship.

I popped my head up for another look. Arno must have hit the droman near the waterline with at least two bolts and probably more. She was definitely slowing—probably scooping water.

Then Gunnlag bellowed an order, and our oarsmen stopped! I didn't realize what that was about for a moment. Arno yelled something in Norse, and Gunnlag looked angrily at him. Arno started talking furiously, and I suddenly realized what was going on. Gunnlag wanted to slow down and disable the other droman; he hadn't realized the blaster was out of charge. Arno was trying to get us rowing again.

When Gunnlag got the picture, he bellowed the rowers back into action. Meanwhile the third droman was coming on, not more than a quarter mile away now. By that time we were less than a mile from the beach, and the Varangians put their brawny backs into it. At a half mile, the droman slowed. She was quite a bit bigger than we were, and probably rode a few feet deeper. Apparently her captain wasn't willing to beach her.

We didn't hit bottom until we were less than fifty yards from shore. When the shallow keel grabbed the sand; the long ship jerked sharply, throwing me to the deck. But our momentum and the oarsmen's last stroke took us ten yards farther, tilting to the side. Then we sat on the bottom, resting partly on the keel and partly on the curve of our left side, the water within two feet of our gunwale.

The droman was still coming, though more slowly now, and maybe three hundred yards back. I could picture her bowmen waiting ready. The Varangians didn't waste time. Grabbing weapons and shields, they piled over the portside gunwale into waist-deep water. The surf was negligible. I followed them, holding my stunner and communicator overhead; we were all ashore within a couple of minutes.

The droman had veered off, out of bowshot. We'd

come through the whole thing without one casualty. There were seventy-eight Varangians on the beach, along with one Norman, one Greek, and one holy monk from India.

PART FIVE

THE BATTLE

TWENTY-THREE

Once ashore and satisfied that we weren't about to be attacked from the sea, I looked around. The wide beach sloped up to a screen of trees—trees that didn't look like any I'd seen before on Fanglith. Or on Evdash either, as far as that's concerned. Their trunks were like thick rough pillars, without any branches at all. At the top, each of them had a broad crown of what looked like very long leaves, maybe twelve or fifteen feet long, that curved out and down. Each leaf came directly from the top of the trunk, which I suppose was maybe sixty or seventy feet tall.

Arno told me it was a date orchard, that the trees were date palms. I knew about dates; I'd eaten them aboard the long ship. After looking around for a minute, we walked up the beach and into the orchard, which was only about a hundred feet wide. Behind it was a field of something that looked like grass and that Arno said was wheat. I remembered wheat from Provence and Normandy, but it had been quite a lot taller there. Later in the growing season, I suppose. On the other side of the wheat field was a row of more ordinary-looking trees.

Eastward about half a mile was a little hamlet of maybe twenty small houses, plus sheds and other out-buildings. On a knoll a little way back of the hamlet stood a castle, not very big but built of stone. I would have seen it from the long ship if my attention hadn't been behind us, while from the beach, the orchard had been in the way.

We all stopped to look it over, the Varangians talking quietly in their singsong language.

"A Saracen place," Arno said to me. "Most of Sicily is peopled by Saracens, and there is no Christian church in that hamlet. If there was, we could see the cross. But this could still be Norman territory. Where Guiscard or Roger conquer Saracen ground, they leave the people to their own laws and religion. It saves no end of trouble.

"From the tower they must have seen our vessel being pursued by Saracen warships, and may have seen us run aground. That they have not sent cavalry to attack us gives me hope that this district is Norman."

He went over to Gunnlag and they spoke in Norse. Some of the other Varangians entered into the conversation; I wished I could understand what they were saying. When they were done, Gunnlag and Arno led us off across the wheat field, ignoring the hamlet and the tower, heading toward the hills. I asked Michael to find out what was going on, and he fell into step with one of the friendlier Varangians who'd been agreeable to his questions before.

The more ordinary-looking trees on the other side of the wheat field shaded an irrigation ditch. We stopped there to drink, then started across another wheat field on the other side. As we walked, Michael angled over to me.

"Some of the Varangians wanted to sack the hamlet," he told me. "Some of the younger ones don't seem very smart; their motto seems to be, act now and let the consequences take care of themselves. But Lord Arno recommended that we reach the hills before nightfall and camp in a place easy to defend. And Captain Gunnlag agreed. They don't want to risk attack in the open by Saracen knights, or get surrounded, trapped, in the hamlet. Or antagonizing the Normans, if this place has surrendered to them and been granted Norman protection.

"Lord Arno believes that if there are Saracen knights

in the castle, they are too few to attack us. But the Saracens use pigeons—a kind of bird—to carry messages from one place to another. The steward of this castle could easily have sent word to some nearby lord that a shipload of Christians has come ashore here.

"Then, by darkness, Lord Arno and some other will go down to the hamlet and see what they can learn—find out if this district has indeed been conquered by Normans."

If the district was hostile—still under Saracen rule—and if the castle's marshal had sent a message to some governor by bird or mounted messenger, would we be attacked that night, I wondered? It seemed to me that if a Saracen force came after us, they'd better be a large force; seventy-eight Varangians plus a Norman knight might give them more than they bargained for.

Plus one Evdashian rebel with a stunner. That should be worth something.

I wished I'd been able to raise Deneen, though. I counted back on my fingers. This would be the fourth night since she'd left for our uninhabited island. At best I couldn't expect her to be powered up again till the sixth, but I'd still try every now and then.

None of us was used to hiking. The Varangians and Michael weren't even used to being on land—not lately anyway—and neither was I for that matter. While Arno seldom walked far, and probably never had; he was born and raised a horseman. So the rugged hills were pretty hard on us. Probably less on the Varangians, though. Rowing, the way they did it, worked the thighs hard, and it certainly worked the heart and lungs.

Of course, the Varangians had a lot more to carry. Each of them wore a heavy sword. Some of them carried a long-handled battle-axe over one shoulder, and others a bow and a quiver of arrows. All of them carried a shield, most an ornamented round shield that Arno told me was Byzantine. But some had a long, rectangular shield slung over their backs, almost big enough to hide behind.

If we were attacked, I'd have to do without, at least

until I could scavenge one from someone who'd been killed—preferably a Saracen if it came to that. Not that I had anything against the Saracens; I might like them better than Normans or Varangians. But I'd committed myself, and besides, I had an "in" with the Varangians, as a holy monk.

After drinking our fill at a brook, we made camp on a hilltop, where anyone would have to walk or ride up a steep slope to get at us. If we were surrounded, sooner or later we'd have to fight our way down to water, but even I could see that the brook wasn't defensible.

One thing we hadn't been able to bring from the long ship was food. My stomach was complaining already. It threatened to be a long night, and tomorrow didn't show much promise either.

Then Arno started back to spy out the hamlet, taking Michael with him because the Greek could speak Arabic. With them gone, there wasn't a man in camp that I could talk to or understand. I very definitely hoped they came back.

Even as tired as I was, it took me quite a while to fall asleep. Which was unusual. The Varangians had bedded down all packed together—for warmth I suppose. To me though, they smelled too bad for such close quarters, and I slept a little way off from them. I was cold and hungry, and my muscles were starting to stiffen up again. About the time it got dark, the moon came up, too little past full to tell the difference just by looking. When I did get to sleep, I kept waking up or half waking up from cold and the stony ground, but I only got up once, to relieve myself.

When it was daylight, nearly sunup, I awoke for good. I was really stiff again, from rowing, and maybe partly from hiking up hills and sleeping on the hard ground in the cold. For the first time, I really looked around. Four or five miles south was the sea, with no trace of warships, although I could make out a couple of what I supposed were fishing boats. In every other direction were rugged hills, mostly bare. Here and there were patches of scrub, and in some of the ravine bottoms there were trees. To the north, the hills rose to become mountains.

Arno and Michael were back, but they were still sleeping so there was no one to tell me what they'd found out. It looked as if something had happened, though; each was wrapped in a blanket. I limped down the hill to the brook and took a long drink, then limped back up, my stomach growling. Water didn't make much of a breakfast. By the time I'd gotten back to the top of the hill, I was warm again, and the worst of the soreness was gone. The sun was looking at us over the next ridge east, and Arno and Michael were both awake.

No one seemed in any hurry to get on the trail.

I went over to Arno. "What did you find out?" I asked.

He grinned and, patting the rock next to him, invited me to sit. "We went to the first house," he said. "I hid beneath a window and sent the Greek to the door with a piece of Saracen silver." Arno hefted the purse at his belt, which held what might be the only money among us now. "He'd lived in Messina when it was still Saracen—there are many Greeks there. He knows Saracan ways and language, and something of their religion—enough to pretend he is one of them, a convert. He told them he'd escaped Varangian priates. And while the Greek talked with them, the Saracans fed him. They'd seen the ship, they said, and later they'd seen the infidel dogs, perhaps a hundred of them, cross the wheat field. The commander of the tower garrison had sent men on horseback to Agrigento and Sciacca to inform the commanders there and ask them to send knights.

"They also told him that the Normans had captured Palermo, and that there is fighting in the west, and over east around Troina."

"How did Michael get away?" I asked. "Wouldn't it have seemed suspicious for him to leave, under the circumstances?"

"It was no problem. They gave him a mat to sleep on and went back to bed themselves. After giving them time to go to sleep, I slipped inside and killed them. Then I ate my fill and we left."

From a purse he hadn't had the day before, he took a few dates and gave them to me. I stared at them a moment before eating, and even as hungry as I was, they didn't go down easily. I could see why Arno might feel he had to kill them, but he'd said it as casually as if it meant nothing to him. And I suppose it hadn't; he *was* a Norman.

"When are we going to start hiking again?" I asked. "Or aren't we?"

"Gunnlag sent archers out hunting. We'll need food. All Norsemen learn archery as boys, and they are used to hunting on foot. And these hills have many goats." He pointed northward toward the mountains. "That's the way to Norman territory, but it seems to be a long, hard march. We'll do better with meat in our bellies."

It was on toward midday when we left. By then we'd eaten a half-grown goat. The shares were small, but they helped. Most of the others were footsore—Michael and Arno the worst of all. The ground was rocky, and I was the only one with stiff soles on his boots. In fact, I couldn't see how their soft-bottomed shoes could possibly last across the mountains. Maybe they could make some kind of shoes out of goatskin, I decided.

After the first half hour of hiking, I got loosened up enough that it didn't go badly at all, but by late afternoon I was bushed again, and hungrier than I could believe! So was everyone else, and we started taking quite a few breaks. Also, it got a lot colder as we got higher up. We'd come to several stone huts, but no one was staying in them. Arno said they might be for herdsmen—that sheep had probably been grazed in these mountains before the Norman invasion. I wondered what sheep ate here. By the looks of the bushes, something ate twigs—perhaps the goats.

Gunnlag had sent scout/hunters ahead of us, and two of them shot a goat each. We cooked them for an early supper, or half cooked them, by a mountain brook, and ate one of them plus the head of the other. The rest would be breakfast. I was appointed to carry it, in a smelly bag made of its own skin. Then we pushed on. By dusk, when we made camp, we'd passed banks of crusty old snow on some north slopes, and I was prepared for a miserable night. Just about everyone but me was limping now from sore feet, though I didn't hear any complaints.

Before I lay down, I went a little way off. "To pray," I told Michael. "Tell the Varangians I'm going off by myself to pray to the angel Deneen." I went out on an outcrop and tried the communicator, but got no one. Just as I'd expected. Tomorrow night would be the sixth. I could reasonably hope to get her on the sixth night. If not, then maybe on the seventh.

After that I went "to bed." This time I didn't let smelly bodies bother me. I lay down against the jam of Varangians to share warmth. I suppose it helped, but it was the coldest, most miserable night I'd ever spent.

What can I say about the next day? Until late afternoon it was basically the same as the one before: hike up and down steep slopes and pick your way along ravines. The country was high and cold, and if a little less rugged, it was still tough going. We were still in luck with the weather, which was sunny without much breeze, but on the other hand, the scouts only killed one goat. One goat for eighty-one of us. Gunnlag stopped early to camp, and a number of men with bows were sent hunting.

If they didn't have some luck, we'd be hungrier that night than the first.

While we lay around in the late sun, we heard a horn off to the south. I asked Arno what he thought it was. He said it sounded like a Saracen war trumpet, but they probably used them as hunting horns too. I asked him what they might be hunting in a time of war like this.

He grinned at me. "They're hunting just what you think they're hunting," he replied. "Us. And the horn means they've found our trail."

He got to his swollen feet and, with only a slight

limp, walked over to Gunnlag to talk with him about it.
By the way Gunnlag looked—standing, staring off toward the sound—he'd come to the same conclusion on
his own. I went off to pray to the angel Deneen again.
Maybe this time. If not . . .

From what I understand about prayer, what I felt
when I called Deneen that evening wasn't much different from what the Christians felt when they prayed to
their God. Again I didn't get any answer. I began to
wonder if, just possibly, my communicator wasn't working. Unlikely. Maybe . . . I didn't like to think about it,
but maybe something was wrong with the *Rebel Javelin*—
something worse than fuel crystallization. No, I told
myself, it's just a night too soon.

And tomorrow night could easily be a night too late. I
decided it was time to turn on my remote again, in case
she called me.

The hunters were back sooner than they might have
been. They'd heard the horn too. Among them they'd
gotten one goat. She'd been gutted, and given to me to
carry because we weren't going to stay where we were.
It didn't appeal to Gunnlag for a defensive stand. True,
it was a high point on a ridge, but an enemy could
charge along the crest at us from two sides with only a
mild slope to ride up. While on the next major ridge
north there was a rounded peak, sort of a knob, that
would be a lot easier to defend.

It was nearly dark when we reached it. By that time
we'd heard horns twice more, the last sounding as if it
came from the place we'd left two hours earlier. I
wondered how many Saracens there were. The Varangians rolled and lugged the available large rocks into a
crescent at each end of our position. Only the ends were
attackable. The rocks didn't make a wall at all; you
could walk between them. But they'd give a little cover
from arrows if you knelt behind them. Then we sat and
squatted in little clusters at the top.

That's when I realized that someone wasn't with us.

"Where's Michael?" I murmured to Arno.

"I've sent him north," he answered. "To see if he can
find some Norman force to relieve us. The Saracens

will assume we've sent someone, but one man is hard to trail by night."

"Can they track us at night?" I asked.

"Saracen knights are like Norman knights in their love of hunting. And the moon will rise before long, with light enough to track a force the size of ours."

That seemed reasonable to me. Piet had taught us to track during our survival training, and we'd followed well-beaten animal trails by moonlight.

"How many of them do you think there are?" I asked.

Arno shrugged. "They think we are a hundred, so they may well be twice that. Quite possibly more. And they are on horses; do not doubt it."

It occurred to me to wonder what use I'd be up there on the hilltop. The Saracens had to be pretty smart about war, or they wouldn't be a power on Fanglith. And if they were smart, they wouldn't rush us. They'd sit down the hill and let us get good and thirsty. They might not even waste arrows on us.

And knowing the Varangians, when they got thirsty enough, after maybe a day without water, they'd go down after some. They wouldn't just wait to die. Then the Saracen archers and swordsmen would get a workout. And whoever won—probably the Saracens—a lot of us would be dead when it was over. Maybe all of us.

The last of the twilight had died, and moonrise was still an hour or two off. It was as dark as a night in open mountains can get without a good cloud layer. Which was pretty dark. "Arno," I said, getting to my feet, "wish me luck."

I unbuckled my belt and took my shortsword off of it, then laid the sword by a boulder. My stunner and communicator I kept.

"What are you going to do?" Arno asked.

"I'm going hunting. We hunt on Evdash too, you know." Then, after rebuckling my belt, I slipped out through the partial crescent of boulders and started south down the mountain.

TWENTY-FOUR

Deneen:

It was still night when we got to the island. I put the *Jav* down near the little stream, at about where we'd been before. A little farther from it, actually, in case a big rainstorm came along and the creek outgrew its banks.

With the power off, we'd be down to basics. And I mean *basics*. Most of our equipment, including kitchen and sanitary equipment, operated off ship's power, while what hand-powered tools we had were designed for working on ship systems and structure. We didn't have so much as a shovel to bury trash with or dig a latrine.

Somehow, I hadn't thought about any of this until we were on the island. Then, for a couple of minutes, I considered going back to the continent and having Tarel and Moise get us some things, but that would mean being on power again for several hours, and there was the possibility that they might get into trouble on the ground. Possibly trouble that could take days on power to handle. Unlikely, maybe, but I wasn't willing to take the risk.

Then I remembered that we had the fire starters from our packs, and the shortsword and dagger that Larn had gotten Tarel in Marseille. Plus stunners to hunt with, and Uncle Piet's survival training. And more than anything else, Bubba was with us as our super watch-canid and master hunter.

We were better off than I'd thought; it wasn't like me

to get all shook up with no good reason. That's when I realized how worried and distracted I was about Larn. Which was kind of dumb, because it didn't do anyone any good—Larn or any of us.

Tarel and I looked around for anything I'd missed that might be useful and didn't require ship's power. Then I shut the power off and we all went out and slept on solid ground—more solid than I was used to.

I lay there for a while with Larn on my mind. Both in Provence and Normandy, and recently on the ship from Marseille, he'd shown a lot of ability, resourcefulness, and ingenuity, which had helped keep him alive. But an important part of it had been—let's face it—*really good luck*. And while luck is very good to have, I'd never felt very comfortable about relying on it. It seemed to me that you couldn't know when you'd run out of it—at least, not until it was too late.

Of course, ability has its limits too, but you at least had some idea of what those limits were. And while you couldn't measure ingenuity or resourcefulness, you knew if you had it or not. Just now, Larn's abilities weren't what I could wish they were. For example, his skill with local weapons was almost nonexistent, and Arno had gotten his stunner and blaster away from him. What he had left was his ability to do the right thing at the right time—duck when he needed to. And that's where ability shaded over into luck, which he might or might not have some of at any particular time.

Or was luck another ability—a kind that people didn't usually recognize as one?

That's the kind of thing that went through my mind for a while after I lay down beside the *Jav*. But in half an hour or so I went to sleep anyway.

We got along through five days and five nights, and it wasn't as bad as I thought it might be—at least not for me. I may have been a little bossy at times—let's face it, I was—but someone had to be in charge, and it was my hat. On the morning of the sixth day, with everyone on board, I powered up and called for a systems check on the computer. Including a check of the fuel slugs.

It could have been worse. Crystallization was greatly reduced, but there was still more than I was willing to live with. I'd have to take her out 700,000 miles and run her in FTL mode for a while—lock her into a loop that would bring her back in-system at the same system coordinates. I told Tarel what I was going to do, and told him to explain as much of it as he could to Moise. They'd gotten to be pretty good friends on the island— buddies you could say. And Moise had learned considerable Evdashian through the learning program, although he didn't understand some of our concepts yet.

So far I'd been impressed with how calmly Moise had reacted to all the strange, and to him far out, things he'd been exposed to since I'd put the spotlight on the pirate ship. I'd wondered a time or two if it was partly because, in his world, they believed in so many supernatural things. Then, when he ran into something real that *seemed* supernatural, it might not be as big a shock.

Now, of course, he knew we weren't a threat to him. But it must have been really weird and scary when strange people had hauled him inside a sort of giant boat, or big steel flask, and whisked him into the sky.

As Tarel started explaining, I headed us outbound and then called the maintenance manual into memory. The entry on fuel crystallization referred to a number of library entries, and now that I had time, it seemed to me I ought to read them. The third one I came to was the one I needed to see. One sequence of events that could lead to crystallization was rare, but it fitted all too well what had happened to the *Jav*.

"Prolonged impacts by heavy blaster charges on a ship's energy shield," it said, "can result in weak magnetization of the power transfer system. Subsequent use of the weapons system, with its translation of the gray force into pulse mode, will initiate crystallization in the fuel slugs."

I had no idea what that meant, but for the moment, I kept reading, hopeful that I wasn't getting into mental quicksand.

"Once crystallization is initiated," it went on, "subsequent low-intensity power use, as in mass-proximity mode, and the resulting resistance to normal matrix function, causes feedback to the fuel slugs, extending crystallization rapidly.

"When fuel crystallization occurs, do the following:

1. avoid using the ship's weapons system until the power transfer module has been changed;

2. decrystallize the fuel slugs; and

3. change the power transfer module."

It fitted. The *Jav*'s energy shield had taken a lot of blaster charges before we'd lifted from Evdash. And I'd discovered serious fuel cell crystallization within twenty standard hours of demonstrating the scout's weapons system for Arno.

Well, I told myself, I know what to do about it now. Fingers on the keyboard, I called up parts storage and asked for a new power transfer module. It replied that power transfer modules were not part of standard parts stock on scouts. That was followed by a list of places where I could get one—any of the three Evdashian naval stations.

I muttered an expression that mom and dad wouldn't approve of.

From there I skimmed on through the rest of the articles, looking for information that might be helpful. There wasn't any. But it seemed obvious that I'd better not use the weapons system again, and in trying to establish a political and military power base on Fanglith, that would be a serious disadvantage.

"Tarel!" I called.

"What is it?" he asked, coming over. I brought the third article back to the screen—the article that explained what had happened. He read it over my shoulder.

"And there isn't any replacement module," I told him. "Any suggestions?"

"We've got hand weapons," he said. "Including blast rifles. Maybe they'll be enough, along with our speed and communicators."

"I guess they'll have to be," I answered. But I didn't

feel very good about it. We couldn't have too many advantages, and we'd lost a big one.

At 700,000 miles I shifted into FTL mode on a ten-hour loop, and before we returned to mass-proximity mode, all residual crystallization was gone. Back at Fanglith I parked above the north shore of Sicily at an altitude of fifty miles. The scanner located the biggest town there, a good-sized city even by Evdashian standards. Palermo was where Larn should be. From where I sat, the moon stood well above the horizon—high enough that its light paled the island. I turned on the radio receiver, checked the communicator channel, and touched the *send* switch.

"Larn," I said, "this is *Rebel Javelin*. Larn, this is *Rebel Javelin*. Over."

He didn't answer. *He doesn't have his remote on*, I told myself. *That's all*. It didn't reassure me a bit. *Why* didn't he have his remote on? It was controlled with a switch on his communicator, and the last I knew, Arno had the communicator. The likeliest explanation I could think of for the remote being off was that Arno had turned it off—whether by accident, or because he'd learned about it.

"Bubba!" I called. He came over to me, meeting my eyes. "I'm going to drop low over Palermo," I told him, speaking out loud. "When we get there, I want you to scan around and find Larn. I can't get him on the radio."

He nodded like a human might, and of course he read the concern in my mind. I already had a scanner view of northern Sicily, and asked the computer for a coordinate overlay, to get the coordinates of Palermo. Then, using voice mode, I ordered the scout to park above Palermo at an elevation of five miles. We headed for it.

TWENTY-FIVE

Larn:

When I started down from the mountaintop, I didn't have any plan, but one started to unfold for me as I went: Backtrack, then ambush the Saracens with my stunner. Not that I could stun many of them; besides its short range, the stunner had a limited charge.

They'd probably send scouts out ahead to find the way, and to draw fire if they got close to any Christian bowmen. I'd ambush them. We'd see what they thought about paralyzed scouts who didn't have an arrow or sword slash on them. If they were superstitious, they might quit till daylight. Maybe they'd even turn around and go home, though that seemed a little much to hope for.

In the dark I couldn't see our tracks, but I didn't need tracks to retrace our route. When Gunnlag had decided to move camp, we'd come down from our initial campsite, crossed a small valley, then climbed along a ravine to its head at a notch in this ridge crest. From there we'd hiked along the crest till it topped off at the knob. Even with the moon not up yet, it would be easy to follow the same route in reverse.

The "notch" was an actual sharp one, with a big rock outcrop on one side. When I turned there to start down the ravine, someone grabbed me from behind, hard, arm around my neck, jerking me back with a rough strength too abrupt to let me use hand-foot art. It took me totally by surprise. Another man moved in front of me, knife ready, and peered into my face. Recognizing me, he spoke quietly in Norse, and the one who had grabbed me let me go.

Gunnlag had posted lookouts; I should have realized he would. "I'm going down the ravine to set an ambush," I said softly in Norman French. They didn't understand me, of course; it would have sounded crazy to them if they had. But it seemed as if I should say something to them. One of them said something back in Norse. No one had understood anyone, but I guess it made us all feel better somehow. I nodded and left them, starting down the ravine with as little noise as possible.

As the ravine got deeper, it seemed to get even darker, probably because it was exposed to less sky and less starlight. Where there were clumps of trees in the bottom, it was darker still. It got stonier, too, with lots of boulders that had rolled down from above. The upslope on my right had quite a lot of clumpy brush and scrubby trees, probably because it faced away from the sun. The other side was pretty bare, as if it faced into the sun and dried out too badly during the dry season.

About halfway down the ravine I came to what seemed like a good place. When the moon came up, visibility would be pretty good in the bottom there—no trees, no tall boulders. And on the brushy side of the ravine, the lower slope was clear along there, a slant of naked rock. I scrambled up it on all fours, to take cover above it between two clumps of stiff-twigged scrub. From there I'd have an open shot at anyone riding up the bottom, at a range of only about twenty or twenty-five yards.

Of course, I couldn't know for sure that any Saracens would come along, but it seemed as if they would. If they hadn't shown up by the first light of dawn, I'd just have to take off for the knob—that or hide out and try to make it to Norman territory on my own. No way was I going to try ambushing a Saracen scouting party by daylight, when they'd be able to spot me. And any who got out of effective stunner range—maybe fifty yards—would be able to sit back and shoot arrows at me in total safety.

Meanwhile, I had some waiting to do, and something occurred to me that I hadn't thought about before: I was going to have to stay awake. If I went to sleep, Saracens might ride past without waking me up. Right away I started worrying. Turning off my remote, I took it out of my ear so it wouldn't interfere with my hearing.

Staying awake turned out to be easier than I'd expected, because it was getting pretty cold again, and just sitting there didn't keep me warm like hiking had. After checking by feel the setting on my stunner—at this range, narrow beam and just above medium intensity seemed about right—I shoved my hands inside my cape to keep them warm in my armpits.

I wondered what Jenoor would think if she could see me here, then imagined that she *could* see me, and what we might say to each other. After a while I dozed in spite of the cold—dozed and wakened, dozed and wakened—and didn't worry about it. In as shallow a sleep as that, I told myself, I'd wake up if any horses came along.

Finally I awakened with a start, and thought sure some sound must have done it—maybe horseshoes on rock. I sat still, hardly breathing, but couldn't hear a thing, and after a couple of minutes decided it had just been nerves. The sky down the ravine was lighter, but it didn't seem to be the graying of early dawn. Besides, I was sure I hadn't slept nearly that long. Moonrise, I told myself. Of course. After a few minutes I could see moonlight shining on the upper slope across the ravine; the moon had climbed above the next ridge east. Now I could see quite a bit better, although my side of the ravine was out of direct moonlight, in heavy shadow.

If the Saracens were going to move that night, they'd probably have started by now. If they'd reached our first stopping place, chance was that they'd followed our trail down off that ridge to camp by the creek in the little valley below it; there were even some empty huts there. And if they'd done that, I told myself, I shouldn't have to wait too much longer.

So I was ready when, maybe ten minutes later, I

heard faint hoof sounds. I lay down on my stomach and crept forward a couple of feet so I could look farther down the ravine. I saw movement, and seconds later a horseman rode out of the shadow of some trees fifty or sixty yards away.

There were three of them, their armor covered by robes—advance scouts I suppose. They rode one behind the other, twenty or thirty feet apart. I let the first ride past my position before I pushed the firing stud. He slumped at once, falling without even grabbing to hold on, and while he was slumping, I shifted my aim to the second. That one was falling too, as I moved for a shot at the third, who had wheeled his horse and was spurring it back the way they'd come. I pressed the stud a third time at maybe fifty yards and saw him reel in the saddle, fall forward, and ride out of sight clinging to his horse's neck.

Then, without even thinking, I let go with my impression of the wail of a Thargonian ghost tiger. It was supposed to be the spookiest sound on the known worlds. Us kids had learned it watching holo-dramas when we were, like, ten years old. And practiced it on shadowy evenings playing "hide from the tiger," a game that's been big on Evdash for generations. Whoever was "it" would make the sound while they hunted for the other kids.

On a still night like this one, I suppose you could hear it for a quarter mile or more. I don't know what the Saracen thought of it, but I'll bet he didn't slow down. I realized I was grinning like crazy.

I didn't go down to check the guys I'd zapped. I was pretty sure the first two were unconscious but probably not dead. The third one was my best product. He knew something had happened to him. He was probably half numb, and when he came out of it later he'd tingle with pins and needles. Yet he hadn't seen anything, no arrow had touched him— And there'd been this terrible noise! Meanwhile the other two horses— first one, and after a moment the other—had turned and clattered back down the ravine out of sight, apparently only buzzed a bit by the stunner.

If the Saracens sent another scouting party, it would probably be bigger, and maybe strung out farther apart. If I was the Saracen commander, that's what I'd tell them to do. But if they were nervous enough, they might bunch up anyway.

They bunched up anyway. Maybe half an hour later I heard their horses. Two had passed me, fifteen feet apart, and the third was about even with me, when I zapped them quickly, one after another, then got up in a crouch and stepped out to where I could shoot at the others. Most were in a confusion of trying to turn back, getting in each other's way. But one was sitting off to one side, looking around, and his eyes locked on me. I zapped him first and he fell like a sack, till a foot caught in a stirrup. His horse was turning, and I didn't want it to drag him away so I flipped the setting to high and zapped it too. It stopped, shuddered, and I zapped it again. It collapsed. I turned the stunner on the hindmost of the others as they galloped off. He fell. The others, three at least, had disappeared, with the wail of a Thargonian ghost tiger, or a reasonable imitation, in their ears.

One thing I did not want was the Saracens to know it had been a man who had ambushed them. I wanted them worried about devils and demons. So I moved along behind the shadowed fringe of scrub to where I could plainly see the man who'd spotted me. Then, with the intensity still on high and the beam at its tightest, I zapped him again.

I didn't feel very good about it. I'd killed men before, in Normandy, but that had been in self defense, or to free Deneen. They hadn't been lying helpless.

It was time to go back to the Varangians, but it didn't seem like a good idea to go back up the ravine. The Varangian lookouts would have heard my tiger impression; they had bows, and they'd be nervous. What I did instead was clip my stunner on my belt and start up the steep slope. The top had to be a spur ridge that would slope upward to join the main ridge ahead.

The side of the ravine was almost too steep to climb; the dirt kept slipping away beneath my boots. In places

I grabbed the scratchy, stiff-branched bushes to pull myself along through the dark, squinting and flinching, hoping I wouldn't get a twig in the eye.

After a while I reached the top, breathing hard from the exertion. I scrambled out of the scrub onto the open crest of the spur ridge, then heard hooves and looked up. A rider had been coming along the crest in my direction, and seeing me, had spurred his horse into a galloping attack. He wasn't more than forty yards away, ignoring his lance, drawing his sword, leaning to strike. My hand seemed to move in slow motion, drawing my stunner, raising it, pointing, not worrying about settings. His horse nose-dived, hitting the ground so heavily I swear I could feel it through my feet. The Saracen hurtled over its head in a billow of robe, moonlight flashing on sword, and I zapped him too as he skidded and rolled. He stopped not more than five yards from me. As I scanned around for any more riders, I was panting from excitement as much as from the climb.

There weren't any others in sight.

The rider was dead. I didn't need to check him out to know that. I hadn't thumbed the intensity back from high after killing the guy in the ravine, and at such close range, I'd really curdled his synapses.

Apparently, after the survivor had returned from the first scouting party, the Saracen commander had not only sent a strong party up the ravine. He'd also sent outriders to bypass the ravine and see what they could see. One at least, and maybe one on the opposite ridge, too.

I took the Saracen's shield; I'd probably need one when daylight came. As I started along the spur ridge toward where it connected with the main ridge, I stayed just below the rounded crest, at the edge of scrub and shadow.

When I reached the main ridge, I kept a careful eye peeled for Varangian lookouts, and called softly as I approached the notch. They didn't show themselves, but I could feel their eyes, and almost their strung bows, their nocked arrows. Nothing happened though, and before long I was at the base of the knob.

It occurred to me that I probably hadn't accomplished much except to delay the Saracens till daylight. And maybe make myself look good to the Varangians. The delay wouldn't allow us to move on farther north— not far enough to do us any good. On horseback the Saracens would catch us before another night fell, even if we moved as soon as I reported in. Where we were camped now was as good a place as any to make our stand.

Maybe I should have struck off north alone, I told myself. *Maybe I should yet*. But instead I started up the last slope toward camp.

TWENTY-SIX

Gunnlag himself was one of the lookouts on the knob, and when he saw it was me hiking up to camp, he went to Arno and woke him up. Gunnlag was curious and the boss, and he needed an interpreter to ask questions through. It turned out that when the lookouts at the notch had been relieved, they'd told him I'd passed through. And I suppose that my carrying a Saracen shield got him especially interested.

"What did you do out there?" Arno asked. He was doing more than passing on Gunnlag's questions; he was curious, too.

"I ambushed a Saracen scouting party," I told him. Arno passed the answer on to Gunnlag.

"With what weapons?"

"With a holy amulet."

Gunnlag's brows knotted, so I went on. "There were three Saracens in the first scouting party. I caused the first two to fall from their horses unable to move. They should still be lying there, alive. The third I caused only to go numb, and let him ride away to his army. I was hidden in shadows, and they were unable to see me. All he could tell his commander was that two men had fallen from their horses without the twang of any bowstring, and that he had gone numb and nearly fallen from his saddle without being struck a blow. And that there had been a terrible sound, as of a soul in torment."

I said all that a sentence or two at a time, so that Arno could translate. After the last sentence, Gunnlag said something and Arno turned to me again.

"He says his lookouts at the notch reported a sound like that."

I nodded. "Then, a while later, about eight more came. I caused four of them to fall; I'm afraid I killed one of them. The rest fled."

When Arno had repeated this in Norse, Gunnlag frowned again and said something more. Again Arno turned to me. "He wants to know why you didn't kill them all."

I shrugged. "I am a holy monk." Arno's eyebrows raised at that, of course, before he passed it on to the Norseman. "And besides," I went on, "when the Saracens find them, their commander will be confused and mystified. All the Saracens will be. Dead men they would understand about, especially if I'd killed them with arrows, or sword or knife. And from what I've heard, Saracen knights have no great fear of death or other men. But what could it be that paralyzes them, and makes such a terrible sound? That will put fear in their hearts, at least while it's dark."

When Arno had finished interpreting, Gunnlag stood, peering intently at me.

"Then," I went on, "I climbed the side of the ravine, and at the top was attacked by another Saracen knight. I regret that I had to kill both him and his horse. There was no time to use more delicate magic, may God forgive me." I motioned with the shield. "I took this from him," I said. "I may want it when daylight comes.

"And Arno," I added when he'd finished interpreting, "tell Gunnlag that if he sends warriors down the ravine to see, they should not kill or rob or even touch the fallen men they find there. If any of his warriors go there, they should pretend to be mystified at what they see. The paralyzed men will remember it, and tell their commander."

Gunnlag pursed his lips thoughtfully. Then, without saying anything more, he went and woke up two of his men and talked to them. They left, carrying shields and swords. Arno and I walked over to the mass of sleeping Varangians. One of the disadvantages of going to bed late, in a situation like that, is that you have to sleep at the edge, where there's not so much body heat.

When we lay down, Arno murmured a question of his own. "Why did you do it? Tomorrow it will make little difference. We are all dead men then, unless God, through some saint, intervenes."

I hadn't even thought about that before. "I did it," I said, "because—because tomorrow some saint may intervene. Or some angel. And I want us to be alive if one does."

It struck me then that he'd asked the question as casually as if he was asking whether I thought it was going to rain. I don't think he put as much importance as I did on the matter of living or dying. Then it struck me that I wasn't making as big a deal out of it as I would have a month earlier, or a week as far as that's concerned.

I closed my eyes. It had been an extra-long day, and I'd hiked a lot of miles. Even cold, and with my stomach grumbling about no food, I went right to sleep.

The first time I awakened—just barely—was when a Varangian I was lying against got up. I was vaguely aware that it was starting to get daylight, then went right back to sleep. The next time I awakened, the rising sun was in my eyes and just about everyone was up. I thought about a drink of water, then remembered there wasn't any. The nearest water could easily be a mile away.

I got up and stretched, noticing that most of the rowing soreness was gone. And I remembered that this was, would be, the day of reckoning. I went over to where I'd left my shortsword the night before and put it back on my belt.

That's what I was doing when I heard the distant halloos. Walking to the south side of camp, I looked in the direction the calls had come from. Two Varangians, lookouts, were trotting from the direction of the notch. Apparently the Saracens were coming up the ravine.

Arno was standing near; now he came over to me. "Gunnlag sent men down the ravine after you came back," he said. "They found two men dead and four men down, unable to move. Apparently you used a higher setting on them than you did on me that time."

He was grinning. I didn't feel like grinning back. A Norman might feel cheerful on a morning like this, but I was no Norman. I recalled the time he referred to—our first meeting, in Provence, on the road from the Cenis Pass. That was the first time he'd tried to take my weapons from me.

The Varangians didn't look glum either. They weren't saying much, but mostly they looked either cheerful or grim; a few looked thoughtful. Most had been mercenaries in the Byzantine army, and the others were probably veterans of battles in other places. I suppose all of them had been close to death at times. Besides that, from what Arno and Gunnlag had said, their whole culture was warlike. That would mean they'd almost have to feel different about danger and death than I was used to.

"Do you still have power in your stunner?" Arno asked.

I nodded. "Enough for a few more shots, I suppose."

Smiling, he fondled the hilt of his sword. "That is one advantage of our weapons here," he said. "They last as long as you can wield them. Unless, of course, they break. And Saracen swords are too light to break Norman blades."

The lookouts had reached the foot of the knob now, and slowed to a walk on its steep slope. At almost the same moment, the first few Saracens rode up through the notch.

Over the next quarter hour, something more than two hundred appeared, maybe as many as two-fifty to three hundred. They trotted their horses easily in a rough column of twos toward us, and I wondered if they'd attack us right now instead of besieging us. When their lead riders reached the foot of the knob, they separated, half of them bypassing us on the knob's steep flanks to the ridge crest on its other side. This put half of them on the south end and half on the north. None stayed on our flanks, which were too steep to ride up, but the Saracens could attack from both ends if they wanted to.

"What now?" I asked Arno.

He shrugged. "They'll probably wait and let us get thirstier."

I was already thirstier than I could ever remember being.

"And maybe try to get the Varangians to use up their arrows," he went on. "But I doubt that will work. These Varangians are no Lombard peasants called to war, scarcely knowing a sword from a spade." He gave me a friendly clap on the shoulder; it was like being hit by a club. "You have never seen a battle like this will be," he told me. "Watch well, while you still live! Breathe deeply of it! Let the sounds fill your ears! And when you go to meet God, keep the memory of it; it may help to pass the time in heaven or hell."

I'd settle for watching the Saracens from a distance. Their horses were noticeably more lightly built and graceful than the Norman destriers, and the Saracen knights were colorful in robes that covered whatever their armor might be.

Then four of them rode partway up the knob, stopping out of bowshot. One, apparently their commander, rode another few feet and shouted to us in a language I'd never heard before. Apparently the Varangians didn't understand it; at least none of them shouted anything back. Then he tried another, which I thought might be Greek. And it seemed to be, because Gunnlag stepped up on a boulder and called back. The Varangians laughed. The Saracen commander, after staring for a moment, turned his horse and trotted back, followed by the other three.

Arno questioned one of the Varangians, got an answer, and turned to me with another grin.

"Gunnlag told him his father eats pork."

I couldn't see why Gunnlag would say that, or why the Varangians had laughed. I'd eaten pork in Normandy, and it had seemed all right. In fact, I'd liked it. Arno, seeing that I didn't get it, explained.

"To a Saracen, that is a terrible insult. Their religion holds that eating pork is a mortal sin."

Frankly, to me it seemed stupid to insult someone who's getting ready to kill you. But maybe Gunnlag figured it wouldn't make any difference, and that he might as well enjoy what he could while he could.

Arno asked some more questions. It turned out that the Saracen commander had offered surrender terms. If we surrendered, we wouldn't be killed. I suppose that anyone who wasn't ransomed would be sold into slavery.

They didn't attack though. Not for hours. The morning wore on, and the afternoon, and I kept expecting it. I hardly noticed how hungry I was. The thirst was something else; it I noticed. A few times some Saracens rode near enough to shoot arrows into camp, and I was glad to have a shield. But that was it. The Varangians didn't even shoot back. They were waiting for the Saracens to get closer, I suppose.

Judging by the sun, it was mid-afternoon when, signalled by trumpets, Saracens at both ends of the knob grouped to attack. Again trumpets blew, and horsemen formed ranks of ten. They blew again, and the ranks started toward us at a walk. There seemed like an awful lot of them. The Varangians nocked arrows. At about a hundred yards, the Saracens spurred their horses to a trot, and at about eighty yards, at Gunnlag's shout, the Varangians sent a flight of arrows at them, followed by another. A few horsemen and horses fell, some to be ridden over. The Saracens had spurred to a heavy, uphill gallop. The Varangians dropped their bows, drew swords and picked up shields, or raised two-handed battle-axes, then moved out together to meet the charging enemy. Several held huge swords that took two hands to use. I stayed where I was, leaving my shortsword in its scabbard, waiting with my shield on my left arm and my stunner in my right hand.

The Saracens hit.

It would have been a lot worse if they hadn't been riding uphill. As it was, they didn't have a lot of momentum, and the Varangian swords and axes cut down horses and men in a melee of violent motion and spraying blood, impacts and bellows. Brown dust billowed; men and horses screamed and fell. Three Saracens broke through, and I zapped each of them before he could wheel to hit the Varangians from behind. After brief minutes, maybe only one, the charge broke. A trumpet blared, and the Saracens in front of us wheeled and rode back down the slope. Some of the Varangians picked up bows and sent arrows after them.

I turned. At the other end of camp the fight was over, too. Gradually, in the relative stillness, my eyes registered the shambles all around. Dead horses, dead men, bloody dirt. Quite a few of the bodies were Varangians, dead or dying, while some of those on their feet bled from slashes. Arno's hauberk was smeared with crimson, but apparently the blood wasn't his.

He looked around until he saw me, then grinned in spite of his thirst. "I saw what you did," he called to me. His voice was hoarse and raspy. "Your 'holy amulet' is a valuable weapon."

I looked at my stunner. The indicator was on red; at the most it was good for three more shots—one, at least. "It's almost used up," I told him.

"In that case," he said, "I suggest you find a sword to your liking—something longer than that." He gestured at my shortsword.

I wasn't sure how much good a sword would do me—any sword—but I hefted a few dropped by the dead. Most of them had blood on the hilts, but I made myself pick them up. The Varangian swords I tried felt heavier than I could handle properly. My arm was strong enough, but not my wrist and hand. The Saracen swords were lighter. I played with one of them, testing; this one I could handle easily.

Then a hand gripped my shoulder, and I turned around. It was Gunnlag. He beckoned me to follow, then led me to the body of a fallen Varangian. Arno came along, curious. Gunnlag picked up the man's sword—one of the big, two-handed ones—and husked earnestly at me in dry-throated Norse.

"He's telling you to use that one," Arno said. "For someone with little skill, the two-handed sword is better. It is for berserkers, or for those who are strong but inept."

I didn't know what a berserker was, or whether I was strong enough to handle a weapon like that one. But inept fitted me pretty well, so I took it and tried a few practice swings. Big as I was by Fanglithan standards, and strong, it was too heavy for me to use effectively, even with two hands. Gunnlag saw that, and looked around at the bodies, then went to one of the largest. The sword he picked up was single-handed but big, with a hilt long enough that I had no trouble gripping it with both hands. I swung it high and then low, and then in figure eights.

Gunnlag was grinning and nodding now, and said something to Arno. Other Varangians were looking on, most of them grinning too. "He says," Arno told me, "that he wishes you'd come to him earlier, when you were a boy, or even a year ago. He says you'd have made a fine Varangian."

I nodded. Not that I was agreeing with him. I was just being courteous, and maybe appreciating the compliment. I wasn't the kind of warrior who would get kicks out of hacking people up. If I was any kind of warrior at all, it was the kind that just wanted to overthrow the Empire and then retire to something more peaceable.

So far I hadn't been paying attention to what the Varangians were doing. Now I did. Some were bandaging the wounds of their buddies with pieces of Saracen robes. A few were killing the badly wounded of both sides, sticking them in the neck with their knives. I could understand that; otherwise they'd lie there and die slowly. But it was something I didn't offer to help with.

Something else the Varangians did was look for any water bags the dead Saracens might have carried. There weren't any; they'd probably left them behind on purpose. After that the Varangians started dragging dead horses to form a crescent-shaped barricade at each end of camp, a little below the brow of the knob. I went out and helped them. It was heavy work. Even as cool as the day was, and as dry as we were, I was soon sweating from it. After the dead horses were all in place, we sort of leveled it off on the uphill side with the dead humans, Saracens and Varangians both.

When we'd finished, Gunnlag prayed over the dead at both ends of camp. Then we sat around and stood around, watching. I felt really bushed, and wondered if we had enough strength to fight off another attack, even behind the barrier we'd built. There were plenty of Saracens left, but only fifty-three Varangians fit to fight. The Saracens didn't seem in any hurry.

It felt like an hour or more that nothing happened. I wondered if the Saracens even planned to attack again. Maybe they'd just sit down there and wait for us to die or come to them. Then some of them made a big show of riding toward us to drink from their water bags, so some of the Varangians started cutting the heads off dead Saracens and throwing them down the hill. Every time they threw one, the rest would cheer, though not as loudly as they would have if their throats hadn't been so dry.

If only Deneen would show up, I thought. Then I realized with a shock that I hadn't tried to call her since early the evening before! Of course she could be expected to call me—but I'd taken the remote out of my ear in the ravine! Fumbling it out of my belt pouch, I seated it in my ear again. Then I spoke into the communicator, my voice rasping over dry throat membranes.

"*Rebel Javelin, this is Larn,*" I said. "*Rebel Javelin, this is Larn. Over.*"

Nothing. How many days had it been? "Damn it, Deneen, I *need* you guys! We're in big trouble here! Tomorrow will be too late!"

Her voice in my ear was the most welcome sound I'd ever heard in my life! "Larn! What's happening?"

It's amazing how much calmer I got, right away. "We're somewhere in Sicily," I told her, "inland, in the mountains."

Arno was staring at me, and I switched the sound from the remote to the hand unit so he could hear.

"Arno and I and a bunch of Varangian warriors are on the top of a mountain, and a bunch of Saracen knights have us surrounded. We haven't had anything to drink since yesterday. They charged us once, and a lot of guys are already dead. And the rest of us will be pretty darned soon. Like maybe in an hour or maybe five minutes."

"We're on our way," she snapped. "Keep talking, and I'll get a read on your location."

"Right," I said. "We've got a great view from up here. Mountains all around. I can't see the sea, though; we're too far inland. The flies are starting to gather around the bodies. The Varangians have been throwing Saracen heads down the hill, and it looks as if the Saracens are getting ready to attack again."

It must have been the head-throwing that got to them. They were forming ranks again, one behind the other, and I got the notion that this time they wouldn't quit. There were about ten in each rank, and I counted nine ranks at our end. I suppose the guys at the other end of camp were looking at the same sort of thing.

I switched the receive switch back to remote, so I'd have my hands free to fight and still be able to hear.

"Hold on!" I shouted to the Varangians. "The Angel Deneen is coming to help us! Hold on until she gets here!"

The first Saracen rank was starting our way at a slow

trot. Then the second. Then the third, the fourth . . .
The Varangians were fitting arrows to their bowstrings.
I hefted the heavy sword. It looked like a race, and I
didn't see how Deneen could get there first.

TWENTY-SEVEN

As we moved out onto the barricade to make our
stand, Gunnlag grabbed me by the arm and shook his
head, pointing back, snapping something in Norse. I
gathered I was supposed to be a backup, along with
several wounded men.

But by standing on a rock and looking between Varangians, I could see the charge well enough from the
brow of the hill, a few paces back. As the lead Saracens
got closer to the barricade, they realized they couldn't
ride over it, while riding uphill the way they'd had to,
they wouldn't have nearly enough speed to jump it. So
a little short of it. They swung down from their saddles
and came at us with swords. One problem the Varangians had was standing up. Dead bodies, especially the
barrel-like bodies of horses, aren't the best footing for a
sword fight. But they had the advantage of elevation,
and slashed at the Saracens clambering up at them. It
was slaughter, and for a half minute or so I thought
for sure we'd hold them, even as outnumbered as we
were.

But the Saracens weren't stupid. The sides of the
knob were too steep for horses, so we hadn't extended
the barricade very far around. Now, on foot, some of
the rear ranks started around to flank us, and the hand-

ful of us in reserve—the wounded and myself—moved to keep them out, while a few of the men on top dropped back to help us.

I can't describe what went on, because after that all I saw was what was close around me. We still had the advantage of position, but there were too few of us and too many of them. I didn't even think of finesse, of strike and parry. I didn't really think of anything at all. I just swung and slashed. Once, through the fog of desperation, I heard a voice howling like an animal, and realized it was me. And the howl was the Thargonian ghost tiger. Then more of the Saracens were on top with us, and more, and then . . .

Then I heard screaming, and realized I was also hearing the *thud! thud! thud! thud!* of a heavy blaster. But there still were Saracens around us, striking with their swords. My blade half cleft a heavy shield, stuck there, and was jerked from my hands. Without even thinking, I snatched my stunner from my belt and fired, then fired again at another Saracen, and threw it at another when it failed on the third shot.

Then Arno was beside me, striding into the melee. Varangians too, more of them now. Because, it turned out, the attacks on the barricades had melted back under blaster fire and the sight of the scout close overhead. The Saracens who'd reached the top were suddenly outnumbered.

"Larn!" Deneen's voice spoke in my ear as I tugged my sword free of the Saracen shield.

I straightened, ignoring her, the heavy sword in my hands, and looked around for more attackers. I wasn't about to be distracted when I needed my attention on staying alive. But I didn't, really. The Saracens were running now, back down the side slope, several falling and rolling, unable to stop themselves. There weren't any left to strike.

I blinked, shaking my head, becoming aware of things around me—other things besides Saracens. It was like coming out of some kind of bloody trance. Then I started counting. There seemed to be twenty-six Varangians left on their feet, most standing momentarily motionless, staring upward. I knew that some of them had to be wounded. I was spattered with blood myself, but as far as I knew, none of it was mine. You might not believe how much blood gets sprayed around in a fight like that.

Gunnlag shouted a hoarse order, and we moved back to the barricade. There were a lot of dead Saracens there, but down the hill I could see a lot of live ones—a lot more than there were of us.

And there was the scout, maybe two hundred feet overhead. I waved at it, then looked at Gunnlag. "The Angel Deneen," I told him, then crossed myself. Arno heard me, and repeated it loudly in Norse; I caught the name "Deneen" when he said it.

A second later the loud-hailer boomed out with about a minute's worth of talk that was a total mystery to me. The language wasn't Evdashian or Standard, Norman or Provençal, or Greek. I didn't even know the voice.

But it sure had the Saracens' attention. And when it was done, we saw them get on their horses and start rounding up the strays—the horses whose riders hadn't, or wouldn't, return. When they were done, they all left, riding along the ridge crest to the notch, where they turned off out of sight into the ravine.

"Larn," said the voice in my ear, "I'm the one who's got a problem now." I'd never heard Deneen sound like that. Tired. More tired than I was. "I just checked the fuel system again. Using the weapons system, even less than a dozen bolts like that, has begun some pretty heavy fuel crystallization. I never imagined it would happen so fast.

"Now here's what I'm going to do. I'll put Tarel and Moise down with you, each with a blast rifle, pistol, and stunner. And one of each for you. Then I'll get to the island again as quickly as I can, and shut down for a few days. We can not afford to get ourselves stranded."

"Just a second," I said. "No rifles. They'll make us too conspicuous. Or just one. Make it one, in case we need some longer range firepower. And a pistol and stunner for Arno, and belt magazines with spare charges."

"All right . . ." she began, but I interrupted.

"And we've had no water for nearly twenty-four hours. Or any food. None of us. Put down a hose; there's one in a locker in the machine room. And send down any food you can spare, if there's enough of it to share among thirty men."

"Right. I'm leaving the pilot's seat to do it."

"Got ya. Larn holding."

A bunch of the Varangians were staring at me, including Gunnlag, who, like Arno and me, seemed unwounded.

"The Angel Deneen is going to let two other holy monks out of the sky ship," I told them, "with special protection for us, to help keep us safe to Christian territory. She has to go back to the heavens."

I figured she'd land and let them out, but she had a better idea—one that would help keep up our image. She lowered to about fifty feet and let Tarel down in a harness. When he was down, she winched the harness back up and let down another guy, who had to be Moise. I realized then who'd been talking on the loud-hailer. Like Tarel, Moise wore a marine jump suit. He was tall for a Fanglithan; I suspect it was from a decent diet when he was a kid.

Deneen's voice spoke in my ear again. "There's some emergency food concentrate in Moise's musette bag," she told me. "All we've got left of it. And Tarel's musette bag has extra cells for your communicators. Water's coming next."

A minute later a hose came down, with a pail taped to it. On my cue, Deneen would release some water, a few quarts at a time. I'd catch it in the pail and pass it around among the Varangians. I drank last, which I'm darn sure the Varangians noticed. It tasted like hose, but it was *good!*

When all of us had drunk a bit, I got some of the cubes of food concentrate from Moise's pack and passed them around, two per man. That wasn't much, but any more might have made us sick on such empty stomachs. After that everyone drank again. Then I retaped the pail to the hose and told Deneen we were done. The hose drew back up into the hatch and disappeared.

The hatch closed behind it, and in a minute or so the *Jav* started to rise, rose till we couldn't see it anymore.

"That's it, brother mine," said Deneen in my ear. "Good luck. And wish me the same."

I raised the communicator to my mouth. "Thanks. You've got my best wishes, for whatever they're worth." And she did. Not getting stranded here might not be as important to me as staying alive, but it ran a close second.

Luck! It occurred to me that, everything considered, we hadn't done too badly on Fanglith, luck-wise. So far. Not for a world like this one. Things had gone wrong, but we were still alive. And that was more than I could say for a lot of Varangians and Saracens.

PART SIX

TREACHERY AND CLIMAX

TWENTY-EIGHT

Actually there were thirty Varangians able to walk reasonably well. Five others could hobble with help. We'd take them with us to the nearest water and leave them there on their own. The Varangians killed the more severely wounded, then all the dead were prayed over.

It had occurred to Gunnlag that I should do the praying. After all, I was the holy monk, the chief of the holy monks. But I told him I wanted him to do it because he was our war chief. I also told him that the Angel Deneen would want him to, over the Saracens and all. And just now what the Angel Deneen wanted was what we did.

I could have pretended to pray, of course, but these guys were dead, and they deserved the real thing. And while he was praying, I found myself feeling really solemn. If there actually was some kind of heaven, the way the Christians thought, and maybe the Saracens, then I wanted them to go there, all of them. That's when I realized that I didn't hate the Saracens, even though we'd just been chopping at one another with swords, trying to kill each other. I only hated the Empire. Interesting.

After the praying, Tarel gave me my weapons and Arno's. I blessed Arno in Evdashian while holding up my crucifix. Actually, what I recited was part of the acceptance formula for initiates into the middle school honor society, modified a little for the circumstances. I didn't know any Christian formulas. Then I gave Arno a pistol and stunner, and a belt magazine of replacement charges for each.

I kept the blast rifle. It would be my symbol as chief monk.

Next I turned to Moise and asked him in Norman French if he spoke Greek.

"Yes, sir," he said, in Evdashian at that. "I also speak your language. Your sister had me learn it with the learning program, and we have practiced it ever since to develop my fluency."

"Good. I'm assigning you to speak it with Arno. He needs the practice. But first I want you to tell Gunnlag Snorrason something for me, in Greek." I pointed. "He's the older Varangian with the red hair. It's best that Arno not tell him, because I'm appointing Arno the leader of this expedition for now. And Gunnlag should get the word from someone else, not from Arno.

"And another thing: As far as these people are concerned, Deneen is an angel of God. D'you understand?"

He nodded soberly.

"Good. And she came down from heaven to bring you to us. You and Tarel. So while you should be courteous to the Varangians, always act as if you're their superior. Is that clear?"

"Yes sir."

"Fine. Now I want you to tell Gunnlag that Arno is a Norman of importance, a liege man of the great leader, Roger of Sicily. And that we will soon be in Norman land. Tell him."

We were the center of the watching and listening Varangians, Gunnlag the nearest of them. Moise turned to him and spoke in Greek. When he was done, he turned back to me for further instructions.

"Tell him that because of that, Arno will be our leader on the march. Gunnlag will still be the chief of the Varangians, but Arno will be the march leader—the march leader of all of us, including us holy monks. Got that?"

Moise nodded. "Yes sir," he said again, and again he

talked to Gunnlag in Greek. Gunnlag nodded with no sign of resentment.

I looked at Arno. "Did you get that too?" I asked in Norman French.

"Yes," he said. "And I shall treat the old Viking like a Norman knight. I have seen him fight, and I love him like a brother."

It seemed to me that things just might go right for a while. For a change.

Progress was slow because of the wounded. As we hiked, Tarel told me what they'd learned about fuel crystallization, and approximately what Moise had said on the loud-hailer. He'd spoken in Arabic, the Saracen language, telling them that the vessel from Allah—Allah was the name the Saracens gave to Fanglith's god—that the vessel from Allah bore the Angel Deneen. And the Saracens were not to molest any further these people they'd been attacking. They should let them leave in peace, or risk Allah's further wrath.

"Was that Deneen's idea?" I asked. "Or Moise's?"

"Deneen knew he speaks Arabic. She does too now, but hasn't practiced it much. She told him to say whatever it would take to keep them from attacking you any more, and he took it from there."

"Umm. You guys get along all right? You and Moise?"

"Oh sure. We're good friends."

I was glad to hear it. I'd wondered if maybe they'd developed some rivalry—if maybe Moise had gotten interested in Deneen, too.

Dusk was settling when we reached a creek in a small valley, another valley with abandoned huts in it. Gunnlag agreed with Arno that we shouldn't camp there though—that we needed to reach a high place. So we drank our fill again, then left the five who needed help to walk, and started up the next ridge. Two of the Varangians keeled over when the going got steep, and three others couldn't make it, so we waited while they were helped back to the hut where we'd left the other five. Then we went on again—twenty-five Varangians, Arno, and three "holy monks from India." It was black night when we got to the top, chewed and swallowed the last of the food concentrate, and bunched up to sleep. The cubes didn't quiet our stomachs, which growled and grumbled, but they'd help us keep going.

The next morning, Arno and Gunnlag sent our four best hunters out ahead, after pointing out the course we'd be taking. Then, after about an hour of lying around, the rest of us started out. The muscles in my forearms had gotten surprisingly sore overnight, and my hands stiff—from using the sword I suppose.

The hunters would be moving slowly, so we moved slowly too. An hour or so later we came to one of them who'd killed and dressed out a half-grown goat. There wasn't any firewood nearby, so we ate most of it raw, keeping enough to share with the other hunters in case they hadn't gotten anything. Goat is tough chewing, especially raw, and bloody raw is the opposite of appetizing for me. But when you're hungry enough . . .

Maybe two hours later we came to another hunter with another goat. This was near the mouth of a ravine where there was scrub, with dead branchwood to burn. So we took a break, half-cooked the goat, and ate some of it, wrapping the rest in the hide. A third hunter saw the smoke and hiked over. He hadn't seen anything near enough to shoot at.

Then we lay around for a while, feeling full, napping in the sun, digesting the half-raw goat meat. We never saw the fourth hunter again. He might have fallen and broken a leg somewhere. We yelled, there and later from a ridgetop, but never heard a thing.

A couple of ridges later I wondered if maybe he'd run into hostiles. Because when we reached the top of this ridge, we could see a lot bigger valley on the other side. Arno said a valley like that was sure to have farms and hamlets, and almost surely a castle with knights.

And these people wouldn't have heard of the Angel Deneen, though hopefully they might be under Norman control.

We talked it over and decided that the Varangians would hike down one of the ravines. It had enough brush and trees to give cover. Tarel and Arno would stay with them to provide firepower. Moise and I would hike along the top of one of the spur ridges that walled the ravine. From there I could provide blaster fire with my rifle, if needed. And while the two of us could be seen from a distance, the sight of two hikers shouldn't get anyone excited. Not when neither of us was visibly a warrior. Neither of us carried a shield, and I'd left my longsword on the battleground.

Tarel turned his communicator on so we could stay in touch.

It was a warmer day than we'd been having. Spring was coming along, and the country wasn't as high as a lot that we'd been through. I was actually enjoying the hike. We paused on a high point, from where we could see a lot of the valley. And Arno had been right: A good-sized hamlet, almost a village, was visible, with a castle nearby. I saw a dust cloud in the valley's lower end, and staring, made out a number of mounted men at the head of it. They had to be military.

I took the communicator from my belt. "Tarel," I said, "this is Larn. Tarel, this is Larn. Over."

"This is Tarel. Over."

"Tell Arno there's a force of cavalry in the valley, riding toward the castle. I can't tell if they're Normans or Saracens. Ask him what he wants to do about this. Over."

"Hold on; will do."

It was two or three minutes before I heard anything more than faint murmuring. Then Arno answered. "This is Arno. We'll continue down the ravine as far as there's cover for us. Then we'll wait until dark. After dark I'll go out and see what I can learn."

"Right," I answered. "Moise and I will keep hiking the ridgetop to near the end. Maybe we'll be able to see more farther on. Larn over and out."

A moment later I heard Tarel's voice again. "Got that. This is Tarel out."

A half-mile ahead, the ridge crest started dropping off more sharply into the valley, giving us a fuller view ahead. The cavalry had ridden to a point almost in line with it. I still couldn't make out details, except I was pretty sure they didn't wear robes. They made me think of men returning home though; they formed a fairly strung out group, about twenty of them. And they weren't making the dust they had been, as if they'd slowed from a trot to a walk. I let Arno know. Then Moise and I sat on the ground and I followed them with my eyes, wishing I had binoculars.

After a minute, I noticed something else. Another horseman, ahead of them and off to one side, had stopped, as if he had gotten off the road for them.

Again I called Tarel, and told Arno what I'd seen.

Arno chuckled. "The people of the country here are Saracens. That the horseman got out of the road probably means that the cavalry are Normans, and that the fighting here is past."

"Do you want to go on out into the valley this afternoon?" I asked.

He didn't answer immediately, and when he did, it was slowly, thoughtfully. "No. We are fed now, and there is no great haste. We'll stay under cover till nightfall."

Moise and I stayed where we were for a while, continuing to watch. The castle was far enough away that we couldn't see what went on when the cavalry got there. Finally we picked our way down into the ravine, and along the bottom till we came to Arno and Tarel and the Varangians.

It was nap time again.

TWENTY-NINE

We did more waking than dozing. And with danger no longer baring its teeth at us, plus the probability that we were out of enemy territory, sitting around made the Varangians restless and impatient. So Arno didn't wait till dark to go scouting; he started out when sunset was coloring the sky.

Even no more than that made the Varangians more cheerful. They liked action—something going on. If not their action, then someone else's. At least something was happening.

While dusk settled, Tarel and I sat side by side without saying much. Being with him made me remember Jenoor, and that made me introspective. Moise had gone over to sit by Gunnlag and ask him questions in Greek; he found the Varangians intriguing. After a while, he came back and sat down by Tarel and me again. Gunnlag, he said, had told him I'd surprised him—that he hadn't thought a holy monk could fight like I had. I'd been like a berserker, Gunnlag had said, howling in battle and wielding my sword with a fury that would do credit to any warrior he'd seen.

Neither of us was clear on what a berserker was, but apparently it was something or someone pretty wild in battle. Moise was impressed with the story, and Tarel even more. As for me, there wasn't much I could say. Even allowing for Fanglithan exaggeration, it sounded like pretty high praise by Norse standards. I couldn't remember much of the fight—general impressions, fragments of image. But I did remember hearing someone howl and realizing it was me, and that I had gone at it pretty hard.

I was big by Norman standards, of course—even by Varangian standards. But the Varangians, like the Normans, had always seemed to me to be a lot stronger and a lot more formidable than I was.

I recalled the times when one or another of them had grabbed me. Arno, on that first day in Provence, when he'd grabbed my wrist and hauled me up onto his destrier. And Varangians a couple of times. They'd seemed terribly strong. Was it because of the way they did things? With hard, abrupt force, the way a warrior might learn to do them? Did they actually think of *me* as physically strong—or at least fairly strong? And was I, in fact, stronger than I thought? I didn't have the hand and wrist strength to handle a Varangian sword one-handed, but maybe the rest of me compared better with Normans and Varangians than my hands and wrists did.

One thing I knew for sure: Fighting with swords was something I'd gladly do without.

It was sometime after dark when I woke up. How long after, I don't know. The moon wasn't up yet though, and it was really black among the scrub trees in the ravine bottom. Guys were moving, talking. Then I recognized the plod of hooves, not running or even walking, but stamping around, and not just one horse but several.

"Larn! Gunnlag!"

It was Arno's voice. I rolled to my feet and moved through the dark in his direction. "What is it? What did you find?" I called.

"You were right!" He said it in Evdashian. "We're here! They are Normans!"

Gunnlag was beside him before I got there, asking questions in rapid Norse, and I had to wait for a minute before I could get any more information. Then the Varangian chieftain turned away and began to shout orders.

Arno turned to me. "The baron holding this district in fief is Gilbert de Auletta," he said. "He has invited us to stay at his castle, and within a day or two he will provide us with an escort to Palermo. Which is no farther than two long days' walk. And for you and me, and perhaps a few others, he will provide horses."

Three of the baron's men waited for us outside the darker darkness of the scrub woods, with spare horses for Gunnlag and me. I had one of the wounded ride mine—a Varangian named Ketil, from a place called Jämtland. He was a huge man, even by Evdashian standards, and one of those who used an oversized, two-handed sword. I'd noticed him early on, not only because of his size, but because of his helmet. It had a nasal on it to protect the nose, and looked to be Norman. Normans had fought Varangians at various times, and I suspected that Ketil's helmet was a trophy from some Norman he'd killed.

Arno hoisted me up to ride with him. He was impressed that I'd give up my horse to a wounded comrade, and I was surprised that he found it admirable. It showed me another side of Arno; if I'd thought about it at all, I'd have expected him to consider my giving up my horse a weakness. The other Varangians regarded Ketil as a savage, which from them seemed to be a term reflecting admiration as well as caution. They all seemed wary of him, as if he was dangerous. Supposedly, as a youth, he'd been a member of a bandit troop in Jämtland that had preyed on trade caravans over the mountains there. He'd even broken a moose to the saddle to ride on, they said. Whatever a moose was.

It was nearly unbelievable that Ketil had walked all the way from the battle site. His calf had a deep cut across the muscle that made it impossible to flex his ankle or push off with the ball of his foot. Try walking on hills that way sometime! And even tightly bandaged, it leaked blood off and on. Yet the only sign of pain he showed was his bad limp. His grim lack of words didn't seem part of it; he hadn't talked much before the wound, either.

He didn't even say thank you, or anything else, when I turned my horse over to him.

Gilbert de Auletta's castle was Saracen-built, of course. It wasn't as large or luxurious as Roger's at Mileto, not by a long way, but it had a bath and gardens. And a dining hall. Eating was our first order of business. The Varangians ate the same way they did just about everything—they gave it a hundred percent. They weren't shy about the wine, either.

Gilbert kept us company while we ate, and drank wine with us. And spoke Greek with the Varangians. In fact, as the drinking continued, it was mainly with the Varangians that he talked. He'd been born in Italy, in Campania, grandson of one of the earliest Norman mercenaries there. Until the invasion of Sicily, he told us, he'd spent much of his life in the Norman effort to drive the Byzantines out of Italy. And he spoke Greek fluently, or at least easily.

Like the knights I'd known in Normandy, he wore his hauberk at the table, but he was different-looking from any other Norman knight I'd seen. Even wearing a hauberk, he had a slender, fine-boned look—like a Saracen, Arno whispered. His face was sharp, and his wrists and hands small. But his hands were extremely muscular, his bare forearms well-developed and sinewy, and when he chewed, the muscles in his jaw looked like stones.

His almost-black eyes seemed to actually gleam with an intensity that made me uncomfortable, but I couldn't fault his friendliness or hospitality.

Arno didn't seem to drink much. He raised his cup often enough, but I never saw him accept a refill. I decided he probably had a reason for that, so I did the same, and in Evdashian told Tarel and Moise to follow my example.

After supper we bathed. The Varangians knew about bathing. I didn't ask whether it was done in their homeland or if it was something they'd learned in Miklagard. In the bath was the only time I'd unslung my rifle from my shoulder, even at the table. And even in the bath I kept it in reach. The Varangians and Gilbert would just have to assume it was some religious instrument.

When we'd finished our bath, a servant showed Arno, Tarel, Moise, and me to a separate room, with actual mattresses, stuffed at least partly with nice-smelling herbs. The Varangians would bunk down in the dining hall on straw. I put my belt, with its weapons, on the floor by my head, and Arno blew out the flame in the bowl of oil that was our lamp. It felt incredibly good to lie on something soft, with no stones digging my back, and my stomach not only full but happy.

Now that I felt comfortable and safe, my mind kept me awake. Tired though I was. First, my attention went to Jenoor. From her it went to the Empire. What was I doing about it? I lay there scratching occasionally and feeling frustrated. So far, all my attention had been on surviving; I hadn't accomplished a thing toward establishing a rebel base. But survival was something, and when we got to Palermo, I'd meet Roger. And Guiscard, if he was there. And if Arno didn't volunteer an introduction . . .

Arno interrupted my thoughts. "Larn," he murmured. "Yes?"

He spoke in slow Evdashian. "I feel ill at ease here, apart from the Varangians. It may be unsafe."

I remembered my feeling about Gilbert. "Why?"

"I do not trust this baron."

"Was there something he did? Or said?" I couldn't help remembering Isaac ben Abraham's words about Norman treachery.

"I'm not sure. But this much I can say, although it falls well short of accounting for my feeling. Gilbert de Auletta was born in Italy, and his father before him; I believe you heard him say it. Some of those early families resent greatly the successes of the sons of Tancred de Hauteville, whom they consider upstart latecomers: They plotted and fought almost constantly against William Iron Arm until his death. And do against Guiscard when they dare. Roger arrived from Normandy only fifteen years ago, and his success here galls them most of all.

"And finally, they resent those newcomers of us who've attached ourselves to Guiscard or to Roger and have prospered by our loyalty."

Dimly I could see him get to his knees, his face a lighter blob in the darkness. "Gilbert may not be one who feels like that, but I do not trust him, for whatever reason. We should go back out among the Varangians."

Neither Tarel nor Moise had gone to sleep yet, so they'd heard all that. Together we got up, belted on our weapons, and left to spend the night on straw in the dining hall. I thought of taking my mattress, but decided it wasn't the thing to do. One of the Varangians was awake, sitting on a table, apparently a guard, and I wondered if Gunnlag was suspicious too. Or whether it was simply standard practice for Varangians among strangers in a strange stronghold.

It was Arno who woke me up. The sun was shining through the windows. I'd have been glad to sleep for two or three more hours, but servants were setting up for breakfast. By daylight, with the busy, ordinary sounds of breakfast being put on the table, our fears of the night before seemed a little silly. To me at least. Breakfast showed me again how the Normans in the south had changed from those I'd known in Normandy. We had fruit as well as porridge and cheese, custard as well as meat and bread and eggs.

I wished I'd brought a toothbrush with me.

The weather had turned almost summery—quite warm, no wind, bright sun, and only a few fluffy white clouds. After breakfast we loafed around outside, napped in the sunshine, snacked on dates and some small wrinkly fruits called raisins, and occasional little cakes with a fruit in them called figs, which I'd tasted first in Marseille. They were brought to us by servants that Arno told me were Saracens.

Like Roger's place at Mileto, and unlike any castles I'd seen in Normandy, the grounds here were landscaped. Like the Byzantines, the Saracens definitely had a stronger aesthetic sense than Normans did, but

I'd bet ten credits that the Normans would pick it up from them. Like they were picking up bathing.

Later, some of the Varangians left on horses to get the wounded we'd left behind in the mountains. Most of the rest were feeling energetic enough to wrestle, and one of them challenged Arno. Arno took him on, and it seemed to me that neither of them was clearly the winner.

Tarel suggested to me that he and I spar for them, using hand-foot art, and see what they thought of it. I turned him down, and told him why. The Varangians wrestled with lots of energy and violence, as well as quite a bit of skill. They didn't hold back. And while he and I were supposedly holy monks, it seemed to me the Varangians might scorn just sparring. They might look down their noses at us for holding back when we "fought" each other. Besides which, hand-foot art was my secret—my weapon of last resort.

That afternoon I noticed Arno and Gunnlag talking alone together in a corner of the garden. They seemed pretty serious. Then Arno came over and started talking to me in Evdashian, piecing it out with Norman French where he didn't know a word.

"We may be in trouble here," he told me. "This morning when Gunnlag arranged for horses to bring the wounded, Gilbert said ten Varangians should go, with ten horses. Each of them could then take one wounded on his horse to bring him back. And Gilbert sent with them three knights as an escort, a symbol of his protection. The Varangians wore no hauberks nor carried any shields. Their horses were old, such animals as pages learn to ride on. Gilbert said he would not have good mounts ridden by men other than Normans trained to ride and care for them, and that old horses would have trouble enough carrying two men each without shields and armor.

"Gunnlag felt uneasy, a little, but Gilbert had been very friendly last night, so he agreed. Besides, it all seemed reasonable enough."

It sounded reasonable to me, too. These warriors

could be paranoid. But I remembered my misgivings of the night before, and Arno wasn't done yet.

"Then, a little while ago," he went on, "I climbed the tower to look over the countryside. A dozen of Gilbert's knights were riding east down the road, on destriers, and carrying lances. But soon they left the road, riding south toward the ravine we came out of yesterday. They could have been leaving on patrol of course, but I have a feeling it is more than that.

"I told Gunnlag what I saw, and he feels as I do. Gilbert may have sent them to attack the Varangians."

"Why would he do that?"

"Last night, I am told, Gilbert asked many questions about you. He must have heard of your power from the Varangians. He may wish to take you hostage."

Like you did, I thought. But there was a difference between Arno and Gilbert, a difference in character that I'd felt the evening before.

"And he knows the Varangians would defend you," Arno was saying. "If he kills ten of them, there will be only fifteen left."

I looked at that. "You said a dozen of his knights seemed to have followed them. And there were already three knights riding escort. How many of the knights would the ten Varangians kill, do you think?"

"The Varangians do not expect an attack. Not by Normans. And they took neither hauberks nor shields. If they were tricked, surprised at close quarters . . . They do not fight skillfully on horseback; it is not their way. They could be killed without killing any of Gilbert's men, or maybe two or three, if they are lucky."

It *could* happen that way. On the other hand, Gilbert's knights could very well have gone out on patrol, with no idea of attacking the Varangians.

"Let me ask you a question," I said. "Would you be willing to get hold of a horse—steal one if necessary—follow Gilbert's men with your blast pistol and stunner, and attack them if they attacked the Varangians?"

Arno didn't have a quick answer for that. I thought of making him an offer that occurred to me, but decided against it. I'd let my question be a test.

After a long ten seconds, he passed it. "I will see about a horse," he said. "A hunting horse. They are faster, and with this"—he patted the holster on his belt—"I do not need a destrier. I'll let them believe I've come out to join them. I'll tell them that Gilbert and I have talked things over."

I unslung my blast rifle and handed it to him. "Then take this," I told him. "It is accurate at a distance."

He looked at me without expression, then nodded. I wished I knew what he was thinking. Not because I feared treachery just now, but because I'd like to understand him better. Maybe this would help ensure an introduction to Guiscard or Roger. Whether it did or not, I owed it to the Varangians.

I took the recharge magazine off my belt and gave that to Arno too, along with a thirty-second short course in how to use the rifle. If I had to do any shooting here, it would probably be at close range; my pistol and stunner should be plenty.

He walked over to Gunnlag then, and they talked for a minute or two. When they were done, Arno left, walking toward the stable. Gunnlag looked toward me and nodded, then strolled toward a bench beneath a fruit tree of some kind. It occurred to me that he and I had things to talk about too. Because if he and Arno weren't being paranoid—if Gilbert did intend to kill the ten Varangians—then he probably had plans to kill the others too.

I got up to look for Moise. He'd have to interpret for us.

THIRTY

We decided that we shouldn't let ourselves be separated, and that we'd keep our weapons with us at all times. He agreed there might not be any danger, but we'd play it safe. Then he called his men together. He didn't say anything about what we suspected; we didn't want any of them to get agitated and maybe do something foolish. Instead, he told them they'd become careless, reminding them that they were among strangers, and they were to stay together unless ordered otherwise. He also warned them not to get drunk at supper.

All in all it spoiled the afternoon. The servants came out again with dates and fig cakes and sweet drinks, and the weather was beautiful, but I couldn't really relax or take a nap. I felt impatient for something to happen, for Arno to come back and say it had been a false alarm. But it was unreasonable to expect him back before the next day.

Last night's supper had been something hustled together late for unexpected guests. This one was a production. Roland de Falaise, in his timber castle in Normandy, probably hadn't even imagined a meal like the one we sat down to. This time the entire Norman household ate with us. The baron and his wife sat at opposite ends of the short main table, while his knights sat among the Varangians at both main tables. His foot soldiers ate separately at two long tables nearby.

Gunnlag didn't look happy with the way we were seated—the knights and Varangians mixed like that—but he let it pass. All the knights, Gilbert included, wore their hauberks at the table, and so did the foot soldiers. And of course the Varangians did too.

I remembered how, in Normandy, I'd thought that the Normans must be real barbarians to wear hauberks at the table. Now I began to understand why: The danger of treachery and attack were always in the back of their minds.

But actually, everything *seemed* fine. A guy in what you might call civilian clothes played some kind of stringed instrument and sang for us while we ate. Pages waited on us. There was fowl of some kind, pickled fruits of several kinds, different kinds of meat . . . And the baron told dirty stories in Greek and Norman.

The only false note was that he never said anything or asked anything about Arno not being there. He had to be wondering about that, unless he'd already taken care of Arno.

That is, it was the only false note until a spiced hot drink was brought out that smelled marvelous. I had an instant suspicion of that drink. And when Gilbert proposed a toast—it was in Greek, but obviously a toast—I took only a tiny sip of it.

Within half a minute, Varangian bodies began to slump. Varangian sank to the table, and Tarel's, and Moise's. But not Gunnlag's; he'd only pretended to drink. His fierce blue eyes burned on Gilbert. The baron and his knights had obviously not drunk either. As for me, it had been a tiny sip too much. I felt a slowness, a creeping, growing numbness.

Gunnlag barked something in Norse, and a few Varangian heads raised weakly. Gilbert smiled and gave an order of his own in Norman French: "Kill only the Varangians!" Immediately, the knights were on their feet, knives in their hands, grabbing handfuls of Varangian hair, pulling heads back, cutting throats. Arterial blood sprayed scarlet. Gunnlag grabbed the knight beside him and they crashed together to the floor as I got slowly up, stunner in my hand.

But standing was too much for me. I began to fold,

my knees giving way even as I started to swing the stunner, my finger on the stud. As I fell, I saw knights collapsing, and heard a woman scream—Gilbert's wife, who hadn't even squeaked at all the throat-cutting. Then I hit the stone floor, and that's all I remembered for a while.

THIRTY-ONE

I opened my eyes and tried to sit up. A pain stabbed through my head—from the drug I suppose—so I lay back and settled for raising my head a little. I was back in the bedroom we'd been put in the evening before. The lamp had been left lit, its yellowish flame flickering above the rim of the bowl, making shadows jump on the walls. My hands were shackled together, and some-one had been good enough to dump me on one of the mattresses. A sour-looking knight had been left to guard me; his hard eyes had caught my movement, and his jaw was clamped with hostility.

He didn't say anything though, and neither did I then. Instead I lay my aching head back down and tried to put things together for myself. The Varangians who'd been in the hall had to be dead now, except maybe, just possibly, Gunnlag. And it was hard to imagine even him getting out of it alive. Gilbert had said "Kill only the Varangians," nothing about taking their chief alive.

On the other hand, it seemed as if Tarel and Moise might still be alive somewhere. If I was valuable—and I supposed that was the reason for all this—then it seemed as if Gilbert would want them alive too, at least for the time being.

I wondered how many Normans I'd zapped before I'd passed out, and whether any of them were dead.

And Arno? Gilbert hadn't asked about him. Maybe he'd been followed and killed. Or maybe Gilbert had decided that if he had me, he could ignore Arno. Which was probably true. Arno had the rifle, a pistol and stunner, and maybe ten healthy Varangians, if he was lucky. With them he could probably get to Palermo all right. He'd have no reason to try rescuing us here. That would be a lot more dangerous than rescuing the Varangians in the mountains.

In fact, I couldn't see anyone rescuing us. Deneen wouldn't be back for five days or more, and she was alone, with no one to put down. Except Bubba of course. And for all Bubba's talents and brains, this wasn't the sort of situation he could operate in.

It was up to me to get out on my own. My hands explored my belt; it was bare. I didn't have so much as a knife, or a communicator if I had anyone to communicate with.

Just having my hands free would be a big improvement, a start. Carefully I raised my head enough to look at my guard again, and didn't see a sign of any key ring. Only his eyes. I suppose Gilbert had the key to my shackles.

"Where is Gilbert de Auletta?" I asked.

The Norman scowled. "Taking care of other business. He'll get to you soon enough."

That didn't sound very promising. I got the notion of Tarel or Moise being questioned, maybe with the help of things like knives or hot coals. I hoped they'd have the good sense to tell the baron whatever he wanted to know.

"How many men did I kill in the great hall?" I asked.

My guard didn't answer, but if looks could kill, I'd have been dead right then. I was pretty sure I hadn't swept much of the room before I passed out, but I'd had the stunner on medium, and at close range like

that, a military model could kill people. Maybe I'd
zapped a friend of his.

I wondered if Arno would still be interested in getting the help of the *Rebel Javelin*. Maybe, when he got
to Palermo, he'd talk to Guiscard, and Guiscard would
come up here and wipe Gilbert out. That was my best
chance, I decided.

But it irked me that I couldn't see any way of getting
out of the situation on my own. I decided to relax as
well as I could and wait, so I closed my eyes. After a
while I dozed, and woke up to Gilbert's voice. A hand
slapped me hard.

Gilbert didn't look too good, or sound too good either, and I wondered if I'd zapped him. That didn't
seem possible. If it hadn't killed him, it would have left
him unconscious for quite a lot of hours.

"Where is the monk called Moise?" he demanded.

"Brother Moise? The last I knew, he was in the hall,
falling off the bench from the drugged drink. Perhaps
the Angel Deneen has taken him into the sky. Perhaps
she will come back and take you next."

He glared more hatred at me than my guard had, and
for a moment I thought he might draw his sword and
convert me into steaks or something. Instead he turned
and left the room without saying anything more.

By that time, my headache was only a shadow of
what it had been. And interestingly, I was actually
feeling pretty casual about the situation. I'd either be
dead tomorrow or alive, and right then I wasn't all that
worried or afraid. Which seemed a bit strange to me,
but I wasn't going to argue with it. Instead I closed my
eyes again, to rest and hopefully sleep some more.

The next time I opened them, my guard was asleep
on one of the other mattresses. The lamp had burned
down to a fluttering glow. Something had wakened me,
and I sat up. Looking around, I couldn't see anything
that might have done it.

Then I felt a draft, and the lamp blew out. The draft
had been from the wrong direction for the window or
door, and it smelled musty. Someone or something was

behind me now, I was sure of it. I could sense something there, and for a few seconds my hair felt as if it were standing up like wires. *It's got to be Moise*, I told myself, and the spooky feeling passed.

Why Moise? And how could it be him?

Then a knife tip touched the side of my neck from behind, and callused fingers touched my face. My heart almost stopped. There was the whispered word, "Who?", in Provençal.

I barely breathed my name.

The hand withdrew, and the knife. "Is the other one your guard?" he whispered.

"Yes."

Dimly I saw my visitor slip past me toward the Norman guard, and kneel. After a minute I heard a long shuddering sigh. My visitor stood again and came over to me. "Come," he murmured. "Your guard is dead."

Now I recognized the voice: It *was* Moise!

I rolled to my knees and got up. "My hands are shackled," I whispered, "but the guard has no key."

"We can free them later," he murmured, then took my arm and turned me around. There was an opening low in the wall, with a faint glow on the other side. Moise led me to it and we went through on hands and knees. The other side was a passage not more than three feet wide. A girl was standing back from the opening, maybe twelve or fourteen years old, holding an oil lamp. I couldn't tell what she looked like because, like most of the other women and older girls I'd seen here, she wore a cloth over her face from the cheeks down.

Moise, still on his knees, pushed the door closed. It was mortared slabs of rock, looking like the stone blocks of the wall but split thinner. It seemed to move on some kind of bearing, maybe stone balls in rounded holes. The slight grating sound of its moving was what had wakened me.

If it hadn't been for Moise's voice, I wouldn't have recognized him. In the lamplight, I saw that he was wearing a hooded Saracen robe and slippers.

We got up then, and Moise said something to the girl, in Arabic I suppose. She answered him, and I followed them along the passage. A few yards farther we came to stairs that led steeply down maybe fifty or sixty steps. At the bottom the passage continued level, its ceiling low enough that I had to stoop a little. The girl stopped after maybe a hundred feet and pointed upward. Moise pushed where she pointed, and a trap-door opened overhead. We helped each other up, and I found myself in a round room with a ceiling that barely allowed me to stand erect. The place smelled kind of like grain smells on Evdash.

A tall, powerful Varangian was sitting there against the wall, hauberk, sword, and all. His legging was cut away from one leg, up to the knee, and his calf was bandaged. "Ketil!" I whispered, and going to him, I shook his hand awkwardly with both of mine. It seemed to me he might be the only Varangian left alive here. I realized then that he hadn't been at the banquet; in fact I hadn't seen him since we'd arrrived at the castle.

I turned to Moise. "How did you get here?" I asked, still softly. "How did *he* get here? And who's the girl?"

"Her name is Layla. She is the daughter of the Saracen who was steward of this castle. He was killed fighting the Normans; so was his master. She and her mother work here now.

"She was told to take care of Ketil, and then the Normans apparently forgot about him. So when she heard that the Varangians had been massacred, she brought Ketil here to hide. After the battle of Misilmeri, her father showed her the hidden passageways and every hiding place. She even knows a hidden way out of the castle. Just above us is a large grain storage vault. Sometime in the past, a false floor was put in it to form this secret chamber."

He stopped there as if that was all of it. "So how did you get out of the hall?" I asked. "And run into her?"

"It was you who made it possible. But first I must explain that I did not even taste the drink. Then, seeing the Varangians falling drugged, I pretended to be drugged too, and let my head drop onto the table.

Before you fell, you killed several of the Normans with your stunner. Unfortunately, Gilbert was only touched by it—he was probably ducking beneath the table as it reached him. I heard some Normans saying that Gilbert could neither move nor speak, though his eyes were open.

"His wife took charge then, screaming orders to the knights who still lived, and the castle's foot soldiers. More orders than there were Normans to carry them out, some of them impossible or contradictory. I felt hands drag me from the room and leave me in a corridor. When I opened my eyes a slit, a minute later, there were only myself and two Normans lying there, and my belt things had been taken. So I got up and fled. I didn't know where to go, so I went outside, intending to hide in the shrubs and plan what I might do.

"But Layla, who was going home from working in the kitchen, saw me leave and followed me. She brought me here and gave me this." He took a sheathed knife from inside his robe. "And brought me the robe as well," he added. "Then a few minutes later, she brought Ketil. I described you to her then, and told her I wanted to rescue you. And Tarel."

"What about Tarel?" I asked.

"He is somewhere with no hidden passage. Only three rooms open on a passage, and by luck, you were in the third of them."

"Ask her if she can think of a way we can get to him and get him out."

"I have. She tells me there is no way short of searching, and taking him by force."

"Okay," I said, then examined my wrist irons. There was no lock. They'd simply been bolted, the nuts turned so tightly they'd been burred. I gestured. "Can Layla get a hammer and chisel? Now?"

Moise turned and spoke to her in Arabic. She shook her head as she answered. "Not tonight," he told me. "She would have to go to the smithy and steal a chisel, and there will be men about, searching for me."

Then Ketil spoke, questioning, and Moise answered in Greek. Next Moise said something in Arabic to Layla, who nodded, raised the trapdoor, and stood waiting, looking at him.

"What?" I said.

"Ketil has an idea for freeing you. We will go and bring something, Layla and I." Then they left, the trapdoor closing behind them.

Ketil and I sat waiting for quite a while, neither of us saying anything. Ketil looked as if I wasn't there, as if he were alone with his thoughts. Grim thoughts. His two-handed sword was in his fists now, fists that looked enormous to me. Finally the trapdoor began to lift again, and Ketil raised his sword in readiness for whatever might appear.

The first head through was Layla's, and Ketil relaxed. A block of firewood followed her, then Moise, who closed the trapdoor.

"There," he said to me. "Kneel down and put your chain on the block."

I got the idea, and knelt. The chain was only about three inches long. When I put it on the block, my wrists were less than three inches apart. Ketil had gotten up. I looked up at him, and my thought, in Norman, was *God, let him be accurate*.

Because the ceiling was low, he got down on his knees. Then he raised the heavy sword as high as the ceiling allowed and swung hard while my eyes squinched shut. There was an impact that jerked my wrists, and my eyes popped open. The chain had been cut and the block half split, and although each wrist still had its iron cuff, my hands were free.

Ketil was examining his blade where it had chopped through the chain, while Layla stared at the block from over the edge of her veil. I turned to Moise. "Now I need a Norman hauberk," I told him. "And a sword. Let's see if my dead guard's been discovered yet."

Tarel:

I woke up on my side in a dark room, with the first headache of my life—a bad one. I was on a stone floor, with my hands tied behind me, and whatever my ankles were tied with was also attached to my wrist bonds, bending my legs back. I was really immobilized. If I tried to move my feet, it pulled on my arms.

Someone was there with me. I couldn't see him because he was behind me, but I could hear him breathing. I was pretty sure it wasn't a guard. A guard would have had a lamp lit, and besides, this sounded like someone asleep, and maybe sick or hurt.

I didn't need a guard anyway, the way I was trussed up.

There were other sounds too, that came in through the window. At first I could hear people talking. Normans. Then after a few minutes I heard someone call from a little distance, and someone else called back. Then it was quiet, with only a little talking a couple of times, farther away in the courtyard. From what I could hear, they were hunting for someone. I wondered if some of the Varangians had escaped, or possibly Larn. Deneen had said Larn led a charmed life; that he always found a way out of things.

My fingers found the cord—it felt like twisted cloth—that tied my ankles to my wrists. If I could get that untied . . . I pulled on it, which drew my legs back farther, until I felt the knot with my fingers. That was the first practical value I'd had from hand-foot art—it makes you flexible. But when I let go of the cord with my hands to explore the knot, my legs wouldn't stay bent that far back, and the knot got away from me.

Now what? I wondered. There was no one to answer, of course. Whoever was in the room with me was behind me, probably also tied up.

So I just lay there for a while, waiting for whatever might happen. But that got boring, so I pulled on the cord until my fingers found the knot again. Then I pulled an inch or two farther, until I'd hooked a couple of fingers of my left hand under a more slender cord that was wrapped several times around my ankles. I held on with my left hand then and began to feel of the knot with the fingers of my right.

It had been pulled up pretty tightly. I've always had strong fingers though; in school there wasn't anyone who could grip me down. Hardly any could even hold their own against me, not even Larn. So I dug and plucked at it, not sure whether I was accomplishing anything or not. After a while, the backs of my shoulders felt like they were going to cramp. But I wasn't willing to let go, because then I'd lose whatever gain I'd made.

Finally, I could feel the cord give a little through a loop of the knot, and a minute later I'd pulled it free. But the knot was still tied; it had been a double knot. I let go and gave my shoulders a rest, rotating them as much as I could. Then I went through the whole thing again, but this time I knew I could do it, and pretty soon the rest of the knot was untied. My ankles were still tied together, but they weren't tied to my wrists anymore. Straightening my legs was one of the biggest treats of my life.

Then I just lay there for a minute, listening. I could barely hear someone talking in the courtyard, pretty far away. The guy behind me was still breathing about the same as before.

Now to get my arms in front of me. I rolled over on my stomach and bent my legs back as far as I could, grabbing my left foot with my left hand, and worked until I'd gotten my hands over my feet. Now the hard part was over; my hands were in front. All I had to do was untie my ankles and I'd be able to get up and move around. Though I wasn't sure what good that would do me; my wrists would still be tied together. But at least it gave me something to do while I was waiting.

Then I became aware that the breathing behind me had changed. I was pretty sure whoever it was was awake now. I also realized that whoever it was must have heard me moving around on the floor, and probably grunting, while I was getting loose.

"Are you awake?" I whispered in Norman.

The reply was in Norse; it was Gunnlag Snorrason! I groped for a moment for the Greek I'd started learning on the *Jav*. I'd had Moise recite all kinds of Greek stuff, with Evdashian equivalents, into the linguistics program for analysis while Deneen had had us in FTL, getting the fuel decrystallized. Then I had run the

Greek-Evdashian data base into the learning program, and had had a session with it. But only one, and I hadn't had a chance to practice with it because we'd gotten into other stuff.

"My hands, feet, not free," I said in Greek. "I try make them free."

He murmured something back at me in rapid Greek that I didn't understand at all. "I no understand," I told him. "Only very very slow."

He muttered something in Norse. I started to work on getting my feet untied. That cord was pulled tighter than the other had been, but after a couple of minutes, it started to give. It didn't take long after that.

Then I turned around and, kneeling, explored Gunnlag's bonds. He'd been tied the same as I had, but it was easier to work on the knots, now that I had my hands in front of me. When I got his ankles free from his wrists, he gave a big groan of relief and said something in Greek that I recognized as "thank you," with some other words added.

His legs and body were so thick that I didn't think he'd be able to get his hands around in front, even with my help, so next I started on the knot that tied his wrists together. It was really tough. With my own wrists still tied, I wasn't getting anywhere. Maybe if my hands had been free . . .

I straightened my back and knelt there in the dark, thinking. We might not have much more time. They were certain to come by and check on us sooner or later, and it could be any minute. Maybe there was something in the room that I could use, something with a sharp edge, or a point . . .

Outside the window, the night seemed less dark now. I decided the moon must have come up. It seemed to come up later and thinner each night. The room was about as dark as before though. I got up, went to the window, and looked out. Fifteen or twenty feet below was a garden. Then I groped my way around the room. I couldn't find any kind of tool, not even any furniture, or anything sharp or rough fastened to the wall.

That left my teeth. With my eyeteeth, I started to dig at the knots that held my wrists.

Arno:

I rode my mount hard. I wanted to catch up with Gilbert's troop before it caught up with the Varangians. The Varangians could be useful to me. I had enjoyed their comradeship, and we had fought well together, side by side.

It was a close thing. Gilbert's men were in sight of the Varangians when I caught up, and the Varangians, unsuspecting, had halted with their escort to wait for them. Gilbert's marshal, Richard de Sele, led the troop. Another Italian-born Norman. It was clear he did not like my joining them. Nor did he hide his sneer when I arrived on a hunter, carrying neither lance nor shield. I told him I'd talked with Gilbert, and had decided to join him.

Less than half a furlong from the Varangians, Richard ordered his troop to charge. Spurring their destriers into a gallop, they raised their lances above their shoulders and drove at the surprised Varangians, who for a moment did not know whether to try running, to fight from horseback, or to dismount. I made the question irrelevant. My hunter easily kept pace immediately behind the troop, and I felled them with my stunner almost as quickly as a breath. All but Richard. He glanced back with a look of shock, then swerved to flee. I finished the others, then changed weapons, and with the blast pistol, shot his horse from under him, sending him crashing.

He got to his feet, drawing his sword and limping badly, scarcely twenty yards from the Varangians. I had spared him deliberately to their tender mercy. Their three escorts, who'd drawn away from the Varangians to be aside from the charge, had seen all that had happened. They milled in confusion now. It went against their Norman fiber to flee, yet what they had seen had overawed them. I settled their uncertainty by charging at them. They turned and fled, riding hard.

It did not suit my plans that they take word to

Gilbert, so I spurred after them. Seeing me in pursuit, one turned aside, spurring viciously. I ignored him, my hunter gaining on the other two, and I killed them both with the pistol. Then I stopped and fired two aimed bolts from the blast rifle at the man remaining. The second bolt took the horse from under him. I trotted to where he lay, the dead horse pinning his legs. He cursed me as I jumped down, and with a dagger thrust I released him from his pain and humiliation.

Then I returned to the Varangians. Their mercy had not sufficed for Richard's life. He lay dead and dismembered by multiple sword blows.

The sun was a vivid orange-red ball half hidden by the westward mountains as we started back toward Gilbert's castle, myself the leader now. It was nearly night when we stopped to eat from our ration bags, and sleep. The Varangians were mostly indifferent horsemen. It would be unwise to lead them down into the ravine until the moon had risen. What there was of it, for it would be scarce half full tonight.

Tarel:

It took more patience than I knew I had, but finally I worked out the knot and got my hands free. I went right to work on Gunnlag's ankle bindings, and I'd just gotten them untied when I heard a metallic sound at the door—someone putting a key in the lock.

I jumped to the wall, where I'd be behind the door when it opened. It swung inward, letting weak light in from the corridor, and I heard a voice speaking Norman.

"Only the Varangian chief is here. You must have put the false monk in another room."

"No, this is the room. Someone else must have fetched him. Or moved him."

"Gilbert isn't going to like this when we tell him."

"Tell him what? We'll look in the other rooms until we find the filthy heretic."

Then the door closed. I heard them take the key out, but I hadn't heard it turned first in the lock. For maybe half a minute I stood there, getting up my nerve. Then I tried the door; it was unlocked. I started easing it open for a peek along the corridor, but I'd only opened it a few inches when I heard a Norman voice, excited but not loud.

"I tell you, the chief heretic, the one who carried the strangely shaped staff, was in there earlier. Shackled."

I felt excitement surge as I pulled the door almost closed. It sounded as if Larn might be loose somewhere. A door thudded shut: the two Normans were in the hall now.

"I helped Charles drag him in there, so I know," the voice went on. "Then Charles stayed to guard him. Now they're both gone."

"All right," the other said reasonably. "Then someone sent and had him moved."

"But only Gilbert would have had him moved. And he thinks the vile dog is still in there."

"Maybe Gilbert forgot. The state he's in tonight, he could forget his *Pater Noster*. Let's look in . . ."

They'd moved on down the hall, and I couldn't make out the rest of it. Then I couldn't hear them at all anymore. By that time Gunnlag was on his feet beside me. It seemed to me that pretty soon the knights would be back, probably with others, and they'd check this room again, plus the one to our right that they'd just come out of. I opened the door wide enough to look out; to the right a little way was a corner. They'd gone around it. To our left was a stairhead that probably led down to the dining hall.

I grabbed Gunnlag's thick arm, slipped out into the corridor, and started down it to our left. Then we heard voices from the stairway, coming up. Instantly I moved to the nearest door and turned the handle. It opened and we ducked in; I closed it quietly behind us.

But before it closed, the weak light from the corridor had given us a glimpse of the room. In it were the hauberks and weapons stripped from the Varangian dead!

It took me about ten seconds to find a knife in the dark and cut Gunnlag's wrists free. The hauberks had to have a lot of dry blood on them, but each of us put one on anyway and picked up a belt with weapons. I'd have given almost anything to have a stunner or pistol in place of the Varangian sword, but it was something, at least.

Then I went to the window and looked out. Off to one side a little way was a bench with an ell-shaped hedge as a screen. The window wasn't very wide, but wide enough, and it didn't have any glass in it. I'm not sure these people even had window glass. I leaned way out—the walls were thick—and dropped my gear. After I heard it hit, I waited to see if anyone came to investigate the noise. When they didn't, I got into the window, let myself down to arms' length, and dropped. Nothing broke when I hit, but it jarred me pretty hard. I got up, grabbed my gear, and moved behind the hedge, where I buckled on my sword belt. Then I heard Gunnlag's gear thud onto the dirt. Half a minute later he dropped too. He must have weighed two hundred pounds, even if he was only about five-feet eight, and I'd guess he was at least forty years old, but he got right up.

We crouched together behind the hedge then. I didn't have any idea what to do next, and if Gunnlag did, he didn't tell me.

Larn:

We pulled my ex-guard's body into the passage and took off his hauberk, collet, gear, and leggings—everything but his helmet; it wasn't there. I'd have to do without it. As far as I could see by Layla's oil lamp, the stuff wasn't even bloody. When we weren't so busy, I told myself, I'd ask Moise how he killed him with a knife without getting blood all over.

After I put them on, Layla led us back along the passage, shielding her oil lamp with one hand. We stopped at the hiding place to pick up Ketil and talk. Ketil put on his helmet. Even lame, he looked ready to fight.

My plan, I said, was to get outside the castle. Then I'd go to the gate, pretend to be a Norman knight, and ask to be let in. They'd never suspect who I was. Inside, I'd try to find out where our weapons were, get hold of some, and see what good I could do with them. Maybe take Gilbert hostage. I wasn't willing to leave without rescuing Tarel. He wasn't just my friend, he was my brother-in-law.

Moise repeated most of this to Ketil in Greek, then had a conversation with Layla. It seemed a lot more than was necessary to tell her I wanted to get out of the castle. When they were done, she nodded, and lowered herself back down through the trapdoor.

"She is going to get some olive oil," Moise said. "To see if we can get your wrist irons off over your hands."

I almost shriveled with embarrassment! I'd forgotten them. I could imagine trying to pass myself off as an envoy from Robert Guiscard wearing irons and broken chains on my wrists.

Layla was back inside of five minutes with a jar of oil, and poured it on my hands and wrists. It was Ketil who held onto the slippery irons while I made my hands as small as possible and pulled. At first I thought it wasn't going to work. Then I decided I'd just have to stand the pain, and jerked hard. In spite of the oil I lost some skin, but the irons came off.

Then we followed Layla a couple of hundred yards farther to where the tunnel ended. There she reached up and touched the overhead, saying something in Arabic. Moise started to push where she touched, to open another trapdoor.

"Just a minute," I said, and looked at Ketil, then at Moise. "I'm going alone. Tell Ketil if he was with me, they'd know at once that something was wrong with my story."

He passed it on to Ketil. I wondered if the big Varangian would get mad, but he just nodded and said something in Greek. Then he took off his Norman-looking helmet and set it on my head. It even fitted pretty well. Looking at it critically, he nodded, then spoke again in Greek.

"He wishes you the blessing of the Virgin," Moise told me.

That surprised me so I couldn't say anything for a few seconds. This was a guy I'd thought of as a savage. Then Moise came up with something.

"Larn, you should take me," he said. "I can help you."

"How?" I demanded. I wasn't in the mood for wasting time in silly arguments. "You can come out with me, but not to the castle gate. You'll have to hide outside somewhere."

"I can help you," he insisted. "I can be a Saracen, or a Levantine Jew. They dress like Saracens."

"How will that help me?"

He didn't answer for several seconds. Then, "We'll think of something," he said.

"Moise," I told him, "that's not a reason."

He surprised me. His voice was hard when he answered. "Then here is a reason. I am going with you whether you like it or not."

I suppose my eyebrows went up at that. "Huh!" I said. "Do you realize we'll probably be dead by morning?"

He nodded soberly.

"Okay," I told him, "we'll go together."

I stuck out my hand and we shook on it. Then he reached up again and pushed up the trapdoor. Unlike the other, this one made him grunt to raise it. I shook hands with Ketil before we left, then bowed to Layla. I didn't know the Norse or Saracen rules of courtesy, but I wanted to do something to express my thanks. Especially to Layla. She'd owed us nothing and put herself at risk. And saved our lives this far, anyway.

Then I pulled myself up through the trapdoor and gave a hand to Moise.

He lowered the trapdoor back into place. We were in a small room. "Layla told me this is a holy place," he whispered.

We left through a doorway with no door in it, that led into a good-sized room lit through large windows by moonlight. I'd wondered what a holy place might be like. In this one, the only furniture was a lectern in one corner, and in the opposite corner, a low platform with a railing and what seemed to be a desk. I suppose they had some meaning, but I have no idea what.

From the outside door we could see the castle some way off.

"Larn," Moise murmured, "there are two things we must consider before we go any farther. Would a knight be out without a horse? And also, you speak Norman with an accent."

He had a point. Two points. The lack of a horse I could probably lie my way around. But while my Norman French had become pretty fluent, and I could disguise my voice, I'd never pass as Norman.

"If anyone asks," I answered, "I was a boy in Provence who was adopted by a Norman knight when my father was killed."

Even by moonlight I could see that Moise wasn't entirely satisfied with that. I wasn't either, as far as that was concerned. But it was the best I could think of on the spur of the moment. And that's what it had to be—the spur of the moment.

"Let's go," I said, and we started for the castle.

THIRTY-TWO

This time the castle wall looked different to me. Bigger. Forbidding. When I'd ridden up to it before, I'd been a guest, and the gate had been open for me. Now I was on foot, an enemy trying to trick my way in.

It occurred to me that maybe no one was on gate duty this time of night.

I'd thought there might be a big knocker or a bell rope, but I ended up pounding on the gate with my sword hilt. After several minutes and some hard pounding, I tried yelling. Finally, someone spoke angrily to us through a slot in what I suppose you could call the gatehouse, a rounded section of wall to the right of the gate.

"What do you want?!"

"I want in, that's what I want!" I disguised my voice by making it higher pitched and nasal. I also made it angry and imperious, because the identity I'd decided to pretend here was an envoy of Robert Guiscard de Hauteville, Tancred's son, Duke of Apulia, Calabria, and Sicily. Someone whom hopefully they wouldn't want mad at them, and wouldn't question too hard.

"I am Laurent de Caen," I continued, choosing Caen because I'd at least been there, even though it had been at night, in a storm, and I hadn't ventured inside the walls. I'd come close to getting killed, too. "I did not come all the way here from the duke," I continued, "and have my horse killed under me, to be kept standing outside in the night."

There was no answer, and I wondered if I'd blown it—irritated whoever it was so badly that he was going to leave me out here. Or maybe said something that had given me away as a fake. It was dangerous pretending to be something you don't know much about, I told myself, especially with people like these.

We waited about five minutes, and I was just getting ready to start pounding again when a small door opened to the left of the gate. A knight stepped out and motioned us in. The wall was about twelve feet thick, and the gate like a dark trap they could close at both ends while we were inside.

But we went in and nothing happened.

I recognized the knight who met us on the other side: Stephen, Gilbert's steward; *seneschal* is the Norman word. He'd been in charge of the banquet that evening, and maybe in charge of drugging the drink. That much gray hair meant a lot of experience and years of weapons practice; in a sword fight he'd take Moise and me before we could yell "mercy." And his narrow eyes didn't look very trusting.

"Caen?" he said.

"Caen. On the River Orne."

"Your speech does not sound like Normandy."

I gave him my coldest look. "I did not come here to relate the circumstances of my childhood," I said stiffly. "Where is your master?"

He didn't answer for several seconds. "He is—not well. Perhaps I can be of service to you."

That sounded fine to me. Although actually, Gilbert and I had hardly spoken to each other, he'd seen more of me than Stephen had, and there was a better chance he'd recognize me. "Perhaps you can," I said. "The duke has sent me to seek the whereabouts of a renegade vassal, Arno de Courmeron, who has trafficked with Vikings preying on Norman shipping. His profit from it will be his head separated from his body.

"Delivery of this Arno to the duke, alive, will be rewarded by a special ducal fief: precedence above all others in the showing and sale of destriers." I was getting into it now; the story was flowing. "Also, ownership of this Arno's well-known herd of brood mares," I went on, "which has been landed at Palermo and is currently in the duke's possession."

I glanced around at the three armed men who stood nearby, then back at Stephen. "Arno is known to have been shipwrecked on Sicily, and is traveling with several dangerous thaumaturgists said to be from India, as well as with a band of Vikings. The duke will also pay well for each of these other miscreants delivered live to him." I turned and gestured at Moise. "This is Isaac, a Levantine Jew employed by the duke to counter their thaumaturgy."

Stephen chewed a lip thoughtfully; he actually seemed to be buying all this. My hopes began to brighten.

"Come with me," he said after a moment. "I will find out if the baron is well enough to see visitors."

He turned and began to lead us across the grounds to the building that was Gilbert's residence. We hadn't gone more than a few steps when someone started yelling near the tower. Stephen paused, staring in that direction; then we heard swords clash. "Come!" he said, and started running toward the noise with his men. Moise and I followed. We turned the corner of a building, saw the fight, and ran toward it. Two men were backed into an angle of the castle wall; one stood in front of the other and was holding off three knights with his sword. In the angle, only one of them could get at him at a time.

It was Gunnlag, and the one behind him was another Varangian! "Hold!" I shouted. "These are two of the men I seek! The duke has first claim to them, for a long list of outrages!"

The Norman who'd been battling Gunnlag backed away. The noise was drawing a small crowd, knights and foot soldiers with blood in their eyes.

And the second "Varangian" in the corner wasn't Varangian at all; it was Tarel in Varangian gear!

"Get a bear net," I said. In Normandy, I'd seen the nets the nobles used to capture bears. "We shall take them alive."

"We have no bear nets here," Stephen said. "There are no bears on Sicily." He turned to the growing cluster of men. "Fetch pikes, staffs, rocks. We will batter them into submission."

"Isaac," I said to Moise in Norman, "speak to the criminals in Greek. Tell them they can save themselves serious injury if they throw down their swords."

Moise repeated it in Greek. Tarel, of course, had understood my Norman French, and tossed his sword out readily enough. Gunnlag could hardly bring himself to let go of his, but he did, dropping it at his feet. That's when I decided to forget about getting some energy weapons back. I'd settle for horses, with Gunnlag and Tarel my prisoners. "Bring shackles," I said. "I'll. . ."

I stopped there, because everyone's attention was shifting from me to someone else. It was Gilbert arriving, drawn like the rest by the noise. His hair was wild and his eyes wilder. He stared at Gunnlag and Tarel, then demanded to know what was going on—why they were still alive.

Stephen explained, and Gilbert's eyes turned to me. "An envoy from Guiscard? From the devil, I'd say. It is the same. Let me see your paper of authorization!"

I struck my forehead—the front of my helmet actually—with the heel of my hand. "In my saddlebag!" I said. I didn't expect him to buy that, but I had to try.

He peered at me then in the pale moonlight. "Don't I know you from some . . ."

He never finished. A floodlight spread around us from above, freezing the action. Then, as I looked up, the action *really* froze. Because someone up above—Deneen, obviously—was playing a stunner over the crowd. I fell, not unconscious, but unable to move.

Overhead, an emergency hooter began to sound, probably to spook the Normans. I hadn't realized the *Rebel Javelin* had a hooter; only a honker, I'd thought. It kept on, sounding as if the scout was settling to the ground. I couldn't see what was happening because I'd fallen on my side, and someone's body lay almost in my face. Seconds later I heard running feet. Someone grabbed me under the arms and raised me partly off the ground. Then I saw—Bubba? Bubba looking at me. Someone started dragging me. I wanted to yell: *Deneen, don't risk the scout, don't* . . . She was handling me as if I were a little kid, dragging me.

None of this felt right, felt real. The stunner must have affected my perceptions. I hadn't known they did that.

Then she was pulling me up the ramp into the scout. And someone else was there, by the ramp, with a blast rifle. *That's* Deneen, I thought. Deneen, slender in jump suit. So it had to be someone else dragging me.

I was laid out in the dark cabin, able to see only upward, and my rescuer ran back out. The cabin wasn't right either. Everything was weird.

A minute later someone else was dragged into the scout, and a voice said, "That's it! I've got Tarel too. Close her up and take her up!"

It was dad!

"Wait!"

I don't know how I got it out, but I said it. Slurred and slowly I had pronounced the word. And again, "Wait!"

"Hold it," he said. "What is it, Larn?"

"Frien's. Don' . . . leave . . . frien's . . . Be . . . killed."

I wasn't sure if he could understand or not.

"Jenoor, blast a couple of bolts against a wall, to keep anyone back who might be thinking of rushing us." I heard a rifle thud out three bolts.

Jenoor! He'd said Jenoor!

"Help me, Aven," he said. "He's heavy and he feels boneless. I need him up on my back." Between the two of them, my parents got me onto his back with my head flopped over a shoulder. He had to move bent over so I wouldn't fall off.

"Larn," he said as he carried me back down the ramp, "We're going over among the bodies. Tell me when I come to the right one. Can you do that?"

"Two," I mumbled. "Two . . . frien's."

"Two," he said. "I got that." We went back among the bodies, pausing over one after another, seeming to take forever. Most of a minute, I suppose. We'd looked at eight or ten before we came to Gunnlag.

"Him," I said.

"Right."

The next was Moise. "Him."

"Is that all?"

"Yes."

There was growling, then an espwolf barked out "Down!" We hit the ground, arrows hissed, and the rifle thudded again, and again. Dad was back on his feet, had grabbed me under the arms, dragging me hurriedly, roughly, to the cutter and up the ramp. I hadn't known he was so strong; I'm not sure he had either. He dumped me and ran back out. I heard shouting in Norman, clashing of swords—clashing of swords?—more thuds from the blaster, and in half a minute another body was dragged in and dropped. The confusion of sounds continued outside, but for then the blaster was silent, and dad was gone again. The blaster thudded twice more, and a moment later once. Dad was back with another body, breathing hard.

"In, Jenoor! Aven, close her and lift!"

There were espwolves aboard, too—more than one.

Not Bubba, obviously. Lady and the pups—pups who'd been half-grown when I'd seen them last, but were near full-size now.

The door shut out the moonlight, and gradually the cabin illumination came on.

We'd be well above the ground now, I knew. The cutter's windows couldn't be opaqued like the scout's could, but we'd be high out of sight in the night sky. I didn't know what to think, what to feel, it had all happened so fast.

Then Jenoor was on her knees beside me, crying all over me, and I didn't worry about it anymore—just lay there with my eyes spilling over. It seemed impossible that she was still alive, and for an empty moment I was sure I'd wake up to find I'd been dreaming again.

After half an hour though, she was still there, and I was functioning well enough to talk better, even though I couldn't move much. By that time, Tarel and Moise and Gunnlag were talking, too. Slowly of course. Tarel had explained to Moise who these people were, and Moise had been explaining to Gunnlag. I was impressed with how matter-of-fact Gunnlag seemed about the whole thing.

I noticed, though, that Jenoor sat near with her stunner on her lap, just in case.

"Dad," I said, "there's one more guy we need to get back there." The words still didn't flow at normal speed, but they were clear now.

"One more? How do we get him?"

"I'm not sure. But I'd like to try to bring him out, too. I owe it to him. He's a Varangian, like Gunnlag. A barbarian warrior. A huge guy, tall, and strong as a gorn."

He didn't answer right away.

I remembered how Arno had recovered from a light stunning, back in Provence. After he got so he could talk decently, it hadn't been an hour before he could get around pretty well. "When I can get around all right," I added, "say in half an hour or so, we can go back. I'll think of a way."

"Tall, you say. Did he fight with a two-handed sword?"

I knew right then what he was going to tell me. I remembered the sound of swords back there. "Yes," I answered.

And he wouldn't even have had a helmet. He'd given me his.

"Larn," dad said quietly, "it's too late for him. Some men came running toward me, from the other side of the cutter, and before Jenoor had a chance to fire, he came out of the shadows and cut them off. He was kind of hopping, as if something was wrong with one of his legs. He killed a couple of them before they cut him down, then Jenoor took care of the others."

I felt a surge of grief! Ketil. Big, mean, ugly Ketil. I couldn't even guess how many men he'd killed in his life. But still, I hadn't felt this bad since we'd raised from Evdash, leaving Piet and Jenoor. It was embarrassing. It took a minute or more before I trusted myself to talk again, and it was dad who broke the silence.

"Where are Deneen and Bubba?" he asked. "We quartered most of the continent between the northern sea and the Mediterranean, looking for the radiation signature of a scout, and had just about decided you hadn't come to Fanglith. Then I remembered you and Arno talking about 'Sicily,' and this island seemed to fit the description. But instead of getting an instrument read on a ship's systems, the wolves got an esp locational on you and Tarel."

"Deneen's got the scout on an uninhabited island in the western ocean," I told him, "with all systems off. She's had serious problems with fuel crystallization, apparently from the scout taking multiple blaster charges on the shield."

"Can you guide us there?"

"Sure. But she ought to be all right for now, and there's something else I'd like to check on first. Arno's back near the castle somewhere. Not in the castle; at least I don't think so. Back in the hills. Hopefully, with about ten warriors. Varangians."

Varangians! It hit me then: Varangians had attacked our ship, taken us captive, killed half a dozen Normans, lost Arno's horse herd for him, and planned to sell us as slaves. And we'd ended up allied with them against—who? Some of Arno's fellow Normans.

Fanglith's a crazy world! I told myself. Well, maybe not crazy, but the rules were awfully strange, so far as there were any. It occurred to me that this was *not* a world for a rebel base. Someday, possibly, but not now. Not for a long time. It was too unpredictable.

Testing my legs and balance, I got to my feet slowly but unassisted. It turned out that standing made me feel better.

"So you want to find Arno," dad said.

"Right. It shouldn't take long."

"Can you find him with the night scanner?"

"Sure," I said, and with my arms half out for balance, I walked carefully to the copilot's seat, next to mom. She smiled without speaking. She looked beautiful, even if her eyes were a little soggy, and I grinned at her. Then I returned us to coordinates five miles above Gilbert's castle. At that height, we didn't need to go hunting for Arno. On the screen I could see a troop of ten mounted men waiting on the road half a mile from the castle. That had to be them, I thought, then spotted a single rider approaching the castle wall. That would be Arno.

I took us down, intending to call him with the loud hailer. But he stopped, so I decided to wait a minute and see what he was going to do. Killing the cabin light, I dropped to 250 feet with the sound receptor on high.

Arno:

It had been good to get out of the dark and rocky ravine, where even with moonlight a horse could easily stumble and fall. In the open valley I'd been able to turn my attention to the castle and what I might find there.

It did not seem to me that Gilbert would have sent ten Varangians out to be killed without having plans to dispose of the others. The question was whether he'd been more successful inside the castle than out.

I hoped that Larn might have foiled him, or at least been spared, and it seemed to me he might well have. For I doubt I have known anyone more favored by fate in hazardous circumstances. But luck is treacherous, and in enterprises like his, or mine, one can meet death as readily as victory, and more quickly.

The wisest course now, it had seemed to me, was to leave my Varangians a little distance from the castle—far enough not to be seen or heard by any watchman on the wall. I myself would halloo from outside and see what I could learn. If the situation seemed beyond salvage, we'd ride the rest of the night toward Palermo and perhaps some friendlier castle along the way. Almost any would be friendlier.

So I had left the Varangians on the dark and silent road and gone on alone until the wall loomed close before me. But not too close; I kept some fifty paces between it and myself, with my pistol in my right hand. Looking upward toward the parapet, I called out: "Halloo, the castle! Who is in command here?"

A watchman answered from atop the wall. "This is the castle of Baron Gilbert de Auletta," he called back. "The baron himself is at home and in command. Who asks?"

That told me part of what I wished to know: Larn and Gunnlag had not overthrown him. It would have been miraculous if they had, of course, unless Larn's sister had returned in their skyboat. There would have been half a score knights left, and thirty or more foot soldiers, after Gilbert had sent his troop into the mountains. In close quarters, even sky weapons would avail little against such numbers, especially in the presence of treachery, which Gilbert would surely attempt.

I ignored the watchman's interest in my identity, and continued my ploy. "I have been told that you have in the castle three holy monks from India, and their Varangian bodyguard. I have a message for them from the Bishop of Palermo."

I was less interested in what he said than how he seemed when he said it. For if my friends had been massacred, he would hardly tell me so. His considerable delay in answering suggested that he might have sent word of me to Gilbert. Thus I backed away a bit, shifting my shield from my saddle pommel to my left arm, turning my horse that my protection would be toward the wall. Bowmen could well be on their way to the parapet.

"Go to the gate," said the watchman at last, "and you will be let in. Then you may speak with Gilbert himself."

I was tempted, but my sky weapons would not protect me from ambush, from being rushed in close quarters. And for the first time, it occurred to me that Gilbert himself would probably have sky weapons now. "No," I said, "I will wait here."

While I waited, I backed my horse another twenty or thirty paces away. If Gilbert did have sky weapons, he'd hardly be skilled in their use, but he might well have learned how to fire them.

Shortly I spied another head above the parapet, and a different voice called to me—Gilbert's. "Who are you to disturb our rest here?"

His words were slow, his voice weak. Even in the quiet of night it was hard to hear him, and it seemed to me that he might have been shot by a stunner. I remembered the symptoms very well, from my first meeting with Larn and from scoundrels I myself had stunned while driving my first herd to Marseille.

"I am Arno de Courmeron," I said. "Your troop of horses came upon a misadventure in the mountains and will not be back. Any you may send after me will suffer the same fate.

"I have come for my friends, to take them to Palermo. If they are within, send them out unaccompanied and we will leave you in peace. Otherwise, Guiscard will send for them, and you will not like his messengers."

I expected either words of compliance, or likelier, some angry retort, but for a moment nothing seemed to happen. Then I felt a sudden tingling, and reined my horse to turn, for I recognized the weak touch of a stunner. It reached farther than my old one had. The beast wheeled, rearing, and half stumbled. Affected as I was, I was thrown from the saddle.

* * *

Larn:

I'd heard the exchange between Arno and the watchman more clearly than they had. And seen more clearly,
too; to our scanner, the moonlit night might as well
have been day.

I'd also seen Gilbert helped up the outside stairs to
the top of the wall, followed by four knights or sergeants; their hauberks were longer than foot soldiers
wore. Two had bows, while the others had pistols in
their hands, and Gilbert gripped a stunner.

They lined up along the parapet, all but Gilbert
keeping out of sight. I didn't waste any time settling
downward to about a hundred feet from them, above
and to the side. Then I slid the door open a couple of
feet, while Arno and Gilbert had their friendly conversation. I did these about as fast as if I hadn't been
stunned; all it took was light motions of the control rod
in front of me, and a touch on the door control.

"Jenoor," I said quietly, "set your stunner on high,
medium-wide beam, and take out the guys on top of
the wall."

"Right, Larn."

As she knelt by the door, I saw Arno go down.
"Quick!" I told her, and the men on the wall fell without another move. Without hesitating, I moved to just
above the parapet. "Dad," I said, "the guys on the wall
have got pistols and stunners. Will you pick them up?
I'd rather not leave things like that with that crew."

"Right," he said, and moving to the widening door,
jumped the forty inches or so down to the wall-top. He
was back in maybe a minute, a pistol in each hand. An
extra stunner was clipped to his belt and another pistol
was shoved under it. "That's it," he said, and I lifted.

A minute later we were on the ground, and dad was
outside helping Arno to his feet. Together they got
aboard and I closed the door behind them for security,
swiveling my seat to face them.

"Are you all right?" I asked Arno.

He looked around, saw Gunnlag and the rest of us.
"Well enough," he said. "At that distance, Gilbert's

stunner only numbed me a bit. And the horse, apparently."

"Good. I have an offer for you. Can you catch the horse again?"

"Probably. If your skyboat has not frightened him too badly." He looked around. "Where is your sister?"

"With our other skyboat," I said, and got him back to the subject. "Here is my proposal. Take the Varangians to Palermo, where they can get jobs as mercenaries if they want, and we'll take you with us to one of our worlds. They need warriors there who learn quickly and can lead."

Dad had been standing behind Arno, relaxed but with his hand on his stunner; he remembered what Arno had tried the last time he'd been aboard our cutter, nearly three years before. Now, as I made my offer to Arno, dad's eyebrows went halfway up his forehead. His Norman French was rusty, but he'd understood.

Meanwhile, Moise and Gunnlag were carrying on a murmured conversation in Greek. I hoped we weren't going to have any trouble from them. It didn't seem likely.

"Otherwise," I went on, still talking to Arno, "you have your rifle, your pistol, and your stunner. We'll leave some recharges with you, and our best wishes."

I could almost see him thinking. His wealth—his horse herd—had been lost. And while he could always start over . . . "I will take the Varangians to Palermo," he said, "and go with you. But I have already promised the Varangians that I will go back with them and pick up their wounded where we left them. And there are people here who would gladly see us dead. Did you kill Gilbert?"

"He's alive, but he'll be out of action for hours. We've got all his blasters and one of his stunners."

Arno nodded. "If I go to Palermo, how will you pick me up?"

"We can find you. Our wolves know how."

I turned to Gunnlag and Moise then. "Moise, tell Gunnlag to go with Arno. He will take the Varangians to Palermo, where there are jobs as mercenaries if they want them."

It was me Moise spoke to instead of to Gunnlag. "I already told him your offer to Arno. He said he wants the same offer. He will go to Palermo with them, but then he wants to go with you to your land. He thinks it must be very different from any land where he has been before. He would like to see it, and fight there. He will swear himself to you if you'd like."

I could see dad looking doubtful at that, and I could understand why. But I knew these men, and I felt some loyalty to them after all we'd gone through together.

"Tell Gunnlag I'll be glad to receive his oath. And after he and Arno have gotten their wounded and gone to Palermo, I will take him with us."

Moise turned to Gunnlag and talked to him in Greek. Gunnlag grinned through his beard, then sobered as he turned and spoke Greek at me.

"He wants to know how you swear a pledge in your land," Moise said.

"Tell him to repeat after me," I said, "and we'll shake hands on it afterward."

Again Moise spoke to Gunnlag in Greek. The Varangian nodded, and looked at me expectantly.

'I, Gunnlag Snorrason . . ." I began in Norman.

Moise said it in Greek, and Gunnlag repeated after him.

". . . being under no duress . . . do pledge by my God and the blessed Jesu . . ."

Gunnlag looked especially sober when he repeated the last of that.

". . . to serve Larn kel Deroop faithfully until my death . . . or until we agree to cancel this pledge. . . . And in the event of the death of Larn kel Deroop . . . to serve such member of his family as is present with us then . . . on the same basis."

When we'd said it all, we shook hands. In the background, dad blew quietly through pursed lips. I'd taken on a big responsibility. Gunnlag knew nothing about the kind of place we were going, or how to live or get along there. But from the little I knew of him, he'd changed lands and careers several times before, and things new and different were like food and drink to him.

Moise broke my thoughts. "Sire," he said to me, and I turned to him. "I, too, would like to go with you."

"Moise, you might not like the world we're going to."

"I believe I would, sire. Tarel has told me something of the worlds among the stars, and of your quest to free them. Here my family is dead, and I have no place. I would like to help you."

Somehow it was a lot harder for me to agree to take Moise than Gunnlag, the seasoned Norse mercenary and occasional pirate. Moise was really a different case, and besides, he made it seem so idealistic. And I guess it is idealistic, but we knew what we were getting into, more or less.

But who was I to decide what he should do with his life? Besides, I'd come here to recruit, among other things.

"Tarel," I said, "you're the one who talked to him about it. If he's willing to pledge himself to you, and you're willing to accept it, he can come along."

Tarel looked flustered. Behind Gunnlag and Moise, I could see dad start to grin. He saw me watching, grinned wider, and winked at me.

Tarel nodded and talked it over with Moise. They shook hands on it; the pledge had been made.

Ten minutes later, with the destrier finally having let himself be caught, Arno was in the saddle, with Gunnlag up behind him, and they started down the road to the Varangians.

PART SEVEN

DEPARTURE

THIRTY-THREE

I piloted to Deneen's island with dad sitting beside me. The others mostly napped. We talked off and on, and dad never questioned my decision to take Arno and Gunnlag, or Moise, with us when we left Fanglith. It was as though he'd go along with it, if I thought it was the thing to do.

I wasn't surprised, but it made me feel good anyway.

The island was quite a bit west of Sicily—about a twelfth of a planetary circumference—so there was still a lot of night left there when we arrived. We could have landed right then, but if we'd wakened Deneen, there'd have been at least an hour more of talk. And we all needed sleep—it had been a long day, and a long, intense night. So we bunked down on the cutter. Only Bubba, Lady, and the pups had any conversation from one craft to the other—silent, of course.

Then we overslept sunrise by more than an hour. By the time we landed, Deneen was walking back to the *Jav* from tending her fish traps. Bubba hadn't said anything to her—let her be surprised, he'd decided. And when she first saw us, at a distance, she was scared. That's when Bubba told her who we were. Close up, of course, she recognized our family cutter easily. There were lots of hugs and some tears when we all got together.

Then mom and Deneen fixed breakfast on an open fire. The high point was Deneen's fish. Mom contributed powdered milk, two kinds of algae bars, and whole-grain crackers. On the cutter they'd been living mostly on condensed rations.

Even with the not-so-great cuisine, it was a party.

After breakfast, mom had Deneen power up the *Jav* and checked its computer for the medical manual and inventory. Then she went into the dispensary and came out a while later with powder that presumably would kill fleas, and some greasy stuff for lice. At least they killed known equivalents on other worlds. The wolves had been scratching; they'd already gotten fleas from us. After a swim and a scrub, dad used clippers on Tarel, Moise, and me, down to the skin. Then we smeared each other. I can see how the grease might kill bugs: It not only stung and burned, it reeked. After half an hour we scrubbed again, and like the wolves, got powdered. Then we put on clean jump suits.

Meanwhile, Deneen had thrown our clothes, and the pallets we'd used the night before, into the *Jav*'s sterilization chamber. When the sterilization cycle was finished, she checked crystallization and turned off the power again. An hour with the power on hadn't set things back too badly.

Then we all strolled over to the ancient hut we'd found on our first trip, and sat around on the tumbled stone walls, dad and mom on one side, the rest of us on another. The espwolves lay in the grass between us.

The first thing I wanted to hear was what had happened to Jenoor. When she'd finished telling us about her rescue, mom and dad wanted our story of the past few months. That took a while, and when we'd finished, dad grinned at us.

"I guess you're probably tired of sitting now. Your mother and I can tell our stories later."

"Dad," Deneen said, "that's not funny. Give! Now!"

He laughed. "All right. When the Federation went Imperial, the underground on Evdash made some contingency plans: what to do when the Empire grabbed Evdash. Your mother and I, having a cutter, accepted the responsibility of getting Dr. Boshner off the planet. So when we left home, we headed for an estate in the mountains west of the capital, to pick him up."

Dr. G.K. Boshner was a tall, white-haired man who was Evdash's most famous refugee. He'd been head of the opposition party in the Federation senate when the Glondis Party threw out the constitution, and part of the Glondis justification for it involved making a lot of accusations against Dr. Boshner. He'd been lucky to get off Morn Gebleu alive, thirty years ago.

"In planning," dad went on, "we assumed that the Imperials would block off-planet escape attempts as soon as they arrived. It would be relatively easy for them. So our plan called for moving Dr. Boshner to a remote hiding place where he could be kept until off-planet patrols were relatively relaxed. By that time, hopefully, something might even be 'arranged' with naval personnel."

Dad glanced around at us, smiling wryly. "But there was one thing we hadn't been prepared for: how quickly the Imperials would take over the national police. I mean, the first day! Even when we heard it on the radio, we hadn't realized how widely Glondisan sympathizers had infiltrated the force. We assumed it would take a few days for the occupation administration to take extensive control.

"We were wrong. We were about sixty miles west of New Caltroff when a patrol floater spotted us, and hit us with a rocket."

He shook his head ruefully. "At that. We were lucky: The rocket was a solid round, not explosive. It holed us, which of course made us totally unspaceworthy, wrecked the life-support system, and caused other damage, some of it to me. I had about a dozen wounds, fairly superficial, from pieces of metal.

"But we could still fly. And a good deal faster than a police floater. Your mother lost them and hid in the anvil top of a thunderhead."

"A thunderhead?" I said. "The turbulence must have bounced you around something terrible, at the very least!"

"I suppose that's why they didn't look for us there. But in the anvil top, we were above major turbulence, and at the same time, effectively invisible to radar. We parked there and drifted southeast with it, to within twenty miles of a place we knew."

They'd been lucky, all right. Then mom had flown them by night to the place, a backwoods hill farm forty miles north of Jarfoss. Dad had lost quite a lot of blood. The people who hid them put the cutter in a hay barn, surrounded it with walls of hay bales, then roofed it over with bales on top of planks. It took months to get repair parts. Commercial sources had been shut down by the Empire, and when they finally got parts, it was from the naval supply depot at Jarfoss—parts never intended for a small civilian cutter. But they made do.

They never knew the pipeline the parts came through.

Dad had thought seriously then about staying on Evdash, and working with the underground, but the Glondis Party had old grudges against him, and there was a price on his head. He'd be a danger to anyone he might work with, a magnet to the political police.

A turncoat police unit, it turned out, had already arrested Dr. Boshner. He was hanged without trial during the first public executions. He'd been tried in absentia, back on Morn Gebleu, nearly thirty years ago.

The Glondis spy network really kept things hairy for a while. The resistance movement lost probably a third of its people the first week, and there was a continual trickle of losses after that. Mom and the people they were with doctored dad themselves, rather than risk getting a doctor. Mom sutured his wounds; his only anaesthetic was homemade whiskey.

Meanwhile a new underground was forming, and bit by bit, contacts were occurring with the old. It was hard to evaluate its size or much about it, because for safety, no one knew the names of more than a few others. But as far as he and mom could see, the nucleus seemed to be the military. And apparently the loyal police, when they'd adjusted to the new situation, started closing their eyes to underground activities as much as they dared.

By that time in dad's story, our behinds were tired of sitting on rocks, but we ignored the discomfort. We wanted to hear the rest. "How did you get together with Jenoor?" I asked.

"Jenoor," dad said, "why don't you tell him?"

"Well," she began, "it was quite a chain of coincidence. The sergeant transferred me to a delivery service van, where the driver gave me a shot to kill the pain. Then he delivered me . . ." She paused and looked around. ". . . at Jom and Dansee Jomber's! Dansee was home when I arrived, and it hit her pretty hard to learn what had happened. Piet had been a close friend of theirs. And I'm sure she assumed that the rest of you had been destroyed by patrol ships, though of course she didn't say that to me.

"They kept me in their basement for three days. The first thing Densee did was clean and bandage my foot. I was sort of on a cloud from the painkiller then, and watched her. It was pretty gross."

Looking at me, she smiled. I was cringing. "The first night, a man came there who was apparently a doctor. He gave me another shot—the first one was wearing off—and repaired my foot. That I didn't watch."

She turned to dad then. "Klentis," she said—not Uncle Klent anymore—"why don't you and Aven tell them the rest? It's more your story than mine."

Dad stood up before he spoke, and rubbed his backside. "You'll just have to wait a minute. My bones aren't as young as yours."

I became aware then of just how sore my own backside was from sitting on rocks. "Let's go sit in the *Rebel Javelin*," I suggested. Everyone seemed to think that was a good idea, so we went in and sat on soft, contoured seats. And at mom's suggestion, Moise went into one of the cabins and napped. So much of what he'd been hearing meant nothing at all to him that he'd gotten groggy, and was having a terrible time staying awake.

Dad, it turned out, had gotten a pipeline to a warrant officer in naval operations at Jarfoss. The cutter had been repaired by then, and the idea was for the WO to get information to dad, to help him decide when to try to get off Evdash. At the same time, Jom Jomber was

looking for somewhere to send Jenoor. And the warrant
officer, one of the few people who knew Jenoor was
there, made a deal with dad. He'd provide him with
information, if dad would take this young girl away.

So mom, in a borrowed utility floater, had gone the
next night to pick up this young girl in a parking lot in
Jarfoss. Each had almost come apart when they saw
who the other was.

On the farm, dad asked Jenoor where we'd been
headed. Naturally she told him Grinder. He knew it
wouldn't be in the astrogation cube by that name, and
when he questioned her about it, she didn't know the
planet's official name. When he told her—Tagrith Four—
she said she'd never heard it before.

And if she hadn't, it seemed probable that the rest of
us hadn't either.

They'd talked it over then, trying to figure what we
might have done, in the unlikely event that we had
gotten out-system alive. And decided the likeliest place
to look for us was on Fanglith. If they didn't find us
here, they'd head for Tagrith Four and hope we were
alive somewhere.

Dad told us frankly that he hadn't had much hope.
But any at all was enough to follow up on.

Their own escape, a couple of weeks later, was a lot
less hairy than ours. It involved a major solar flare and
undoubtedly some deliberate "failures to notice" by
patrol scouts. Failures that could be blamed on instrument and radio problems caused by the flare. The
Imperial cruiser had left the system by then.

And Bubba told us then why he'd been so quiet and
moody after we left Evdash. It was more than the food,
and being separated from Lady and the pups. Most
espwolves, by their emotional disposition, can handle
that kind of thing pretty well. His bigger problem was
that he had a secret from us—a very heavy secret, from
me especially.

"I knew Jenoor alive out there on ground," he said.
"Alive, wounded. I also knew it suicide to try get her.
So I said nothing." He looked at me, holding my eyes
with his. "After that, I not tell. I know you. You go mad

if you know we left her there like that. You tear your hair out. After you shoot me."

"No, Bubba," I said. "No way would I ever shoot you. No way! Tear my hair out, yes. And I might have said some terrible things to you, until I got my senses back."

His eyes never faltered. "Anyway," he went on, "I not tell. But it hard to have such a secret. I never felt like that before. Like guilt. Worse than grief."

Jenoor went to him and, kneeling, hugged him. "Bubba," she said, "you seem wiser and wiser to me all the time. You did the right thing, the only right thing." Her eyes were brimming when she stood up. "And look how it turned out."

Bubba grinned at her. "Espwolf live around people, get more and more like them. Even sentimental."

Which made me wonder, not for the first time, what it would be like to be an espwolf.

After Bubba's confession, we talked about what we'd do next. Mom and dad both considered that Fanglith was no place to try developing an anti-Imperial base. We'd keep it in mind as a last refuge, but that was all.

They got no argument from anyone, me least of all.

Now we *would* go to Grinder, just the way Piet had intended. It had at least one smuggler base, dad said, dug into a mountain. We could get the *Jav*'s power transfer module rebuilt there. Grinder had a false but carefully nurtured reputation as an abandoned world, in a system where the sun was supposed to be heating up. A planet with a worsening climate, where hardly anyone, if anyone at all, still lived. It was at the blurry edge of explored space, without commercial resources and far from any trade route. And with far too few people left to maintain technology, any human remnants would have degenerated to primitive survivalism.

So the story went. But Piet had been there, and knew what the real situation was. There actually weren't a lot of people on Grinder, but enough. They'd retained the technology that counted, and they taught it. They all belonged to a single culture that placed a high value

on independence, they were resourceful, and they regarded themselves as one people.

And what they knew of the Glondisans, they didn't
like at all.

What they were short on was organizational and military expertise. Dad was experienced at organization,
and had made a study of military history. "You," he told
me, "are the one with some experience."

I didn't consider my military experience to amount to
much, and it didn't seem like the kind a rebel movement would find useful, but dad disagreed.

"Larn," he said, "I'm not trying to tell you that what
you've gotten here on Fanglith amounts to a military
education. It doesn't. But you've learned to adapt, in-
novate, and survive. And you've also proven yourself
resourceful, able to face death, and a survivor.

"A formal military education probably only touches
on the tactics we'll need, anyway—tactics we'll develop
on our own. Mostly, any actual insurgency will have to
be guerrilla warfare for years—probably lots of years—
both on colony worlds and the urbanized central worlds.
Chances are we'll never wage formal warfare against the
Empire."

He grinned then. "You realize what you've done,
don't you? You've recruited a couple of specialists in
military thinking: Arno and Gunnlag must have an in-
grained, almost instinctive feel for tactics. What they
need is to be educated in technological weapons and
equipment. And about the enemy.

"Meanwhile, with your education and having grown
up in a technological culture, plus your experience now
with warlike primitive cultures, you're the obvious person to work with them. To help translate Norman and
Varangian wisdom into tactics and military organization
that can work for us.

"So we'll call your return to Fanglith a training operation and recruiting mission," he added, then stood.
"And frankly, I can't think of a better place you could
have gone for that than Fanglith." He turned to mom.
"Aven, let's you and I take a hike on the beach. We've
been penned up all too long."

* * *

That afternoon, Jenoor and I took a long hike into the hills and didn't return till nearly dark, getting to know one another again. We stayed six days on the island, giving Arno time to get the Varangians to Palermo and hired out as mercenaries—those who were interested. It also gave the *Jav*'s fuel cell time to fully decrystallize.

Then, power on, Deneen checked to make sure the scout's astrogation program included Tagrith Four. The plan now was that when we left Fanglith, Jenoor, Deneen, and I would fly the *Rebel Javelin*, taking Gunnlag, Moise, and the two pups. The *Jav* had quite a bit more room than our family cutter.

Arno would go with dad and mom and Tarel. Bubba and Lady would keep them company. I was willing to take Arno, but I'd told them about his romantic interest in Deneen, and we agreed it might be awkward if she was cooped up with him for sixty-eight days flying to Grinder. And while neither Deneen nor I brought it up, of course, it seemed to me it might be easier on Tarel if Deneen was with us on the scout, instead of with him on the cutter.

We would transfer Arno's fealty to dad; Arno would agree to that if he really wanted to leave with us. The way Arno's mind worked, you swore fealty to someone and then you were pretty much loyal unless you came up with some incentive to double-cross them and some technicality to make it all right. Which I didn't expect from him under the circumstances. And the espwolves would know if he got treacherous ideas.

Meanwhile I'd have Gunnlag to educate. I looked forward to it. Compile a data base of Norse and Standard, run it through the linguistics program, and have him learn Standard; we'd use it now instead of Evdashian. Evdashian was an offshoot dialect of Standard used only on Evdash, and chances were we'd never see Evdash again.

On the evening of the sixth day, the scout and the cutter lifted for Palermo. With the wolves scanning, we located Arno and Gunnlag, and put Moise down with a

communicator to arrange the pickup. By communicator, I told Arno to arrange for a couple mule-loads of
food and take it to the pickup point, outside Palermo.
I'd have preferred three or more loads, but we didn't
have storage.

Larger spacecraft would have been nice, for the
biovats if nothing else. As it was, we'd have to ration
pretty strictly on the long trip to Grinder.

THIRTY-FOUR

It took Moise and Arno two days to get the food we
needed and get it to the edge of an orange grove a
couple of miles outside the city. Actually, Arno was
nearly broke, way too poor now to buy that much food.
But Gunnlag had received a bounty from Guiscard for
bringing his Varangians to the recruiter, and that had
been enough. (Guiscard and Roger never had enough
Norman foot soldiers, and were always looking for high-
quality mercenaries.) Arno had borrowed the two mules,
and one of the Varangians had gone along to take them
back to town.

Bubba okayed the pickup scene, so dad landed the
cutter to get the food and the two warriors. Then we all
got together on a hill a few miles southeast, got everything distributed, and said goodbye to one another.

The goodbyes were hard, believe me. We wouldn't
see each other again for sixty-eight days. But there was
no way around it, and at least Jenoor and I were together.

*   *   *

Sixty-eight days in FTL gave us a lot of time to talk—about what might be, how we'd like to have things turn out (and why), what problems we might run into, and even occasionally about what might have been. To give Gunnlag practice in Standard, we had him tell us about his people and others, the places he'd been, things he'd seen and done . . .

Moise too. Although he was a lot younger, and had less to tell, there was more than you might think, and it was more interesting than he realized. Fanglith and its people in general were marvelously interesting—I'd only seen a small sample myself.

Their stories strengthened our conclusion that it wasn't the place for us. To coin a phrase: It's an interesting place to visit, but I wouldn't want to live there.

We worked on Gunnlag's and Moise's education. If you want to develop a better understanding, more insights, into your own culture, try educating someone in it who's from a totally different culture. That can be worth a whole series of university courses to you. Gunnlag, like Moise, was marvelously adaptable and had a quick mind. And of course, they each had some unusual and surprising ways of looking at the things we told them about.

But the most meaningful talks, for me, were some between Jenoor and me in the privacy of her tiny cubbyhold cabin or mine. (There were no cabins for two on the scout.) Talks about the future. And once again, I—we—knew too little, had too little information to plan with, beyond the next step or two, or in broad, vague terms. That kind of planning we could do.

At first, we considered the possibility of settling down as sort of "backup revolutionaries." Not get involved too deeply. That way we could live a semi-normal life, enjoy some stability, raise a family.

But it seemed as if that wouldn't work. Now that the Glondis government had gone Imperial, it was the road to slavery and regret. Fifteen years earlier, when my parents had fled Morn Gebleu, things had been different. And they had children. Now the Glondis Party had consolidated its power on the central planets and was moving to control all the human worlds. We faced a spreading Empire, not a Federation.

So what kind of future could we have together?

We'd had each other, very briefly, and we'd lost each other. It was the wildest luck that we were together again. When I'd thought Jenoor was dead, life had gone on for me. And while she'd had a lot more reason to think I was dead than alive, life had gone on for her, too.

It really had; life had gone on.

So we made a pledge—a pledge subject to change if experience showed us it should change. The revolution would come first with us. We'd be together, work together, enjoy together, as much as we could. For as long as we could. Without clinging to it, without sacrificing the revolution to it. We'd be willing to lose each other, and hope it didn't happen.

Meanwhile we wouldn't worry about it any more than we had to. Life was for living, and hopefully for accomplishing something valuable with. And eventually for dying. For non-revolutionaries, as well as for us. We'd live it while we had it, as ethically as we knew how.

That's the way it sorted out for us—at first only intellectually, but more and more at the gut level, the emotional level, as we got used to our decision.

And that's how it was that, when the *Jav* came out of FTL mode, Jenoor and I could stand holding hands and feeling good about things as we gazed at the bright blue-white bead of Grinder a couple of million miles away. We had work to do and a life to live there. And who knew where else before it was done.

TRAVIS SHELTON
LIKES BAEN BOOKS
BECAUSE THEY TASTE GOOD

Recently we received this letter from Travis Shelton of Dayton, Texas:

I have come to associate Baen Books with Del Monte. Now what is that supposed to mean? Well, if you're in a strange store with a lot of different labels, you pick Del Monte because the product will be consistent and will not disappoint.

Something I have noticed about Baen Books is that the stories are always fast-paced, exciting, action-filled and seem to be published because of content instead of who wrote the book. I now find myself glancing to see who published the book instead of reading the back or intro. If it's a Baen Book it's going to be good and exciting and will capture your spare reading moments.

Another discovery I have recently made is that I don't have any Baen Books in my unread stacks—and I read four to seven books a week, so that in itself is a meaningful statistic.